IMPERFECTION

A devious murderer confounds detectives in this gripping mystery

RAY CLARK

THE
BOOK
FOLKS

Published by The Book Folks

London, 2020

ISBN 978-1-913516-98-7

www.thebookfolks.com

"Man, by the very fact of being man, by possessing consciousness, is, in comparison with the ass or the crab, a diseased animal. Consciousness is a disease."

Miguel de Unamuno

Chapter One

Detective Inspector Stewart Gardener ran across New Briggate before mounting the steps leading to the Grand Theatre two at a time. At the top he banged on the glass doors with his right hand whilst displaying his warrant card with his left.

They were quickly opened by a man as tall and gangly as a stork, whose eyes were so intense that Gardener thought he was staring into a double-barrelled shotgun.

"DI Gardener."

"Good grief, that was quick! I only rang a few minutes ago." The man extended his neck past the entrance and asked where Gardener's car was.

Gardener glanced behind him. Two constables pulled up and parked in the loading bay. The town centre was pretty quiet: too late for shoppers, too early for the club crowd, and the theatregoers were already inside.

Gardener waved them up the steps, and all three men entered the building. "Can you close and lock the door, please?" the SIO ordered the man holding it. "And then tell me who you are?"

"Paul Price, theatre manager. Where are the others?"

"On their way." Gardener glanced around the foyer. Members of staff huddled desperately together, some on the ground floor, others on the stairs leading to the circles. The room went quiet as soon as he entered, all eyes turning toward him.

Gardener addressed the young constables, pointing to one of them. "I'd like you to stay here and guard the entrance." To the other, he said, "You walk all the way around the outside of the building, take a note of all the exits, including the windows."

"How did you get here so quickly?" asked Price.

The manager had already developed a habit of interrupting Gardener, something he didn't appreciate. He was annoyed enough.

"Let's stick to what's important, Mr Price. I need to see the crime scene. It has to be secured, and I can't do that standing here."

Price turned tail and did as he was told, but his expression told Gardener that he was used to giving orders, not taking them.

Gardener was escorted down a long, narrow corridor with cream-coloured walls that smelled of disinfectant and polish. On his right were the dressing rooms; each door was closed. On his left, a notice board displayed information about performance times, future productions, safety regulations, and very probably everything else anyone needed to know about the theatre. To the right of the board was a set of double wooden doors leading to the stage. Behind them, Gardener could hear the frenzy of panicked voices.

As he entered, he was greeted with a mixture of smells: antique leather, make-up, sweat. On his left was a man with a pale complexion standing next to a mixing desk. From his right, a powerful breeze blew into his face. A huge roller shutter door at the back of the building was open. He wasn't pleased.

"Close that," Gardener told Price.

He then surveyed the scene before him. The safety curtain had been lowered. Stage left was an old two-seater leather settee with a narrow rug placed in front of it. On top of the table next to it was a decanter of wine with glasses. Two small tables elsewhere on the stage had brassware and candlesticks, all of which had been neatly coated with cobweb spray.

Gardener glanced at the backdrop: an oak-panelled library, displaying shelves crammed with a selection of leather-bound, dusty tomes. Hung at strategic intervals, posters advertised films in which tonight's guest actor, Leonard White, had had starring roles. A log-effect fire created a comforting ambience. The whole thing reminded him of the old Universal horror films of Boris Karloff and Bela Lugosi.

Especially the corpse at the end of the rope.

Chapter Two

"Has anyone touched the body so far?" Gardener asked Price.

"No."

"So, no one's checked to see if he's dead?"

"Looks pretty dead to me," said Price.

Gardener had to agree with him. "How long has he been there?"

"I don't know."

Gardener removed his shoes, left them by the stage doors. From an inside pocket he produced a pair of gloves and paper slippers. Pulling them on, he walked over to the body and checked for a pulse. There wasn't one. The corpse was dressed in a black evening suit, white shirt, black bow tie, and black waistcoat. His complexion was ghostly white, anaemic; not that Gardener expected a picture of health.

Glancing beyond the body, Gardener noticed a scenery board with an open door frame. Two more people had arrived. He peered up at the ceiling to search the rafters and saw the beam with the rope attached to it, but nothing more. He glanced over at the roller shutter door that had now been closed by Paul Price, doubting very much the killer was still on the premises.

He scrutinised the whole area, then turned and shouted to the crowd. "I want everyone to stay exactly where they are. Do not wander around, and do not come on to the stage."

Walking back to meet Price, he produced his mobile and called Steve Fenton, the Crime Scene Manager, explaining that he wanted him to run an ESLA. He also needed Scenes of Crime as quickly as possible.

Price piped up. "Excuse me, this is my theatre. What's an ESLA?"

Gardener faced him. "You're wrong, Mr Price. It's a crime scene, so now it's my theatre. And you wouldn't understand."

"Don't patronise me. I do watch the crime shows on the TV."

Gardener smiled. "Very well. ESLA is the Electro Static Lifting Apparatus. It looks like a sheet of tin foil. Once we've rolled it over the stage, we'll attach wires to either end where a machine will then pass a charge through it. That will lift all the dust exactly as it's laid out on the floor. We can then take it away for examination, which will give us very precise details of foot marks, which can then be compared against any suspect's shoes we might recover at a later date."

Price glanced at his own feet and then to Gardener. Judging by his expression, Gardener thought the theatre manager's heart had stopped. "Well, I've never seen that on Midsommer."

"My point exactly," replied Gardener. "Now, can we get back to business? What happened?"

"When?"

Gardener wasn't sure whether or not his temper was shorter than usual, or if everyone he'd met so far was stupid. "Can you take me through what happened from the beginning of the show?"

"Oh," replied Price. "Well, not much. The place was full, the lights dimmed, and then a voice came over the PA system–"

"Live or recorded?" interrupted Gardener.

"Does it matter?"

"Live or recorded," he repeated.

"I'm really not sure. I suppose it sounded live, now I come to think of it."

"Did you recognise the voice?"

"No, but it could have been any one of my staff."

"And it might not have been. Was it in the script?"

"I never saw the script. I have no idea what was planned."

"Was the show being recorded?"

"No."

"Where were *you* when it happened?" asked Gardener.

"Sitting with your father," replied Price. "The first box in the dress circle to the left of the stage."

Gardener suddenly remembered his father's presence. The reason he had made it to the theatre so quickly was because he was sitting in a coffee bar around the corner, intending to pick his father up after the show. "How is he?"

"Shocked, like the rest of us."

Gardener wanted to see his father, Malcolm, but at the moment his professional capacity wouldn't allow that. "Carry on."

"Well, after the voice – before the curtain was raised – we saw fog creeping out from underneath. The curtain rose, but Leonard White was nowhere to be seen."

"Where should he have been?" asked Gardener.

"On the settee I assume, but as I've said, I never saw the script. Suddenly, there were a couple of explosions and lots of lighting before a voice screamed out something I didn't catch… and then the body simply dropped… and just sort of dangled there."

"Did you come on stage immediately?"

"I think so."

"Think isn't good enough, I need to know," replied Gardener.

"Well… not straight away. I left my box and came down the stairs and telephoned the police first."

"So, when you entered the stage, did you see anyone?"

"Only my stage manager, Steve Rogers."

"Where is he now?"

"I think he went in the direction of the roller shutter door."

"Was it open?"

"Yes."

As if to back up Price's story, a door to the side of the steel shutter opened and a man wearing jeans and a plain black T-shirt came through it.

"Are you Steve Rogers?" asked Gardener.

"Yes."

"Stay there, please. Where have you been?"

"I stepped outside for a bit of fresh air." He glanced at the corpse. "It's not every day you see one of those."

"Did you see what happened?"

"Not really," replied Rogers.

Not really. What did that mean?

Gardener heard voices on the other side of the safety curtain. Judging by their impatient comments, he would have to say something.

"Can you get me a microphone?" he asked Price. "When I've finished talking to the audience, I'd like a word with your stage manager."

The man behind the mixing desk, a few feet from Gardener, handed the mic over as he approached the curtain. He stepped around it and walked to the middle of the stage. A hush fell over the crowd. He stood in the centre, unsure what to say, realising that although every one of these people was a possible witness, they were also suspects.

From the stage the theatre was different, particularly as the house lights were on. It was cavernous, and as he gazed upwards, much higher and more daunting than he had ever noticed before. He couldn't imagine what it took to tread the boards night after night, performing in front of others. He glanced toward the box where he understood his father to be sitting, and nodded.

He focused himself, then addressed the restless crowd. "Ladies and gentlemen, I am Detective Inspector Stewart Gardener." He flashed his warrant card, aware that no one could actually tell whether or not it was genuine. "I realise how inconvenient all this is going to be, but I have to ask that every one of you remain in your seats until you are told otherwise. I'm afraid there will be no show tonight as planned. I'm sure that most of you will have guessed what you've seen is real. It was, and the whole building is now a crime scene. In due course, each and every one of you will be asked your name and a few other details. So, please do not try to leave the theatre before we have spoken to you."

He couldn't help but notice the concerned expressions; whether it was for themselves or the death of the actor he wasn't sure, but knowing the depth of human nature he could guess.

As he turned to leave, the people seated in the front row tried to question him. He ignored them and returned backstage, thankful of the approaching sirens.

He glanced at Paul Price. "Can you confirm for me that the dead man is Leonard White?"

Price simply nodded.

Chapter Three

Back on stage, Gardener switched off the microphone and handed it back to the sound technician. He found Steve Rogers where he'd left him, near the roller shutter door. The fact that it was open when he'd arrived had really bothered him. If the murderer had used it as a means of escape, he could be anywhere by now.

"What time did you start work?"

Rogers glanced at his watch. "About two o'clock this afternoon."

"I know we're in a theatre and people come and go, but have you seen anyone suspicious lurking around the place, anyone who is not connected to the production?"

Steve Rogers shrugged his shoulders. "No one I can think of. I mean, it's only a one-man show, we don't need much in the way of staff."

"When was the last time you saw Leonard White?"

"The dead man, you mean?"

"Is there anyone else called Leonard White around here?"

"No, sorry... er... when I came in, just after two."

"Where was he?" asked Gardener.

"In his dressing room."

"And?" pressed Gardener.

"I was on my way to see Mr Price, but I knocked on his door and introduced myself. He had his back to me, facing his mirror." The stage manager stopped as if that was the end of the sentence. Like a wind-up toy, he suddenly started again. "He, er, just nodded and said something, but I didn't catch what it was."

The technician was provoking Gardener. It wasn't that he was slow, but he didn't seem to realise how important his information may be. Even more annoying was his habit of protruding his bottom lip and blowing upwards to clear a lock of hair which kept falling across one eye; the option of having his hair cut had obviously escaped his attention.

"Did you see him after that?"

"No. I passed by his dressing room at around four, but the door was closed."

Gardener thought back. That was when his father must have been there. He recollected his father mentioning Leonard White's mood: the actor had seemed subdued, not his usual self, but nothing further had been said.

"Do you know Leonard White?" asked Gardener.

"Not really."

There was that phrase again. You either knew the man, or you didn't.

Gardener and Steve Rogers were disturbed by the arrival of his partner DS Sean Reilly, the Home Office pathologist Dr George Fitzgerald, DCI Alan Briggs, and a team of SOCOs. A number of constables remained by the stage doors, craning their necks to see what had happened. All his team had already donned their protective paper suits so as not to contaminate the scene.

Gardener quickly took Briggs through what he'd found. The DCI listened without interfering. A sharp rapping on the roller shutter door attracted their attention.

"I imagine that's Steve Fenton with the ESLA gear," said Gardener.

Briggs shouted over to Steve Rogers, "You, open the door and let him in."

The DCI, a physical bear of a man originating from Liverpool, had held the position for a little over a year, having taken it shortly after the death of Gardener's wife. In the early days, neither he nor Gardener had seen eye to eye. Time had settled their differences, though, and both officers now held a great deal of respect for each other.

Briggs had a huge barrel chest. Little could be seen of his face due to his thick black beard and moustache. A few inches shorter than Gardener, he carried his authority well. In Gardener's opinion, Briggs' only failing was his short temper; during those outbursts he spoke extremely fast, never fluffed his words, and grew in confidence with each one spoken.

As the senior officer, Briggs allocated the tasks. He asked Gardener's second-in-command Reilly to interview the two stagehands on the other side of the auditorium. He then stepped outside the stage area, calling Colin Sharp over.

"Colin, take a number of uniformed officers and cover all the exits. Go to the entrance and set up tables. Sort out a couple of digital cameras for the officers, mouth swab kits, and personal description forms. I want names, addresses, and any available ID. After that, send them to a table for a DNA mouth swab and get the officers to write down all details, including what they're wearing."

Sharp sighed. "Looks like we're in for a long night, sir. Are we allowed to take their DNA?"

"Not by law," replied Briggs. "You'll need to ask their permission, sign a form. Explain to them it's only for this investigation. After that we'll destroy it. If anyone gives you any trouble, call me and I'll come and sort it." Sharp nodded before leaving. Finally, Briggs organised a roof search with the use of a helicopter.

Moving back to the stage, Briggs asked. "Who found the body, other than the entire audience?"

"Still trying to determine whether the first person on the stage was Paul Price, or his stage manager Steve Rogers," replied Gardener. "As soon as I got here, I checked that Leonard White was dead, then went out and spoke to the audience."

"Where have you been since then?"

"Over there to talk to Rogers." Gardener pointed to him.

"In that case," said Briggs, "you stay here with Fitz until he's completed his examination and the body is removed. I'll interview Steve Rogers."

Gardener and Fitz had to wait for the SOCOs to finish the ESLA before approaching the corpse. During that time, Gardener asked the sound technician to check all of the equipment to see if it had been tampered with. He requested all tapes – whether they belonged to the theatre or not – to be taken away for analysis.

Fitz eventually donned a pair of surgical gloves. "So, what happened?"

Gardener repeated what Paul Price had told him.

"Was this how you found him when you came backstage?" asked Fitz, checking each of the man's joints.

"Yes."

"Let's cut him down, then."

Gardener ordered a couple of uniforms to cut the rope from the beam but to save the knot. He also wanted photos before they made the cut.

The pathologist inspected the skin around the neck. "The rope marks on the neck don't bear the inflamed edge of a vital reaction."

"Meaning?" inquired Gardener.

Fitz sighed, clicked his tongue. "There are no signs of a struggle, which suggests it wasn't suicide."

When the body was finally on the floor, Gardener leaned nearer. "I know he's dead, but why is he so pale?"

Fitz produced a thermometer from his surgical case, removed the actor's trousers and underpants, and placed it inside his rectum. After a short period of time he removed it, noting the reading, before reaching into the bag for a razor blade.

Gardener felt hollow inside. How was he going to break the news to his father? Leonard White had been a close friend.

"I can't believe all this has happened in, what..." – he checked his watch – "...four or five hours."

"It hasn't," replied Fitz, slicing the right thigh of the corpse.

"It must have done," protested Gardener. "I came to pick my father up at four o'clock. We exchanged a few words."

"Not with him you didn't." Fitz pointed to the thigh. "Leonard White's body is stone cold. The reason he's so pale is because he has no blood. At a guess, I'd say Leonard White has been dead since yesterday."

Chapter Four

Once the body had been removed, Gardener and Reilly decided to interview Paul Price.

The SIO glanced curiously around the manager's office. It was small, sparsely furnished, and disorganised. A desk had been placed in the middle of the room without a moment's thought to the symmetry. Along the left wall, Paul Price's computer was perched incongruously on another small desk that could barely be seen due to a mountain of paperwork. A couple of wall-mounted shelves on the right contained an assortment of files without labels. The decor consisted of a carpet that had probably been left over from a production when the theatre had first opened. A pale green emulsion covered the walls. It was extremely warm, but despite appearances smelled fresh: lavender, and something Gardener couldn't put his finger on.

Sean Reilly was sitting in the only chair available. He had a notebook and pen in his hand. Paul Price leaned forward and removed a bottle of whiskey and three glasses from one of the desk drawers.

"For emergencies, you understand," he offered, as if excusing himself. "Would either of you two officers like a drink?"

"No, thank you, Mr Price," said Gardener. "We're on duty."

The manager poured himself one before very quickly draining the glass. He then poured another, placing the bottle back in the drawer, along with the two unused glasses. Sitting back in his chair, he sighed very loudly.

Gardener closed the office door and leaned back against it, arms folded. "Has a murder ever occurred in your theatre before?"

Price sipped his whiskey, clasping the glass with both hands. He was dressed in a pale blue suit, white shirt, and blue tie. He had a large head with a round face, dark blue eyes, and a pencil thin moustache. What hair remained around the sides was still black. Gardener suspected his nose had been broken and reset, and then broken again. On the bridge of his nose, a line suggested glasses were an everyday item, but he had chosen not to wear them. His frame was abnormally thin and emaciated, and the white spots on his teeth and fingernails indicated a lack of calcium within his diet.

"Not to my knowledge."

"How long have you worked here?"

"Over thirty years. In its 127-year history, the theatre has only had six managers. I took over from the late George Green in 1994, who'd taken the position in 1963 after his father had vacated."

"You did say *late*," interrupted Reilly.

"Yes."

"Be no good calling him, then."

Price didn't reply. He merely continued to sip the whiskey.

"What are you actually responsible for, Mr Price? What do you do?" asked Gardener.

"I'm pretty much a one-man band. I look after the general running of the theatre. I book all the shows, take care of the marketing, supervise the team that works for us, oversee the finances, and I cover all the health and safety as well. It's a very demanding position." Price let out another heavy sigh before draining the contents of his second tumbler of whiskey.

Gardener wondered what all the sighing was about, and how many whiskies he was going to drink before the night was out; in fact, before the interview was concluded.

"I take it then that you booked Leonard White?"

"Yes. I had the details of his nationwide tour. His films were good, so I thought it would be interesting to hear him talk about his life."

"Did you book him through an agency?"

"PMA Promotions in Manchester."

"Did you actually know him as a person?"

"No."

"Do you know if he was married?"

"I think he was, but I'm sure the agency will be able to supply that sort of information."

"How much have you seen of him today?"

"Not at all."

"Pardon?"

"I haven't been here. I've had meetings all day, didn't get in until about five o'clock."

"And you didn't see him then? Didn't think to go and introduce yourself?"

"Well, as a matter of fact, I wanted to, but as soon as I arrived I had a number of phone calls to make, and that took me well past six o'clock. There was little point after that. But I'm sure my staff looked after him in my absence."

Gardener changed topics. "Who owns the theatre, Mr Price?"

"A consortium. There are four of us who have an equal share of twenty-five percent."

"Any financial problems?" asked Sean Reilly.

"I don't think that's any of your business, but since you ask, none whatsoever." Price sounded appalled by the last question, though Gardener couldn't think why.

"It *is* our business and we're curious," said Reilly. "Get a few money problems, you never know what folks will do."

Price jumped out of his chair. "I hope you're not suggesting one of my partners would be involved in something like murder."

"You know them better than we do."

"We're not suggesting anything, Mr Price. We're merely conducting an investigation, and we have to explore every avenue." Gardener paused. "Now, back to the questions. No financial problems. Has anyone approached you wanting to buy the theatre? Perhaps someone who wants to demolish it and build a supermarket?"

Price resumed a seated position, poured himself another whiskey.

Gardener was pleased to see that he didn't drink any.

"No."

"What kind of a staff turnover do you have?"

"Very small. Despite the fact that it's a consortium, we're actually family run. All the owners are related to each other, which is why I took exception to your earlier comment."

"You can't think of any disgruntled ex-staff member with a grudge to bear?"

Price stared hard at both detectives. "This is not an inside job, if that's what you're thinking. Nearly all of the people who work for the theatre retire. As I've said, we're all happy to work here."

Gardener doubted that very much. "If you say so."

The DI changed topics again. "Let's talk about the general public. We all know that it can't be easy dealing with them. People tend to complain about all sorts of things. The price of tickets, seating availability, have you experienced anything of the sort recently? Received any intimidating letters? Complaints about the standard of shows, for example?"

The manager snorted and then laughed. "You really do watch too much Agatha Christie. Do you honestly think someone is going to murder for the price of a ticket?"

Gardener had had enough of Price's demeaning manner. "You'd be surprised why one person decides to murder another. But it doesn't really matter what I think. The information I extract from others is far more important."

Gardener moved away from the door, leaning over Paul Price's desk. He spoke slowly and methodically, his anger having reached its peak.

"Now, as I've already said, we're conducting a murder investigation. I don't think you realise how important it is. So, when I ask you a question, I would like a straightforward answer, not some snotty-nosed derogatory remark filled with sarcasm. Or, for that matter, your opinions. That way, we'll all be through a lot faster and still be friends."

Price's expression would have stopped electricity travelling through cables.

Gardener continued. "And where tickets are concerned, I'd like to see your bookings for the whole of this year." He then added, "Last year as well."

"Why?"

"So that we can check any last-minute cancellations, advanced bookings made at the start of the season for a reduced rate, see if a new customer has suddenly started appearing at Saturday afternoon matinees when he normally attends evening performances.

"You see, Mr Price, whoever killed Leonard White knew this theatre. He managed to not only get *himself* in here, but a dead body as well, not to mention concealing it somewhere. Perhaps he's fooled your staff into thinking he has a connection with the theatre.

"I want to know everything about this place. Attempted break-ins, trespassers, threatening or strange phone calls, obsessive fans, mysterious events at previous performances by earlier theatre groups, everything! Whatever you know about this theatre, I want to know."

Gardener stood back, folding his arms again. "And for that matter, I'm going to make it my job to find out everything you don't know."

A resounding knock on the door broke the tension. Reilly stood up, but Gardener opened it and was met by his colleague, DC Colin Sharp.

"Sir," said Sharp. "We need you on the stage."

"I'll be down in a minute."

He turned back to the theatre manager. "Well, I think I've outlined everything I want, Mr Price. I'll leave one of my officers on hand to collect the information as soon as you have it."

"Just hold on, I can't do all that by myself."

"Why not?" Gardener replied. "You seem to manage everything else."

Gardener opened the door to leave, and then turned back. "Two more things. The theatre will be closed until further notice. Second, I'd like a list of all your meetings for today, names and contact numbers."

"I'm a suspect now, am I?" asked Paul Price.

Both detectives left without answering.

Chapter Five

Albert Fettle was a small stump of a man with a rotund belly that stretched a pair of brown braces almost to breaking point. His legs were too small, his shoes too big. He was bald, had blue eyes, and wore a pair of wire-rimmed glasses, which he kept pushing back up his nose. His mouth was cavernous, because his teeth were small and stumpy like him. He walked with a limp, his voice was high pitched, and his accent broad West Riding. He was dressed in a checked blue and red lumberjack shirt with rolled-up sleeves and brown pleated trousers.

"Detective Inspector Stewart Gardener and Detective Sergeant Sean Reilly, Mr Fettle."

Both men showed their warrant cards. They were standing in the corridor leading to the stage. Three of the dressing room doors were open and being searched by SOCOs.

"Aye, I remember you, Stewart Gardener. You won't remember me, though. Caught you and your mate one time nicking wood from behind my shed."

Fettle pointed at Gardener but chose to stare at Reilly. "He were bloody selling 'em by the bagful. Took me ages to find out who it was." The old man smiled and turned back to Gardener. "You made good on yourself, though."

Gardener vaguely recalled the incident and smiled. "I'm sure you must be mistaken."

"Like hell," replied Fettle.

"So, what have you got for us, Mr Fettle?"

From further down the corridor, DC Sharp called to his superior officer. "Sir, we're having trouble with this door. It's locked."

Reilly glanced over. "Whose dressing room is it?"

"Leonard White's."

"Go and find a spare key, somebody must have one!"

Fettle piped up again. "Well, do you want to know, or don't you?"

"Know what?" asked Gardener.

"Christ, Gardener, how the hell did you make a copper if you can't concentrate on the job in hand?"

"There is rather a lot going on at the moment."

"I saw Leonard White walk out of the building. He left the theatre through the stage door."

"When?"

"Just after half past seven. I'd been for a leak. I wondered what the hell were going on. Then I heard a lot of noise from the theatre. Only it can't have been Leonard White, can it? He were dead by then, so it must have been your killer." Fettle snorted. "Bloody perfect disguise, I can tell you."

Gardener was about to ask another question when Sharp shouted "Jesus Christ!" as the dressing room door was opened.

Reilly immediately made his way to the room. "Boss, you'd better come and see."

"There's never a dull moment." Gardener turned to Albert Fettle. "Stay here, I need to ask you some more questions." He then brushed past Sharp into the already crammed small dressing room with Fitz, Reilly, and Alan Briggs.

At the back of the room stood a table. Above that, a mirror had been fixed to the wall. Perched on the table were eight one-pint glasses. Each one was mostly full with a substance resembling raw liver. The bottom section of each glass, however, was a clear serum.

"What's going on?" asked Gardener.

"At a guess, I'd say we've found Leonard White's blood," replied Fitz.

Gardener stared at the glasses, horrified. "It doesn't look like blood."

"That's because it's clotted. It's been in those jars quite a while. Like I said on the stage, I think the victim was killed yesterday. And that's not all," said Fitz. He pointed to the wall above the mirror.

The colour of the scrawl was slightly lighter than the congealed blood, but Gardener suspected that's what had been used to write it:

For long weary months I have awaited this hour.

Chapter Six

Gardener was standing in the garage, staring at the stripped Bonneville motorcycle.

The place was a tip as usual, with spare parts all over. A variety of engine parts sat in a cardboard box, transmission parts in another. At least he hoped they were, and not mixed up. Two wheel rims leaned against one wall, ready for cleaning. Almost every other part of the bike was in a random location he was yet to recall. There were photocopied pages of the service manual tacked to every wall. He was pleased that he'd eventually sent the frame to Jeff Harrison – the enthusiast he'd met in Rawston – to have it professionally cleaned and protected.

His CD player was blaring out *Holding Out For A Hero* by Bonnie Tyler, the excessive drum rolls reverberating around the small enclosure, rattling the door and anything else that was loose. He could feel the beat on the floor under his feet.

He allowed himself a brief moment to think about Sarah and that fateful night in Leeds. She had been holding out for a hero – her husband – but he couldn't find the necessary superpowers to save her. He hadn't felt like a hero then, and he didn't now.

The track changed to *Cold As Ice* by Foreigner, which led him into thinking about the case.

It had been a long night. Technically speaking, he was still on duty: he'd only come home to grab a shower and a fresh change of clothes. He was tired, and his bed would have been a better option, but he didn't have that kind of a job.

Everyone had finally left the theatre at four o'clock in the morning. Gardener and Reilly had returned to the station to set up the incident room. He'd called Mike Sanderson and asked for HOLMES to set up their equipment to compare the first of the witness statements.

The building had been sealed and closed, and a search team put in place. He had kicked off the ANACAPA chart by placing Leonard White's name in the centre. He glanced at his watch: 7:30. He was hoping to return there shortly, when they would hopefully have all the photographs up as well.

Gardener had been disturbed by what he'd seen. A body at the end of a rope was typical enough in his line of work. The lack of blood was the real problem, and he'd been distracted by that fact when trying to interview Paul Price.

The first thing that had run through his mind was, "why?" Why had the killer removed it? A fleeting thought of Jack the Ripper came to mind; he had tried writing letters to the police using the victim's blood. He'd failed because it had hardened in the fountain pen. Had the killer placed the blood in the eight one-pint glass jars in the dressing room simply to write the message? How had he done it? Gardener suspected there was more to it, that it was all a part of some perverse game, especially considering the quote on the wall.

Then came the startling revelation that someone who closely resembled Leonard White had calmly walked out of the theatre as all the commotion was unfolding. In fact, resemblance was probably far too weak a word. By all accounts, the disguise was so good, it had completely fooled people. He wondered how many had actually seen him. So far, only Albert Fettle had come forward.

The connecting door to the kitchen opened, and Gardener immediately caught the mouth-watering aroma of grilled bacon. His taste buds tingled. He would normally prefer a healthy option, but he hadn't eaten for almost fourteen hours, so anything was better than nothing.

His father appeared in the doorway. "You okay, son?"

Gardener turned off the CD player, then turned to the old man. His complexion was still ashen. He was wearing the same clothes he'd worn for his night out, so he obviously hadn't slept either. Malcolm's posture was stooped. Gardener realised his father was no spring chicken. The bad news must have hit him hard. We all take our parents for granted, Gardener thought. *We think they will be with us forever.*

He said he was fine, and they both walked into the kitchen. Chris, his son, was grilling the bacon. Mugs of tea were already on the table, as were placemats and plates. The room was warmer than the garage, and the music somewhat different. Spook was sitting in the corner wolfing down some scraps of bacon fat, paying little or no attention to anyone or anything apart from the snack.

"Come on, Dad," said Chris. "You have to eat." He backed up his statement by serving his father first.

Gardener smiled. No matter how good, bad, or indifferent times were, family meant everything.

The telephone shrilled. Gardener answered it. Colin Sharp informed him the photos were back, and they were waiting to set up the incident room. He said he would be there shortly.

Chapter Seven

Every muscle in Janine Harper's body ached, or at least it felt that way. Although her headache had subdued to a mild pounding sensation, her arms and legs felt heavy, and the stomach cramps were becoming unbearable. It was a symptom she recognised all too well: the first full day of her period always started – and finished – the same way.

Adding to her explosive mood was the fact that she had had a violent row with her boyfriend Carl the night before. He was immature, and didn't care about her feelings, or her moods – a typical male.

She sighed and glanced around the room, holding a clipboard in her left hand, a pen in her right. Stocktaking was a job she disliked at the best of times. She worked in a retail outlet for theatrical supplies. A lot of the products they stocked were small, consumed a lot of space, and took an age to count.

The room was clean and tidy, the decor easy on the eyes: plaster-finished walls in two different colours with a border separating them. The strong parquet floor supported at least a dozen racks of Dexion, which contained everything from bottles of acetone, aluminium powder, collodion and spirit gum, to flexible plastic skin, curling irons, eyebrow pencils and foam rubber – even obscure products like fishskin, a thin, tough, transparent material made from the stomach lining of animals used mainly in olden day theatre for building up layers of skin on the face or body.

Janine made it to the top of the ladder when the doorbell suddenly chimed. She grimaced, slamming the clipboard on the shelving. The pen bounced upwards before finally landing somewhere behind the cabinet.

Brilliant, thought Janine, glancing at her watch. *And it's only nine o'clock!*

She descended the ladder two steps at a time, and wished she hadn't. Janine lost her footing, slid the rest of the way. At floor level, her left foot gave way. She keeled over and hit the Dexion before hitting the ground. Her ankle hurt from the collision, her hands burned from the ladder slide, and her back felt bruised. Janine picked herself up, dusted down her clothes, and set off towards the shop faster than she meant to, which left her feeling a little nauseous. She really didn't need today.

On reaching the entrance leading into the shop, she saw something else she didn't need.

The creep.

Standing with her back to the wall, Janine wanted to cry. She felt closed in. Why of all days was she going to have to put up with him today? He was such a pompous bastard. He barely spoke, and when he did, it was always that soft nasal drawl. He had the ability to make her skin crawl simply by staring at her. He had a face that only a mother could love; one she wanted to punch, continuously.

Janine summoned up the courage and stepped through the doorway, her greeting forced. "Morning."

He, of course, made no reply, but simply continued to gaze in her direction.

Janine wondered if he ever slept. The bags under his eyes were huge. The wrinkles in his forehead were deep. His skin resembled an elephant's hide. He had a long, scraggy beard and bushy eyebrows, and he desperately reminded her of someone.

The man was dressed entirely in black, from what she could see: fedora, shirt, jacket, trousers, socks, as well as a pair of the most expensive shoes she had ever laid eyes on. In fact, despite his appearance, Janine would say that none of his clothes were cheap. They all appeared to have been cut from the finest cloth. She simply couldn't understand why anyone chose to make such a fashion statement. But that was actors for you – an eccentric bunch if there was one.

"My order is on the counter," were his only words.

He continued to glance around the shop as though he was bored, occasionally lifting an item from the shelves, clicking his tongue if it didn't meet with his approval. He ran his finger along the ledges, rolling his eyes.

The cheeky bastard was checking for dust.

She started to pick at her fingernails, wishing he'd go to hell. Ignoring his glare, she searched underneath the counter for a pair of scissors. It was time she trimmed them. A complete makeover with a wild night out on the town was what she really needed. Having found them, she walked across the shop behind the counter, dragging a bin with her.

She was about to make the first cut when the creep stood stock-still and stared at her. It was perhaps the most disturbing expression she had ever seen. The depth of his eyes was limitless.

Janine suddenly thought of a saying her grandmother often used, about a person having an "evil eye". She believed such a person could inflict disease or death simply by a glance.

Her fear increased, and her stomach contracted. She suspected it had nothing to do with her period. She'd always known that the man was strange, but he'd never frightened her to that degree. Janine even wondered if the heating in the shop had stopped working, as a chill crept up her spine.

"What on earth are you doing, girl?" He dragged the sentence out as if his life depended on it.

Janine lowered her head, noticed she was at the point of cutting the nail on her forefinger. The scissors were open, at the ready. For a reason she couldn't explain, she felt ashamed. Perhaps it was the tone in the creep's voice: the demeaning manner in which he'd addressed her. Another stomach spasm resulted in her mood flipping as quickly as his. "What's it to you?"

He lifted his head to the point where he must have struggled to peer down his nose, but he persisted. "Young lady, how you pass your time is of no consequence to me, but there is a certain etiquette one should follow."

"What the hell are you talking about?"

And with that, she cut the nail. A quick snip, and it fell into the bin.

"Oh my good God," he exclaimed, gripping his walking stick a little tighter. "She's done it," he said, as if he wasn't actually talking to her.

Janine snipped another, wondering if they had started a game, clearly delighted at having unsettled *him* for a change.

"Stop it at once, you stupid girl," barked the creep. "Don't you realise what you're doing?"

"I'm cutting my nails for Christ's sake–"

"Never on a Friday!"

Janine stopped mid-cut. He had managed it again. His expression and the tone of his voice had made her feel inadequate.

"What are you talking about?" asked Janine, a little more placidly.

"Don't you know anything about fingernails, young lady?"

"Not as much as you, evidently," she replied, wishing she hadn't.

"White specs on the nails of the left hand, signify gifts on the thumb; friends on the first finger; foes on the second; lovers on the third, and a journey to be taken on the fourth."

He reached out and placed her left hand in his. His touch was so cold, Janine wanted to retract, but didn't for fear of sending him over the edge.

He stared intently. "Second and fourth, foes and a journey. To have yellow speckles is a great sign of death." Glancing up, he held her gaze. "You must never cut the nails of a child under a year old. The mother should bite them off, or the child will grow up to be a thief..." He stroked her left hand with his right, his gaze distant as he rambled. Janine felt repulsed by his attention, but had neither the power nor the nerve to withdraw.

"Cut them on Monday, you cut them for health. Cut them on Tuesday, you cut them for wealth. Cut them on Wednesday, you cut them for news; on Thursday, a new pair of shoes. Cut them on a Friday..." – his eyes met hers again, and he lowered his voice yet further, speaking even slower – "...you cut them for sorrow. Cut them on a Saturday, you see your true love tomorrow."

The creep then whispered, which she found even more disconcerting. "Cut them on a Sunday, the devil will be with you all of the week."

Janine flinched. The man was seriously fucked in the head. What the hell was he talking about, cutting your nails on different days of the week? She wished the manager, Mr Cuthbertson, were here. But he was even more of a creep. He would revel in what was happening. She tried to think of a way to persuade the eccentric thespian to leave. He had suddenly grown very quiet, but he was still staring at her, still holding her hand, and still stroking it, for God's sake. She pulled away quickly, the draft whizzing past the list he'd left on the counter, blowing it to the edge.

He continued to stare at Janine for what she thought was a long time. He didn't appear to be gazing *at* her, more *inside* her. She felt her breath quicken. Her heart pounded against the inside of her chest. Her muscles weakened, and she became aware of how full her bladder was. When he finally spoke to her, the tone of his voice was soft and menacing.

"You smell unwell, Janine."

Eventually, she found the nerve to speak, but the voice didn't sound like hers. "How do you know my name?"

He didn't answer.

Her entire body felt as if it had been enveloped in ice. Her skin started to itch, and her vision had dark shadows around the edges. What did he mean, she smelled unwell? Surely it wasn't because it was that time of the month? She'd taken every precaution. Always had.

"Fear, Janine," he said, as if he'd seen inside her head. "I can smell fear. Are you frightened of me?"

She saw his lips part, but it wasn't a smile. "No," she managed to lie.

He let go of her hand. Smirking, he turned to leave the shop. "If you say so."

Chapter Eight

Gardener and Reilly met outside the mortuary.

For a Sunday morning in late March, the weather was acceptable: blue sky with a little cloud, the sun low, the breeze taking away any warmth.

Reilly glanced at his partner. "Like the new image!"

Gardener smiled. After a shower, he'd changed into a new pair of designer jeans and Ben Sherman shirt, finished off with a pale grey suit jacket. It was the fashion these days, Chris had assured him. He'd wanted his dad to change his image, bring himself more up to date. Gardener had readily agreed, feeling that the time was right.

"Not really my idea, you can blame Chris for that one."

"A young man with taste."

"Maybe he can start on you next." The pair of them laughed. Gardener replaced his hat. It was time to work.

"So, what are we dealing with, boss? Why hang a bloke after you've killed him?"

"Maybe he's trying to prove a point."

"What point? The man was already dead."

"He's trying to tell us something, Sean. There's a reason to what he's doing, as far as he's concerned anyway. He's drained the blood for a reason. He very obviously killed the man for a reason. We just have to find out what it is."

Reilly shook his head. "I've been thinking about what he might have done leading up to that. Did he leave him alive, and let him watch his life drain away? But once he'd done him in, he packed him up, moved him, hung him in front of an audience, and then calmly walked out of the place dressed as the man he'd killed. Why? It was a hell of a risk."

"Impact, Sean. Everything he's doing is meant to shock. The first is for the audience. They have no idea anything has happened. Consequently, they think they're watching an execution, which, to all intent and purpose, is part of the show. The second is for us. We have a corpse with no blood. The next is for anyone who sees him walk out. And the final shock is ours again, we get the blood back."

"A control freak?" asked Reilly. "Is he doing it all because he can? It's a great way to cover your tracks, so it is."

"That's all part of it, isn't it?" said Gardener. "He can do anything he wants if we don't know who he is. If he's so good at disguising himself, how the hell are we going to stop him?"

"The same way we usually do. We wait for him to make a mistake."

The pair of them entered the building, walking down the corridor leading to Fitz's workroom, the resonant sound of their heels bouncing off the walls. Gardener nodded to the receptionist as they passed. "You know, I can't believe that someone could be so good with make-up that he could fool everyone around him."

"Wouldn't take much if you didn't really know who he was supposed to be," replied Reilly.

"My dad did."

"What do you mean?"

Gardener turned to face his partner. "My dad went to see Leonard White at the Grand Theatre yesterday afternoon. He spent an hour with him."

"And he didn't notice anything?"

"I haven't spoken to him yet. I've only had an hour at home, and that was before I came here. It doesn't look to me like he's had any sleep. I thought maybe we could both talk to him later."

"Has he not said *anything*?"

"No. The only time we spoke was when I picked him up from the theatre. He was really quiet, so I asked him what was wrong, and he said he didn't know. He told me that Leonard wasn't himself, he was very subdued."

"Did your dad ask him what was wrong?"

"He did, but he said his friend wasn't very talkative, which was unusual in itself. But he also said that Leonard seemed worried about his wife... and how she was going to take the news."

"What news?" Reilly asked.

"That's just it, he didn't say, even though my dad tried to get it out of him. He said he seemed depressed. My dad had the feeling something awful had happened, and his friend couldn't bring himself to discuss it."

"Still, it doesn't really matter now, does it? We already know that your dad *wasn't* talking to his lifelong friend," Reilly said.

"Frightening thought, that one."

Both men turned and continued toward the steel silver door at the end of the corridor. Reilly opened it, allowing Gardener to walk in first. Theatre No.1 was a narrow building, long and low with strip lighting, accommodating four steel gurneys. Only one was occupied. Fitz stood behind it, facing Gardener, talking to DCI Alan Briggs. The pathologist wore gloves and a green surgical gown. His mask had been lowered. A microphone hung above his head.

The smell of formaldehyde was overpowering. Gardener had never become accustomed to it.

"Morning," said Fitz. "You're just in time."

Before Gardener had a chance to reply, four wall-mounted speakers powered out the opening bars of Puccini's *Tosca*, which was quite possibly the only opera that Gardener knew. After the loud opening, the volume dropped to a more acceptable level. "For what?" he asked.

"The next piece of the puzzle," said Briggs, nodding to Fitz.

"I'd like you to take a look at this."

Fitz had obviously been at work some time – the bottom half of Leonard White's body was already naked. The pathologist pointed to the bruising on the inside of the dead man's left thigh. "The killer has pumped the blood out through the femoral artery. While he shows a small amount of medical knowledge, he's not as good as he'd like us to believe. If you look here..." – Fitz pointed – "...there's extensive bruising where he's probably jabbed away with the syringe until he's found the artery."

"Looks like he's had a game of darts," added Reilly.

"The blood in the pint glasses. Was it Leonard White's?" asked Gardener.

"I've taken samples for analysis. I think it's safe to assume it was." Fitz paused before continuing. "I can't see where all this is leading. He's drained the man's blood, and then given it back to us. There are no broken bones. If you look at the hands, all the fingernails are intact, which suggests no sign of torture. There seems to be a sense of purpose to what he's done, but it's not obvious."

"A ritual?" asked Reilly.

"That's more your territory, Sean," said Briggs. "You ever come across anything like this?"

"No."

"I don't think it's a ritual," added Gardener. "If he'd kept the blood, maybe."

"Was the blood drained while he was still alive?" asked Briggs. "I saw a film like that once."

"It's possible," said Fitz. "I know the film you're thinking of, *The Abominable Doctor Phibes* with Vincent Price."

"Sounds about right," said Briggs. "But that was just a film. Is it possible to do that in real life?"

"Nothing surprises me with the criminal mind," replied the pathologist. "You can do anything if you're so determined."

"Interesting comment," said Gardener to Briggs. "If the killer is a master of disguise, maybe the film world is somewhere we should start looking for clues."

Briggs was about to speak when Fitz interrupted. "There's something on his chest," he said, with a sense of urgency.

Fitz had removed Leonard White's evening jacket, revealing a starched white shirt. Allowing time for photographs, he then quickly took away the aged actor's final item of clothing. He lowered the microphone ready for his report.

"We have a message on his chest," said Fitz, examining more closely. "It hasn't been written on top of the skin, but burned into it, and very possibly while he was still alive if the blisters were anything to go by."

Gardener leaned forward, reading:

> *Man cannot hide from his sin*
> *As the past will always reveal*
> *One has paid while others remain*
> *But be warned, a deal is a deal.*

Chapter Nine

Briggs finally broke the silence.

"I can't work out whether he's a psychopath or a genius. If you're nuts, you don't leave puzzles that have been very cleverly put together with an obvious meaning."

"The puzzles are inconsistent," said Gardener, stepping back from White's corpse. "The verse on the body is something he's made up. The writing on the wall in the dressing room read more like a quote to me."

"From anything you recognise?" asked Briggs.

"No," replied Gardener. "But let's be honest, it could be anything."

"What's he trying to tell us?" Briggs asked.

"The fact that he's harboured a grudge for a long time?"

"Maybe," said Briggs. "And he'll make us work to prove his point. The key to the investigation hinges on the clues he's offering."

Each man stepped outside the room, leaving the pathologist to finish his job. The quicker he did that, the quicker they would have their report.

"You see, that's where he shows his intelligence," said Reilly. "That verse on the old guy's chest was something he created. He knows what he's doing, and it's been well planned. He knew who he wanted and where to find him. What he's doing now is making us play his game. It's cat and mouse. Are we clever enough to catch him?"

"If he killed Leonard White the day before," said Gardener, "he must have known about the tour and where he was staying. So, *we* need to find out where he was staying. After he'd killed him, he went to a lot of trouble to impersonate him and make a public spectacle of the whole thing, before quietly and confidently walking out of the theatre."

"How did he get him into the place and do what he did without being noticed?" asked Reilly.

"I think it's an inside job," said Briggs. "Let's face it, he managed to blend in, and he must have known his way around the theatre, particularly that one."

"Paul Price seems to think not," replied Gardener.

"Doesn't matter what he thinks," said Briggs. "He doesn't want it to be an inside job because it looks bad on him and his theatre. What's your opinion on Price? Is he capable of murder?"

"Anyone's capable of murder," replied Gardener. "I think he's hiding something. The only thing he was bothered about was upsetting the smooth running of the place. Never mind that some bloke's just been killed on his stage in full view of everyone. But my gut instinct tells me he's not involved."

"All the same, we'll have him investigated," said Briggs. "And the rest of them that run it. If word gets round, no one'll work there."

"I'm not sure about that. I don't think anyone is trying to bring the theatre into disrepute," said Gardener. "I think it's personal. Leonard White, and others according to the verse on his chest, has upset someone. That someone is out for revenge. Here's one to think about. Leonard White was in his seventies. The others probably will be too, so how old is the guy we're looking for? I can't imagine someone that old being able to do everything he's done single-handed."

"Well, from what we've seen, boss, he was able to blend in and get others to help him without them knowing. Even if he is as old as them, the real problem is still identifying him. If he's a make-up specialist, where the hell do we start? For all we know, he could have crept back into the theatre last night and watched us. We might have even interviewed him."

"We'll have to go through White's past with a fine-tooth comb, and that won't be easy," said Briggs. "He's been around a long time, spent a lot of his life in different parts of the country. His wife will be able to help us there. She rang me just before I went in to see Fitz to say she was at The Queen's Hotel."

"Sean and I are going to talk to my dad," said Gardener. "He and White were friends, have been for quite a number of years. He's also a big film buff, never away from the cinema. Maybe he'll remember something that will help."

"That's interesting," replied Briggs. "If that quote on the dressing room wall is from a film, your dad might recognise it."

"Bit of a long shot there, sir," said Reilly.

"I don't doubt it, but every now and again the long shot pays off."

"We'll certainly give it a go. But it's been a hell of a shock to him. I don't want to put him under too much pressure."

"Okay. Well, if you need any help, if you're uncomfortable, you only have to ask."

"Thanks."

"Right," said Briggs. "You go and speak to your dad and then get to The Queen's to see Val White. I'll get one of the lads to organise the incident room, and the rest of them on the statements."

Chapter Ten

Gardener had made two coffees and one herbal tea while Reilly sat with Malcolm at the kitchen table. The room was long and wide, and had fully fitted Scandinavian pine units running its entire length with concealed strip lighting. The walls and the floor were tiled to match the units.

For Gardener, the kitchen was a room with pleasant reminders of Sarah. Everywhere he glanced he saw something on which he could reflect: several small clay-figure animals she had made herself; an oil painting of her parents' cottage – her first and last attempt; a wall clock in the shape of a tulip, reminding him of their romantic weekend in Amsterdam. He placed the coffees on the table, sitting opposite his father.

"Look, Dad, I appreciate there's never a good time, and I know it's been a terrible shock, but we have to talk to you about Leonard White."

The expression on Malcolm's face softened. "Of course. I'm sorry about yesterday, Son."

"You don't have to apologise. What happened at the theatre was pretty horrific by anyone's standards. If it wasn't for the fact that we have an investigation to run, I'd respect your privacy to grieve a little longer."

"Thank you. You can ask me anything you want, but I don't know how much use I'll be."

"You'd be surprised how many people say that, Malcolm," said Reilly.

"How well did you know him, Dad?"

"Perhaps not as well as you might think. We didn't meet properly until the mid-Seventies. Pretty much after his days at Hammer Studios."

"And you'd never met before then?"

"No. I'd seen his films. You know me, Stewart, I've always loved films. Deep down, I'd have given anything to be an actor."

Gardener didn't need reminding of his dad's love of the cinema. He had managed to take Chris once a week for as long as he could remember. "So, when and why did your paths cross?" he asked.

Malcolm pursed his lips. "I think it would be late '76. He formed part of the local watch committee."

"What's a watch committee, Malcolm?" asked Reilly.

"Every town has one, or used to, anyway. When you make a film, after its final edit, you send it to the British Board of Film Classification. They issue a certificate. Once it's distributed, the local watch committee for the area then vets the film. They have the power to make further cuts, and even issue another certificate. Well, that's what we did, watched the films and either approved or disapproved."

"How many made up the committee?" asked Gardener.

"Four."

"Can you remember the other two?"

Malcolm thought long and hard. "Sorry, Stewart, it's a long time ago."

"I realise that, Dad, but you'll have to try to remember. It's a possible link. A long shot, maybe, but we have to investigate everything."

Malcolm took another sip of coffee. "I'm pretty sure one of them died a few years ago, in a car crash. I will try, Stewart, it's just, with everything that's happened..."

"It's okay, Dad, take your time." Gardener changed topics. "What about his wife, did you ever meet her?"

"Occasionally, social functions, town hall duty, that sort of thing. Val, I think her name was."

"How did she strike you?"

"Full of her own importance, didn't seem to care about anyone but herself. I always got the impression that she thought she was above us all. To be honest, I don't think she had two farthings to rub together when she met Leonard. I never thought it would work. They were like chalk and cheese. I think she married him for his money, I certainly can't think of another reason. She always made me feel uncomfortable."

"But you wouldn't take her for a murderer?" asked Reilly.

"No... well... you never really know, do you? I can't say I liked her, but I wouldn't speak ill."

Gardener thought his father had handled the question well. "Where did they live?"

"Horsforth. Big house, it had a name but I can't remember it, something Manor, I'm not sure what."

"Can you think of anything that happened during those years? Anything scandalous, a serious incident that someone might want to brush under the carpet?" asked Gardener.

"Stewart, Leonard White was as straight as a die. He worked for Hammer Studios for years, alongside all the big names like Peter Cushing and Christopher Lee. He told me himself that he'd wanted to leave Hammer for a long time. He'd been concerned about their policies. They went through a period of making vampire films, full of nudity and lesbianism. He wanted out." Malcolm took a mouthful of coffee and asked, "Why the question about a scandal?"

"What we've learned so far points to revenge. Leonard White appears to have been killed because of something that happened in his past. Now that could be anything at any time, it's a big playing field out there. I just thought, if you knew something, however insignificant you might think it is, it could help."

"What about his wife, any scandal involving her?" Reilly asked.

"I'm sorry, I don't know her well enough."

Gardener wondered how his father was really coping with the kind of pressure they were putting him under. He felt guilty. He didn't like what they were doing, but they had a job to do. At least they were conducting the interview in the comfort of their own home and not the station, with tape recorders.

"The thing is, Malcolm, someone's playing games with us," said Reilly.

"Why? What's he doing?"

"We shouldn't be telling you this, Dad, but when we managed to get into Leonard's dressing room the other night, there was a message on the wall. I think it's a quote, but I don't know where from."

"What did it say?" asked Malcolm.

Reilly took out his notebook. "'For long weary months I have awaited this hour'."

"Certainly sounds like a quote," said Malcolm.

"Do you recognise it?" pressed Gardener.

"No. Could be anything."

"We were also left a verse, a puzzle perhaps. He's taunting us, leading us to believe there'll be more." Gardener paused. "Let's go back to something you said yesterday afternoon. After I picked you up from the theatre, you were pretty quiet. You said that Leonard White wasn't himself. He seemed worried about what his wife was going to think. Did he elaborate? What was it that would concern his wife?"

Gardener studied the once solid features of his father he had come to depend on. He was seventy-five years old, but his normal healthy complexion carried a haunted, defeated expression. The lines in his face were deeper, the eyes darker, lifeless. "I don't know, son."

"Can you remember the exact words he used?"

"Not the exact words, no. He kept saying Val wasn't going to like it. She wouldn't forgive him. I had no idea what he was talking about, and he wouldn't tell me. He was obviously in some sort of trouble, but I don't know why. Maybe it was something he couldn't forgive himself for. Therefore, *she* wouldn't forgive him."

"And you didn't pick up on anything in the conversation?" asked Reilly.

"No," replied Malcolm. "I mean, at his age, I didn't think it was another woman. I couldn't imagine him having money problems, so I couldn't think what else it could be."

"You don't think someone was blackmailing him?"

"It's possible, but if they were, he wasn't letting on. Maybe that was it," said Malcolm.

"But he never gave you an inkling? Not one bit of evidence about how much trouble he was in?"

"No, nothing. He didn't really say very much. As I told you, he was quiet, subdued, not himself." Malcolm waved his finger in the air. "I'll tell you what *was* strange. When I got there, Leonard ordered tea for us both. When it arrived, he never touched his, just left it on the tray. He never touched a drop."

"What's so unusual about that?" asked Reilly.

"He was legendary for halting productions just so as he could have his cup of tea. It was like a ritual."

Gardener and Reilly stared at each other.

"Is there something you're not telling me?"

Gardener sighed. "Did you ever consider, at any point, that you were talking to someone else other than your friend?"

Malcolm lowered his cup to the table. "What are you trying to say?"

"Are you *certain* you were talking to Leonard White?"

"Of course I was. Who else could it have been?"

"That's what we'd like to know."

Malcolm's grave expression disturbed Gardener. "Are you trying to tell me that someone was impersonating Leonard White and I couldn't tell?"

Gardener took his time answering, unsure how his father would take the news. "It looks that way, Dad."

"Surely to God no one could be that good, Son."

"That's what we thought. But we've had it confirmed that Leonard White had been dead somewhere in the region of twelve to twenty-four hours when he hit that stage. I'm sorry, Dad, really I am."

Malcolm left the table without saying anything else.

Chapter Eleven

The room at The Queen's was large and airy, well-lit with adequate heating. The beige carpet matched the drapes and the bed linen. The antique furniture added an air of elegance.

With her bleached blond hair tied up, too much face paint, and an excess of fine jewellery – none of which complimented her leopard skin top – Val White was exactly what Gardener had been led to believe: common, and unsuited to the luxury that life, or more to the point her late husband, had provided for her. His only complimentary thought was that she carried her age well.

As soon as Gardener and Reilly displayed warrant cards, she had called for room service. When the refreshments arrived, she told them to help themselves – and do the honour of pouring her a cup of tea – while she continued to smoke a cigarette through an eight-inch filter-tipped holder. She never once asked them anything about her late husband.

Gardener was surprised. The woman must have been as hard as granite. His heart went out to the aged actor. It was sad for someone to have achieved his level of status, for it all to go unrecognised by the one person he'd chosen to share his life with. She didn't, and probably hadn't, reciprocated the emotion when he'd been alive. Eager to press on and satisfy his curiosity, Gardener opened the conversation.

"Would you like to tell us about your late husband please, Mrs White?"

"Not much to tell really, cock."

"I doubt that. He was a fine actor, travelled extensively, and led such a full life, probably seen more than most people could even dream about. There must be something to say."

"I'll not argue with that summary," she replied. If her expression was anything to go by, she must have left her enthusiasm back home in the Lake District. Her answers were blunt, emotionless. "But you're talking from a personal point of view," she continued. "I shared his home. Your view is from the public eye. As you say, a fine actor, well liked on the silver screen. Off screen, not the husband I'd hoped for."

Gardener thought back to what his father had said. Val White certainly had a talent for making people feel uncomfortable. Despite the heating, there was a distinct chill in the atmosphere.

"If that was the case, why stay together?" asked Reilly.

"I had my reasons."

"Money being one of them, I shouldn't wonder," he said, cutting to the chase.

Val stared at him. His comment had hit a nerve. "Maybe." She maintained her self-control. "You're entitled to your opinion, cock, it's a free country. Not everyone's relationship runs to what's expected."

Gardener sensed a real difference of opinion building, not to mention an instant dislike between Val White and his partner Sean Reilly. That was nothing new; most people didn't like his abrupt manner. He had an unerring ability to see through people. He had an excellent technique for ruffling feathers and obtaining the information he wanted when interviewing.

"So, there is something you can tell us," continued Gardener. "Why wasn't he the husband you wanted?"

"My home life was what I made it. He was never there. When he was, he might as well not have been. We hardly ever talked, rarely went out as a couple, unless it were a social function of some standing. Quite frankly I played second fiddle to everything, especially his life on screen. The film industry was his mistress."

I wonder why, thought Gardener.

"Let's start at the beginning," said Gardener, eager to maintain a better balance. "Tell me how you met, where you went from there. I need to build up a picture. Someone didn't just kill him, they went to great lengths to make a public spectacle out of an extremely gruesome murder, which suggests an enemy, and a very personal one at that."

"Doesn't surprise me."

"Why?" Gardener asked.

"He was pompous. I've known people stop him in the street for an autograph, and he'd turn 'em down flat. Nothing and no one ever seemed good enough for him."

That wasn't the impression his father had given Gardener, but then again, he wasn't married to the man.

You had to be much closer than a friend to claim you really knew someone.

"It would take more than a disgruntled autograph hunter to do what was done to your husband."

Val White finished her tea and poured another without offering Gardener or Reilly. If she had been a party to all the gruesome details, she was not letting on. "I dare say. He was born in Blackpool in 1940. He had three sisters and one brother. They're all dead. He left school at sixteen and joined the RAF. After leaving the services, he landed a job in the theatre. A talent scout spotted him in 1959, and he went down to work London's West End. He was there until 1964, then he landed a small part in a film."

"All sounds very condensed."

"It's short and sweet because I don't know a great deal about his life before we met."

"Where and when did you two meet?"

"I think it were the late Sixties, because by then he'd settled into films at Hammer Studios. But he'd taken a part in a play back in the West End. The whole thing went on tour and we met here, in Leeds. I went to see the play with a friend. She had backstage passes, and Leonard and I met at the party thrown afterwards. It was the last night, you see."

"What first attracted you to him?"

"He was very confident, knew what he wanted out of life, outspoken... and he had money." As Val White had made her last comment, she smiled at Reilly. "Six months later we were married and bought our first home."

"Where?"

"Horsforth, on the A65 going out towards Rawdon. You can't miss it, big grey house set back from the road, black and gold wrought iron gates guard the arched entrance, grounds full of poplar trees."

"My father mentioned that, but he couldn't remember the name. Can you remember who you bought it from?"

"Not really, although the name Ashington rings a bell. I think that's what it was called, Ashington Manor."

"It's not that important. I suppose I'm clutching at straws, trying to find a link where there isn't one. What happened next?"

"We stayed up here in the house for a couple of years, but then the film bug got him again. He went back to Hammer sometime around 1966 to work with Christopher Lee in one of his Dracula films. And he stayed there for the next ten years. I hardly saw owt of him."

"Any family?"

Val White took a sip of tea and lit a fresh cigarette. "No." Her expression softened. "I would've liked a couple of kids."

"Judging by the circumstances in which he died, he must have made an enemy for himself. You said it didn't surprise you. Can you elaborate?"

"I'm not sure I can, cock. I've no idea who he saw and what he was up to in the ten years he was at Hammer. I'm basing my comments on his attitude."

"Did your husband ever conduct any private business deals, either in or out of the film world?"

Val White was obviously thinking about the question as she inhaled deeply on her cigarette and blew out smoke rings.

"None that I'm aware of."

"There's nothing in his past that you can think would generate such a callous act of revenge?" pressed Gardener.

"We've all got skeletons, Mr Gardener. Just because I can't think of anything doesn't mean they're not there."

There really was very little to go on. Gardener had a conflicting picture. According to his father, Leonard White was an icon, a straight man whom you could trust with your life. He felt the same way about his father. Whatever the old man had told him, Gardener had no reason to distrust. But then, had he really known Leonard White?

As for his wife, she couldn't abide to be in the same room. Why was that? What was she hiding? What had Leonard White done that had so turned her against him? He needed to find the root of the problem. "So, what happened after Hammer?"

"He sort of retired. We had enough money for him not to work again."

"But he did work again, correct?"

"Oh, aye. He couldn't help himself. He formed part of a local watch committee here in Leeds."

"My father was on the same watch committee."

"Really? What's his name?"

"Malcolm Gardener."

"My God! Are you Stewart? You always were a good looker."

Gardener blushed, but the name drop apparently proved effective. Maybe now she was going to open up, say what was really on her mind.

"What a small world. Well, I'm pleased to see you've made something of yourself."

Eager to continue, Gardener repeated his point. "The watch committee, what can you tell me about it?"

"Not a lot." Her attitude had softened. "I was never that involved."

"Did you meet the other members?"

"I did. There was your dad, and a bloke called Fletcher. I think he was a writer. No idea where he is now. And then there were Jack Harper; don't know what he did. A historian, something like that. I don't know where Fletcher is, but Jack Harper was killed in a car crash a few years back."

"Yes, my dad mentioned that, he just couldn't remember their names."

"Oh well, there you are, then. Something's come out of this morning."

"There was nothing involving the other members of the committee that may have caused ill feelings towards your husband? No scandals? No major disagreements?"

"None I can think of, but I'm sure if there were, your dad would remember."

Gardener was beginning to feel frustrated. Despite the fact that Val White hadn't liked her husband, she had still not provided any real evidence, or a reason to kill him. "What about the years after the watch committee?"

"We sold the house in about 1979 and moved to the Lake District, where I live now. Leonard continued working in theatre until he officially retired."

"Who did you sell the house to? Can you remember?"

"I certainly can. It was one of his friends in the film business. A director. Corndell, his name was."

"Do you know if he still lives there?"

"No, he doesn't. We had a letter from his wife, apparently he died four months after buying the house."

"So *she* might still live there?"

"It's possible, she'd be getting on a bit now, though."

Gardener glanced at Reilly. "It's worth a visit." Then to Val he said, "I take it then that your husband came out of retirement again."

"A couple of years back, playing small parts in small theatres. Earlier this year he was persuaded to go on a national tour to talk about his life in films."

"Who persuaded him?"

"His agents, a company in Manchester called PMA."

"How did he feel about that?" asked Gardener.

"He loved it."

"So, it wasn't something he was forced into doing because he needed the money?"

"You must be kidding, cock. Leonard was worth a fortune. Money were the last thing on his mind. He did it because he loved it."

"Where was he staying for the Leeds gig?"

"Same place he always stayed while he was here, The Manor House in Skipton. Big luxurious place on the road going out to Keighley."

"Same place? Was he a man of routine?"

"I wouldn't say so. He liked to do certain things in certain ways."

"Such as?"

"Well, it was more when he went on stage, really. He was very superstitious. Most thespians are. He would never have live flowers on a stage, something to do with flowers having a short life, and it would reflect on the performance. He didn't like whistling on stage. That was to do with the early days of theatre, when dock workers were often scenery change men and whistle calls went wrong. But other than that, no."

"So, he never had a cup of tea at the same time every day, or did anything else at a certain time in a certain way because that's the way it should be done?"

Val White thought about the question. "Not that I can recall."

"When my father came to see him last week, he said that Leonard wasn't himself. He seemed worried about something, and that you wouldn't understand. Any ideas what that might be?"

"Like I said, we didn't get on very well, we didn't talk much. If he did have a problem, he never told me about it."

"You obviously knew him pretty well, you'd been married a long time. Despite not getting on, any reason to think he'd been acting strange lately?"

"No."

She'd answered a little too fast for Gardener's liking.

"Who checked his post while he was on tour?" he asked.

"Well, I did, of course."

"Nothing unusual there? No threatening letters, or phone calls?"

"No. His post was mainly fans wanting signed photos, asking the usual questions. Would he ever go back into films? Was his stage show coming to their area? We had the odd bill, but there were nothing that carried any warnings about him being killed, or blackmailed, or anything else."

Reilly gave her time to sip her tea and take a drag on the cigarette before his next question. "Where were you last Thursday night, Mrs White?"

"Come again?" Judging by her expression, Gardener suspected she was puzzled by the question, as if Reilly had no right to ask her about her private life.

"It's a simple enough question," retorted Reilly. "Where were you on the night your husband was murdered?"

"Back home in Kendal."

"By yourself?"

"No."

"Who were you with?" Reilly persisted.

"I don't think that's any of your business."

"We would like to establish your whereabouts," said Gardener. "Do you have an alibi?"

"You think I murdered him?"

"No, we don't think that," replied Gardener. "But unless we can eliminate you from the list of suspects..."

"Why the hell would I murder him?" demanded Val White.

"He *was* worth a fortune," said Reilly.

"And it were all mine, alive or dead." Val White stubbed out one cigarette and then immediately lit another.

"But we don't know that, do we? For all we know, you arranged to have him murdered because he wasn't prepared to leave you all his money. You made it plain that you didn't get on."

Gardener noticed her mood switch very quickly. "That's as maybe, but I'm not a murderer. I was at home in Kendal, all night."

"All night?" asked Gardener.

"Yes."

"But not alone?" questioned Reilly.

"No. I was with a man called Anthony Thompson, if you must know. He's been my lover for at least ten years." Val White smiled. "Well, seeing as you want to know everything, your perfect Mr White wasn't very good in that department."

Chapter Twelve

It was late. Gardener was tired and hungry and keen to start the incident room meeting.

The whole team was there, not to mention a number of local PCs for support. They'd all pulled together and done an excellent job preparing the incident room. The bulletin board was littered with crime scene photographs. A table in front of the board contained items of evidence in clear sealed bags. Briggs opened the meeting.

"Right, let's have some order. I know it's been a long day and we're all tired, but we have quite a few things to talk about. Stewart will take over, he'll tell you what little we know and what actions need addressing."

Gardener stood up. Dispensing with formalities, he went straight in. "Leonard White's death is a bit of a mystery. We think he was alive and well on Friday. He was not due on stage at the Grand Theatre until Saturday, but we suspect he was picked up early from his hotel and taken somewhere secluded, given a sedative, and his blood drained. The next time anyone saw the actor, he was dangling from a rope in front of his audience, despite already being dead. In his dressing room, we found eight glass jars of what looked like raw liver. Although Fitz is still waiting for the results, there's no reason to think it wasn't White's blood."

Gardener paused to take a sip of water. "Sean and I interviewed his wife Val this morning. She gave us almost nothing to go on. By all accounts, Leonard White was the conscientious type who went to work, did his job, came home, put his money in the bank, and enjoyed what he did without creating enemies... or so she says.

"She can't think of anyone who would want to kill him. She knows of nothing in his past to suggest otherwise. Checking his career will be a big job because he's travelled all over the UK, if not the world. We need to ferret out his friends, if he had any locally. Check his bank accounts, insurance policies, see if anyone stood to gain anything from his death aside from her. What Val White knows may be open to question because her husband spent so much time away from home.

"Include her in the search. I want to know where she goes, what she does, who she sees. Despite the fact that Sean and I don't like her, neither of us suspects she actually murdered him; or for that matter, *had* him murdered."

Thinking about the interview, Gardener was unhappy. He wasn't sure who or what to believe. The fact that she disliked her husband was obvious. Why was another matter. Whilst she was probably innocent – having said everything he had was hers, dead or alive – she was still a suspect, though he had no doubt her alibi would check out. She had given no indication of bad business deals, people crossed or enemies made, but something in the man's past must have triggered that attack.

Malcolm had painted a different picture, and he was quick to realise that it could affect his father and the remaining members of the watch committee, should that eventually prove to be the connection.

"Before we spoke to her this morning, I had a rough idea where the couple had lived when they were here but little in the way of details. Val White thinks the house was called Ashington Manor. Might have a different name now. It's out on the Horsforth Road towards Rawdon, big grey house set back from the road. Someone please check that out. Find out when White bought it, who from, and how it was paid for. And who lives there now."

Gardener updated the ANACAPA chart as he went along. The whiteboard was full of straight lines and arrows pointing all over the place; it resembled a map of the London Underground already.

"So, there we have it. Just because his wife doesn't know about any misdemeanours, or claims not to know, someone does. One thing we have picked up is that he formed part of a watch committee between 1976 and 1979, a group of people who vet films and decide on the certificate before they're shown locally. It's an area worth concentrating on. My father, Malcolm Gardener, was on that committee. The only other surviving member apart from him is someone called Harry Fletcher, at the time, a local writer. He shouldn't be too hard to find. Look close, dig deep. I can't help wondering if there was an incident connecting the watch committee."

"Has your dad said anything, Stewart?" asked Briggs.

"Nothing that helps us with the investigation. It's all been a bit of a shock."

"And he can't remember anything involving the watch committee?"

"No. He couldn't even remember the names of the other two. But, as I said, I don't think he's on top form."

"Okay, so let someone else take a statement from him when he's calmed down a little. One of our lovely WPCs, maybe? I'm sure he'd like that."

Gardener nodded and continued. "Val White gave us another lead. Her husband always stayed at a hotel called The Manor House in Skipton. Sean and I will be going there tomorrow. I'd be surprised if we didn't have a few leads to follow after that."

The SIO glanced around the room. "Does anyone have any questions?"

"You seem to have ruled Val White out," said Thornton. "She obviously has an alibi."

"Yes," said Gardener.

"And her lover will no doubt back it up," said Reilly.

There were a few nods and glances, but no one offered anything further on that score.

"Is there any particular reason for hanging the man after he was dead?" asked DC Sharp.

"None that I know," replied Gardener. "Other than to cause a stir or make an impact of some sort. I want someone to take the rope and find out everything you can. Is there anything special about it? What was it made from? What type of a knot is it?"

"Do you think there's any real relevance to the rope and the knot?" asked Bob Anderson, Thornton's partner.

"Could be," replied Gardener. "We can't rule out anything. I think we're going to have a lot of problems with this one. The killer's obviously very intelligent, and from the knowledge we've so far gathered, we think he's an expert in the art of disguise. He fooled my father, who had been a friend of Leonard White for a number of years. He fooled the theatre staff, because he somehow managed not only to get himself into the building, but also the corpse of the aged actor. So, it seems he's someone who knows the background, has very probably worked in theatre, perhaps even The Grand. Maybe he's worked with Leonard White himself."

Gardener turned to Steve Fenton, the Crime Scene Manager. "Steve, it says in your report you found traces of aluminium powder in the dressing room. Any idea what it is?"

Steve Fenton's physical features were similar to his superior officer's: short black hair, slim build. Gardener had long since become accustomed to Fenton's eyes, which differed in colour from day to day. At first, the contact lenses had confused him.

"Yeah, we found hairs on the table in front of the mirror. It was used in olden day theatre apparently, to whiten or grey the hair. From what I've found out, it's bloody hard to wash out, and if you got it on your face, it would darken the make-up and still wouldn't wash out."

"Another reason to support our man's theatre background," said Gardener. "If he's using material from the olden days, is he as old as Leonard White? If so, how could he manage to do all he's done by himself? Does he have an accomplice?"

Briggs stood up. "Anyone picked anything up from the witness statements?" There was a buzz of conversation, but the general answer was negative. It was far too early. "I issued a press statement before coming in here. I couldn't tell them anything, so I just appealed for witnesses to come forward. I suggest some of you carry on checking that. Speak to the HOLMES lads as well, see if any of their information has thrown up a lead worth following."

Gardener turned to Fenton. "Fingerprints?"

"None."

"He was probably wearing gloves," said Reilly.

"Either that, or because of his theatrical background, he's developed something to hide his prints," said Fenton.

Gardener continued. "I need a couple of you to check out any shops in the city that specifically sell theatre and stage make-up. You could broaden your search by using the internet. Whoever is doing this may not necessarily buy it locally, may not even live locally."

Gardener pointed to the board. "And then we have the puzzles." There were a number of photographs, many of them contained the same picture, but taken from different angles. The verses were also highlighted in large print. "The one found on the dressing room wall reads like a quote." He walked closer and read it out aloud. "'For long weary months I have awaited this hour'." He turned and addressed his officers. "Any ideas?"

"Judging by those words," said Thornton, "someone has a serious grudge."

"I didn't mean that so much, I was thinking more about the overall context. A needle in a haystack maybe, but we need someone to follow it up. Is it from a film, a play, a book, or has our intelligent psychopath made it up? Can you all honestly say you've never come across those words before?"

"I've already checked this out," said Colin Sharp.

Gardener glanced at the officer.

Sharp continued. "I believe it comes from the 1925 film version of *Phantom of the Opera*."

"Where did you find it?" asked Gardener.

"Usual place, the internet. But the reference I came across was from a book called, *Smirk, Sneer And Scream*."

"Who wrote the book?" asked Reilly.

"Someone called Mark Clark."

"Add him to the list of contacts," said Gardener, "we may need to speak to him."

"So, is it a random comment?" Reilly asked, "Or is it there for a reason?"

"I can't see it being random, stuff like this never is," said Gardener. He addressed Sharp, "was there anything else?"

"There was a lot more to the paragraph, so I'll have to study it, see what it's referring to and whether or not it sheds any light."

"So, that opens up more avenues," said Gardener. "As Sean said, is the comment a random one in so far as he's seen it in the film and it simply fitted with what he wanted to do, or does it really mean what he wants to say?"

"It strikes me as being the latter," said Sharp. "I'm liable to agree with what Frank says, this guy is holding a grudge and that film happened to have the right quote."

"Okay," replied Gardener, "so what does it say about our man?"

"He's intelligent," said Dave Rawson. "He's obviously well versed, knows his films, spent a lifetime in or around them, and he'll make us work for a result."

"Okay, so we need to keep digging with that one," said Gardener, "the second quote – or verse – would certainly suggest a grudge."

He turned back to the board and the verse. "This had been burned into Leonard White's chest while he was alive, judging by the blisters on the skin. Fitz suggested a caustic pencil was used, which would have been extremely painful. Sean and I are of the opinion that it's a taunt. Whilst we haven't unearthed any evidence of a disagreement between Leonard White and anyone connected to him so far, there obviously has been one.

"'*Man cannot hide from his sin, as the past will always reveal*'. It's obvious our aged actor has done something he shouldn't. I think you're right, Frank, someone definitely bears a grudge. And it's not just against Leonard White. According to the message, there are others. '*One has paid while others remain, but be warned, a deal is a deal*'."

Gardener allowed time for more questions, but his officers were tired, so he quickly brought things to a halt. He raised his hand to the board. "Actions for tomorrow. I want answers on the rope, and any shop in the city that stocks theatrical products, and any information. Colin can concentrate on the dressing room wall quote, the *Phantom* film, and Leonard White. I also want someone checking out Paul Price and his theatre. Again, there was nothing to suggest he was directly involved, but you never know. I want someone listening to the tapes we pulled from backstage. Something might come to light. And we also need the results of the ESLA.

"We need to pull out all the stops if we're going to prevent another death. So, we have a few things to be going on with, but by no means everything. Sean and I will be in Skipton tomorrow. Hopefully, we'll have something more to add."

Chapter Thirteen

The room resembled a dungeon. The walls were painted matt black, the ceiling grey. In each of the corners, running the length of the walls, were huge cobwebs artificially created by him, despite his loathing of the creatures that spun them.

His mind was instantly cast back to a particular morning. The big black spider was halfway down the wall when he discovered it. Judging by the direction in which it was heading, he suspected the only place it could have come from was behind the wardrobe. He'd felt tense, uncomfortable. His whole body had shivered, his breathing had grown heavier, and within seconds he was sweating.

Where had it come from? More to the point, where the hell was it going?

He and spiders didn't mix. The thought that the monster had been hiding behind his furniture generated absolute revulsion within him. He'd hated spiders for as long as he could remember: all too aware of commonly held beliefs about them being carriers of disease. But he knew other things about them as well – like the fact that it was unlucky to kill a spider. If you were sweeping and came across a web, you should not destroy it till the spider was safe, when you could sweep away the web; but if you killed the spider, it will surely bring poverty to your house. Thereby creating another problem.

To ensure the safety of the spider meant he had to leave it. So, it was still in the room. He couldn't sleep knowing it was permanently at large. If he did manage to drop off, it might creep out and watch him – run all over the place. Even across his face. Couldn't have that.

Then again, he knew there would always be a spider in the room if he grew ill. A long-standing cure for ague or fever was to imprison a spider in a nutshell and then wear it as an amulet. Question was, how would you imprison it in a nutshell if you didn't like them in the first place?

He shuddered again before continuing with his inspection. Bare boards lined the floor, treated and stained light green. But it was not dirty! The display was merely for effect. It was, in fact, spotless and smelled of lavender.

Lining each of the walls – either side of a collection of mannequins – were posters of his favourite film star Lon Chaney in a variety of different disguises. The Phantom. The Hunchback. The Ape Man, from the film *A Blind Bargain.* The Vampire, from *London After Midnight*, his own particular favourite, now a lost film, no copy in existence save his own. Littering his worktops and shelves were a whole selection of make-up effects.

Standing in the corner was a full-length mirror with a light attached to the top. He was, at present, admiring his finest creation from that favourite film. He was dressed in a black beaver hat and a black Inverness coat. His face had the pallor of death. His hair was long and straggly and came down to his shoulders. The eyes terrified even him. He had darkened his eyebrows and fixed a wire ring like a monocle, allowing a hollowed-eye expression. The teeth had taken him an age, but had been worth the effort. Both upper and lower sets were sharp and pointed, and were as real as he could make them. His grin was fixed and further emphasised by shading in the upper corners of his mouth.

He was a genius, of which there was no doubt. Perhaps not quite in the league of his idol. But then, who had been? In his opinion, however, it was more than good enough. It would allow him into places undetected. Carry out the most heinous of crimes without being caught. Grant him permission to continue his work to the fullest. Eyewitness reports would be considered inadmissible, and would therefore do him no harm. They would not give up his true identity. Only he knew that. And once he had completed his mission, without being caught, he would disappear into the night.

He was not a serial killer. He did not have an insatiable appetite to wipe out and destroy as many people as possible. The killing spree would not continue when he'd done what he needed to do. What he was doing could not be tied to religion, nor did he belong to any satanic cult. His plan was not to go down in history alongside the likes of Jack the Ripper or The Boston Strangler or Dennis Nilsen or Harold Shipman.

It wouldn't take long and the police wouldn't catch him. They had no idea now, after victim number one. And they would have no idea by the time they discovered the others.

Why?

Simple! They didn't know who he was. And they were not going to find out!

Nor would anyone else, even after the next victim, whose demise was going to be very different. Victim number two would eradicate any pattern, and perhaps lead them in the wrong direction.

And at the moment, that was all that mattered.

Chapter Fourteen

Skipton's Manor House Hotel was a two-storey grey stone building, sitting in acres of luscious green woodland, enhanced by dark wood, leaded windows, a traditional grey slate roof, and creeping ivy covering the exterior. Each window adorned an intricately hand-crafted window box containing a colourful array of plants. The gravel drive leading to the hotel encompassed a circular fountain and ornately carved bushes.

Gardener admired the view, and could only find one word to describe it: elegant. It was the sort of place he would expect an old country gentleman – or perhaps a retired actor – to have stayed at. The building spoke of money. Set against the background of a clear blue sky in a late March Monday morning, the view was picture postcard perfect.

Reilly left the car and stood beside him. "You're in a good mood, boss, for a Monday morning with the case from hell."

Gardener turned to his partner. "My Christmas present was delivered this morning. I was just leaving the house."

"The King and Queen seat?"

"Chris and Dad had the box ripped apart before I knew what day it was."

"Was it worth the money?"

"I'd say so. I've never seen anything like it." Gardener widened his arms to indicate the size. "It's really deep, and finished in black leather with big round buttons. It's the first new part for the bike." Gardener's eyes glazed. "And my dad had the foresight to have mine and Sarah's names stencilled into the sides. It's brilliant."

"Can't wait for a wee demo on this bike of yours," said Reilly, rubbing his hands together.

"You'll probably have to fight my dad for the first test drive."

"Shouldn't be a problem," said his partner. "By the time you've finished it, your dad will have his own set of wheels, so he will, with its own seat, and handles for you to push."

Gardener laughed. The Irishman was probably right.

"Anyway, let's get back to the case from hell."

The Manor House entrance hall was a mixture of marble and a highly polished wood veneer, with the fresh smell of pot-pourri, no doubt well hidden. The oil paintings were expensive, almost certainly originals. As was the receptionist.

They flashed their warrant cards. "Detective Inspector Stewart Gardener and Detective Sergeant Sean Reilly." Gardener tipped his hat. "We'd like to ask you a few questions if we may?"

"Oh my God, not another."

"Another?" asked Reilly.

"Yes, another!" His reply was terse. "I know you people have a job to do, but so have we. I have a hotel to run, and you keep swarming in and closing down rooms. Well, I'm sorry, but it's simply not good for business."

"Neither is murder," said Reilly.

Gardener studied the man. With his smooth complexion and neatly combed dark hair, he estimated an age in the late twenties. He was very slim and wore a pale blue suit with a shirt and tie to match. The man had exceptionally white teeth, manicured hands, and eyes to compliment his attire.

"Can you clarify that statement, Mr Sparrow?" asked Gardener.

Sparrow glanced down his nose at the name badge on his jacket, wishing it in hell, judging by his expression. He seemed dissatisfied with the familiarity it caused.

"Yes, Mr Gardener, I can and I will. We have already had a visit from the police regarding the unfortunate death of Mr White. He was by himself, and spent approximately two hours in the room. Alone." Sparrow spoke as if he severely resented the police and their business, whilst continually moving his hands and arms as if to express those feelings. "And they told us we were not allowed to rent the room out to anyone until the investigation had been closed. And furthermore, he covered the bloody door with Scenes of Crimes tape, so that everyone else staying here would know."

"Did he ask you for a current guest list?"

"No. Should he have done?"

Gardener glanced around. "Is there somewhere we can talk?"

"Well, I am rather busy at the moment."

"So are we, Mr Sparrow. And we are *real* police officers, and we would like a current guest list. I also want someone to take over the reception desk while you tell us everything you know. What he looked like, his name, where he went, where he said he was from..."

Sparrow's expression became grave. To his credit, he arranged for Gardener's requests to be carried out immediately. Two minutes later they were sitting in the hotel bar, which was equally as quaint but with an interior design slightly different to the rest of the building, wooden ceiling beams, red velvet curtains, and carpet. Classical music played low in the background.

"What was his name?" asked Gardener, seated comfortably in a leather Chesterfield chair.

"Inspector Burke."

Gardener glanced at Reilly, who simply shrugged.

"What's wrong?" asked Sparrow.

"Can you give us a description?"

"He was tall, well built. Stocky, but not fat. His hair was grey, combed back, and he had long sideburns. He had quite big ears, and the most appallingly wrinkled skin. The man had clearly never seen a tub of moisturizer. He was dressed in a suit that was almost as wrinkled as his face, probably came from an Oxfam shop. There's enough of them in the town."

Sparrow sighed more than necessary, glanced at his manicured hands frequently before making another comment. "His nails were disgusting – bitten to the quick. To be perfectly honest, he reminded me of a 1930s film star."

How interesting, thought Gardener, that Sparrow's comment should be linked to the film world. Gardener was beginning to feel the killer had not only left them a bunch of puzzles and clues to follow, but he was clever enough to stay a step ahead of them.

"We will need to see the room," said Gardener. "But for now, let's concentrate on Leonard White. Who picked him up last Friday?"

"Well now, he *was* something. Very smart chauffeur, peaked cap, blond hair, good looking, slim, *he* should have been in films."

"Did he say where he was from?"

"I think the company was called Executive Cars."

"Did he give you a card?"

"No. Now there's the strange thing, you see. It wasn't Leonard's usual choice of limousine. Different company altogether."

Gardener noticed the first name terms, and the fact that Sparrow's attitude had changed somewhat. "Who *were* the usual company?"

"Star Limousines in Leeds."

"Did he offer an explanation for the change of companies?"

"He most certainly did, Mr Gardener," said Sparrow. "After I phoned his room, Leonard came down. He was quite confused at being picked up a day early. With no engagement on the Thursday night, all he wanted to do on Friday was relax in the hotel and go for short walks in the countryside. The driver told him that his wife had had a serious accident and the car had been laid on to take him all the way back to a hospital in the Lake District. Despite the driver being quite calm, there was an edge to his manner." Sparrow paused, and then added, "Lovely fingernails, I have to say."

"Which hospital?"

"I don't believe it was mentioned."

"Did you notice the registration of the car?" asked Gardener.

"I'm afraid I didn't, but at that point I didn't suspect anything."

"So, what happened next?"

"Well, Leonard seemed quite concerned. He wanted to go back to his room to use the phone and to pack. The driver said there wasn't enough time. The old man was beside himself with worry. I told him to keep calm, when I had the time I would pack his things and send them on. Leonard is a regular of ours, you see."

"And have you?" asked Reilly.

"Not yet. Inspector Burke arrived first thing yesterday morning and told me not to disturb the room. And I had to leave it exactly as it was, after *he'd* left."

"So off they went, just like that, Leonard and the chauffeur?" questioned Reilly.

"Yes. The driver said Leonard could use the phone in the car to check on his wife's condition."

"Did *you* think to phone anyone?" asked Reilly. "The limo company, any of the hospitals? Leonard White's agent?"

"I'm afraid I didn't. I do have a hotel to run."

"So, you just let them go without asking for identification? Afterwards, you did no checking?" pushed Reilly. "If he was such a regular customer, I would have expected a little more courtesy towards him. Surprising, really."

"What is?" asked Sparrow.

"The fact that you didn't," said Reilly. "You don't seem to have missed much else, Mr Sparrow."

The receptionist didn't answer, preferring instead to study his nails.

"Let's see the room," said Gardener.

"Of course."

The three of them left the bar and walked up a wide, sprawling staircase with a well-polished banister and a luxurious wool carpet. A door opened into a small square lobby, the entrance to three of the hotel rooms.

Gardener took a pair of gloves from his jacket pocket and removed the scene tape. He opened the door. An entrance hall led to the bathroom on the right. The main room – beyond glass doors – was enormous, possibly the largest Gardener had ever seen for a hotel.

"Jesus Christ!" said Reilly. Obviously the biggest he'd seen as well.

It must have been forty feet long, and the window on the far side took up almost the entire section of wall, affording a panoramic view of the sprawling gardens and the breathtaking valley that lay beyond. He saw smoke from a steam train – probably the Keighley and Worth Valley Railway. Everything was to hand. A TV, DVD, stereo system. A bed that was even bigger than king size. A trouser press, tea and coffee facilities, everything you could want, and probably everything you were unlikely to need. And the room was spotless. Clean, nothing out of place.

Gardener and Reilly immediately began checking wardrobes and drawers, which were all empty.

"I don't understand," said Sparrow.

"I do," said Gardener.

"No one has been in the room since Inspector Burke."

Gardener turned to stare at Sparrow. "There is no Inspector Burke."

"He was probably the feckin' limo driver as well," added Reilly.

"Who was?" asked Sparrow, agitated.

Gardener turned and stood in the centre of the room, before walking over and staring out of the window, across the valley.

"What are we missing, Sean?"

"A message?"

"So, where is it?"

"Would you gentlemen mind telling me what this is all about?" pleaded Sparrow.

Gardener faced him. "You've been taken in, Mr Sparrow. Inspector Burke does not exist, neither does the limo driver or, for that matter, Executive Cars. It's all been an elaborate set-up." He turned to Reilly with an expression of bewilderment. "Where would you put the message, Sean, if you were him?"

"I reckon he's going to make it more of a challenge. He'll leave puzzles, but we'll have to dig for them."

Gardener glanced beyond his partner. "Step to your left, will you, Sean?"

As he did so, Gardener stared at the TV. He kneeled down, noticing that the DVD power light was still lit. He switched on the TV, and pressed the play button on the DVD. The machine came to life and the screen was filled with their first image of the man they were searching for.

"That's Inspector Burke!" shouted Sparrow. The officer was exactly as Sparrow had described.

Gardener studied the background behind the actor, but there was nothing he recognised. The room was nondescript.

Burke spoke. Whether the voice was his own or dubbed was anyone's guess, but the message was loud and clear.

"Now you've allowed the dust to settle, best pay a visit to Albert Fettle."

Chapter Fifteen

Later in the day, Gardener and Reilly entered the theatre through a stage door located in a small side street off New Briggate. The steps leading down took them to the room where Albert Fettle kept himself hidden for most of the day. The silence in the building was haunting. Every sound they made created a resonant echo.

Gardener glanced around Fettle's makeshift home. The decor had been neglected. The walls were covered with a heavily smoke-stained flowered wallpaper, which had been out of fashion for so long it was almost in again. A table stood in the middle of the room, covered with magazines relating to the entertainment world, and an empty butter container that now doubled as a lunchbox. Other than that, there were two cupboards: on top of one were tea making facilities; at the side of the other, a wastepaper basket.

"Now then," said Fettle, from an area that neither detective could initially pinpoint. He materialised from a dark corner, a partially eaten sandwich in one hand, and a mug of tea in the other. His rotund belly was still adding pressure to the brown braces. His bald head currently had a black mark running right down the centre, and today's attire was a checked black and red lumberjack shirt with the same brown pleated trousers and black brogues.

"Not much for me to do round here these days, apart from the odd spot of cleaning."

And the odd spot was all it seemed to be, thought Gardener. "Won't be for much longer now, Mr Fettle."

"Caught him, have you?"

"We're still making inquiries."

"You haven't, then. You'll never catch him if he's that good with a brush and paste."

"Perhaps you should have a go," said Reilly.

"Just stating facts, son. Anyway, don't stand out there, get yourselves in here and have a pot of tea, I could do with a fresh one now. I dare say you've come to ask a few questions, see if I can remember owt?"

"You could say that. How are things here at the moment?"

"Bloody awful!" he replied, switching on the kettle and digging out a couple of clean mugs from the cupboard, without actually finding out whether or not they wanted a drink. "Like I said, there's nowt to do."

"Should give you plenty of time to remember things, then," said Reilly. "Mine's two sugars."

"You've a sharp tongue, for a leprechaun."

Gardener and Reilly chuckled.

"How long have you worked here?" Gardener asked.

"A good forty years," he replied.

With the kettle having come to the boil, Fettle poured the tea and brought it across to them. He then brought over the tray containing milk and sugar.

"Help yourselves, lads."

"How would you describe the atmosphere?"

"Good, or else I wouldn't have stayed. I've enjoyed myself, I've no intention of retiring, and Mr Price is happy to keep me as long I want to be here."

"How do you get on with him?"

"Fine. He can be a bit temperamental, but can't we all? So long as we do our job we have no problems from him."

At last, thought Gardener: two people who agreed with each other. But it didn't help the investigation. "So, you've known him as long as anyone else. How would you describe him?"

"How do you mean?" asked Fettle.

"What's he like to work for? What is he like outside work? The usual stuff."

"He's not a murderer, if that's what you're hinting at. He's a good bloke. Pays us wages on time, doesn't grumble if you have a day off sick. He often pops down to see how

I'm doing. No, if you're looking for a scapegoat, Gardener, he's not your man."

"Pleased to hear it," said Gardener, moving on. "Let's go back to last Saturday. What time did you start work?"

"I was here early that day, I wanted to have a chat with Leonard White. Started work about eight in the morning." Fettle finally finished his sandwich, and scooped up another from the lunchbox.

"Anyone else around at that time?"

"Cleaners."

"No one else?" inquired Gardener.

"I don't think so, box office staff, maybe."

"Anything strange happened around here recently? You've not received any odd phone calls, threatening letters from anyone?"

"Well, if we had, I wouldn't know about 'em. I don't get involved in that side of it. It's my job to greet the people who come through that door and down the stairs." Fettle gestured with his eyes.

"So, you were here when Leonard White arrived?" asked Gardener.

"Aye, I was that."

"Which was what time?"

"After his mysterious trunk had been delivered."

Gardener's senses went on full alert. "What trunk?"

"Bloody great big thing it were. Van were outside the roller shutter door at the back of the stage. Bloke had dropped the tailgate on the stage and slid the trunk out afore asking me to sign."

"Any slogans on the van?" Reilly asked. "Any advertising?"

"There were nowt. It were just a white one."

"What did the driver look like?"

"He was wearing a black cap. Had a cig in his mouth, but it wasn't lit. He were quite big, around six foot I'd say, same build as your mate here. He wore a pair of dark brown overalls and he walked with a limp, 'cause I wondered how the bloody hell he'd managed to move the trunk, but it was in front of me almost afore I'd signed."

"Did he say where he was from?" asked Gardener.

"No, in fact he didn't say much, apart from, 'sign here'."

"Did he say where the trunk had come from, or who'd given him instructions to deliver it here?"

"No. The trunk was big and black, quite old, had Leonard White's name on the side of it."

"What happened after you'd signed?"

"He jumped back in the van and took off."

"Did you notice the registration?" asked Reilly.

"No. I don't normally take deliveries." Fettle took a bite of his sandwich and a slurp of tea.

"Who does?"

"Stagehands, mostly."

"So, how did you find out about the delivery?"

"Van pulled up outside here first." Fettle pointed to the grimy, frosted window that formed part of his room. "Then the door at the top of the stairs opened, and someone shouted 'delivery for Leonard White', and that were it. He were back in the van and driving down the bottom afore I could say owt else."

"So, by the time you arrived on the stage, everything had more or less been done?"

"Aye, I signed and he took off."

"Was the tailgate still down, or had he lifted it back up?"

"Back up."

"Did you inspect the trunk, open it up to see what was inside?"

"No, but it were locked anyway, bloody great padlock."

"Was it heavy? Did you try to move it?"

"No, just left it."

Gardener had wondered how the killer had managed to smuggle Leonard White's body into the theatre. It was pretty obvious now. "How soon after did Leonard White arrive?"

"A couple of hours, maybe."

"Did he ask about the trunk, or did you tell him?"

Fettle chewed another bit of his sandwich and swallowed before answering. "I told him. Nice pot of tea, this." He took another mouthful.

Gardener noticed Reilly was halfway down his cup. He tasted his own – wasn't bad.

"Did White seem surprised?" Reilly asked.

"No, just pleased that it were here."

"Did you offer to go backstage and help him with it?"

"Aye, as a matter of fact, I did. But he said it were okay, he wouldn't need it straight away, but he'd give me a shout when he needed some help."

"Did his voice sound like Leonard White?"

"Can't say as I noticed. I think so."

"What happened next?"

"Well, I carried on in here. A couple of hours had passed, and I went backstage to see if he needed that hand and it was all clear. There was no trunk and no Leonard White. I gave him a shout but no one answered. I went back to his dressing room and knocked on the door, but he never answered that either."

"Did you check anywhere else?"

"Only to see if he was with Mr Price, and he wasn't. But it's not unusual for actors and actresses to take a break. Sometimes they go outside for a smoke, or a walk. They don't always leave out the stage door."

"Was he alone when he arrived?"

"Aye, he was."

"Did he seem okay to you? Not out of breath, or looking worried about anything?"

"No, he were fine. Didn't say much, which I thought were unusual, 'cause I've met him afore and I knew him to be a bit of a talker. And I'll tell you what else were unusual, shall I? I thought the trunk was a bit too much for a man who'd had hip replacement, which is why I went to offer my help. Not that I'd be much use to him anyway, 'cause I'm getting on a bit now. I am still younger than him, though."

"So, you have no idea what happened to the trunk?"

"Come to think of it, no. It were too big to just hide in a corner, but I never saw it anywhere afterwards."

Gardener glanced at Reilly, who in turn nodded. "Where is it?"

Reilly glanced at Fettle. "Could it still be here?"

"Probably. No one came to pick it up."

"Any idea where?" Gardener asked Fettle.

Fettle chewed on his sandwich, gulped more tea. "Could be anywhere."

"Where do you store the props and the scenery you're not using?" asked Gardener.

"We have a couple of different rooms."

"The sort of place that someone would only know if they had worked here?" pressed Gardener.

"I suppose so. As I've said. I've been here forty years. Whoever this bloke was, I didn't recognise him."

"Well, you wouldn't, would you?" said Reilly. "He was disguised."

"But no one's that good. I don't care how good you are, you can't imitate someone so perfectly. You'd have to slip up somewhere."

"I think you'll find you're wrong," said Gardener. "We might all be in for a surprise with this one. Can you show us the rooms?"

"If you think it'll help."

The detectives followed Fettle into the labyrinth of the theatre. For a man with a limp, he could walk at a fair pace. The two storage rooms he showed them were located either side of the stage, down a flight of steps. Though the rooms were full of dust-encrusted furniture, neither one contained the trunk they wanted.

"Are there any more?" asked Gardener.

Fettle stood and thought. "Well there is, but they're way down in the basements. I don't think anyone's been down there in ages."

"I'll bet you're wrong about that as well," replied Reilly.

Each man trooped down to the very bottom of the theatre. It was cold, and Gardener could see his own breath. The first room they came across was at the end of a corridor. There were no physical signs that it had been used recently.

Fettle pulled a bunch of keys from his pocket and tried a few before selecting the correct one. The door opened with a loud crack, and a dank smell penetrated their nostrils. The room was small, and other than posters from previous productions, there was nothing of any interest.

Fettle locked the door and took them back down one corridor and into another. He reached the door, produced the keys, and tried all of them. He stood back and scratched his head, puzzled. "Surely one of the keys has to be here."

"Maybe it's not locked," said Reilly. He used a pair of gloves and tried the handle.

To Fettle's amazement, but not Gardener's, the door opened. Standing in the middle of the room was the big black trunk. Leonard White's name was stencilled on the side – no padlock.

Gardener also produced gloves from his pocket as he moved to the chest, and lifted the lid. Inside the trunk was a long coil of rope. On the inside of the lid a piece of paper had been attached. Judging by the texture, it was a little thicker than normal paper, and had an elaborately designed scroll top and bottom. The outer edges of the paper were blue, but the scroll was beige and flecked with brown spots, the finish resembling a cup of cappuccino.

As Gardener had figured, a message had been left:

I imagine you're used to this now
And you're probably wondering, just how?
Perhaps you should focus in order to be true

And more to the point, ask who?

I've invited you in, but beware, my world is big
Not long now, before the next gig.
You should study your city and seek out a shop,
The next of my chosen will be a big shock.

I'm enjoying myself, playing this game,
And it would be all too easy to give you a name.
It's time to detect, and study the clues,
Be sure to keep up, otherwise you'll lose.

"He's a crafty bugger, is this one," said Fettle. "You'll have a job and a half if you don't know what he looks like."

Gardener sighed, frustrated. "Give forensics a call, Sean. Let's have them check this out. Do you recognise the rope, Mr Fettle?"

The old man was about to reach inside, but Gardener stopped him. "Looks like one of ours."

Gardener picked it up. One end had been cut. It didn't take a genius to realise that the other section had to be the one used to hang Leonard White.

He had evidence bags in the car. He dropped the rope, left the lid open, and turned to walk back out of the room. Before doing so he glanced at Fettle.

"One more question, Mr Fettle. Have you ever heard of an Inspector Burke?"

Fettle appeared deep in thought. "Inspector Burke," he repeated. "Can't say as I have. What makes you ask?"

"Just curious," said Gardener.

Chapter Sixteen

Early evening back at the incident room, Gardener was still shocked by the apparent ease with which the killer had carried out his actions against Leonard White. The man had oozed confidence, as if being caught was completely unheard of. Or equally as bad, the prospect of capture didn't bother him. Perhaps it was a mission. Maybe when it was over he would do one of two things: disappear forever, or hand himself in.

The little to no evidence was frustrating, and it was beginning to feel like a conspiracy that no one ever noticed anything: vans, registration plates, logos. Gardener's only consolation was the few items he and Reilly had managed to collect. The DVD of Inspector Burke, the new puzzle, and the rest of the rope. He was well aware of the mounting pressure to find answers, not to mention the person responsible.

Gardener addressed his team. "Sean and I have uncovered some disturbing evidence relating to the case. If and when the press get hold of it, we're going to come under intense scrutiny from the public, particularly if he kills again. We know that whoever the killer is, he either bears a strong resemblance to White or he's a master of disguise. The receptionist at The Manor House near Skipton said Leonard White was picked up on Friday by a chauffeur from Executive Cars, who had used the excuse that his wife had been taken ill and the car had been laid on for him. We've checked and there is no such company. So, where did the car come from? And where is it now?"

"What make of car was it?" one of the assembled officers inquired.

"The receptionist doesn't know," replied Gardener. "The hotel doesn't have CCTV, they don't feel the need. We have a guest list, so I'd like a couple of you to follow it up, see if anyone can help."

Gardener continued with the briefing. "The following morning, yesterday, the staff at The Manor House had a visit from the police." He let the remark sink in while glancing around the room, studying the expressions of his team.

"I know what you're thinking, you're trying to work out if anyone else has been there apart from us. Well, it wasn't any of you. It was, in fact, an Inspector Burke."

"Inspector Burke?" repeated Briggs.

"Sean." Gardener glanced at his colleague and passed over the disc. "Will you do the honours?" As the DVD played, Gardener was amazed that he hadn't realised the small segment of film had actually been recorded in black and white.

"Is that him?" said Briggs.

"Looks like it," replied Reilly.

"He looks familiar."

"The actor, you mean?" asked Gardener, wondering what Briggs was thinking.

"Yes." But his superior didn't elaborate. "He must be bloody confident to play tricks like this. And he's thought it out as well. Any idea where that is?"

"No," said Gardener. "If you look closely, the background is out of focus. Maybe our lads can clean it up a little bit. Even if they do, I don't think it will show us much."

"What did Fettle have to say?" asked Briggs.

Gardener told them, and then held up the two clear plastic bags. One had the rope, the other contained the latest puzzle, which he'd now copied and pasted to the ANACAPA chart.

"I want that trunk back here," said Briggs. "He's taking the piss! All right, you lot, let's have some answers. This bloke's far too confident, and he's gonna make mugs out of us if we're not careful. And what's that supposed to mean? 'Perhaps you should focus in order to be true'?"

Gardener made his suggestion. "He's very well organised. Everything's been planned down to the finest detail. He's suggesting we do the same." He turned, directing a question to junior officer Patrick Edwards. "Have you looked at ritual killings and murders involving draining the blood?"

"I have, sir, but I haven't learned much. I've studied books in the library, and the internet. I've done a small report for you." Edwards placed it on the table in front of Gardener. "I don't really think it will help us."

"Keep digging. Don't rule anything out," said Gardener, suddenly turning his attention to another member of the team. "Colin, what do you have on Leonard White?"

"I'm waiting for copies of his legal documents, but nothing seems untoward. His solicitor confirmed that in the event of his death, everything he owned would be left to his wife. As for her, she seems pretty straightforward on the face of it, but I haven't been looking long enough, yet."

"Okay. Thornton, Anderson, what about the rope?"

"There's nothing special about it."

Gardener held the evidence bag aloft. "I think we'll find it's the other half of the one in this bag. We'll get forensics to check it out for prints."

"But the knot threw up something interesting," replied Anderson. "It's known as a sailor's eye splice. Not too complicated to form, but pretty effective at holding something in place."

"Which takes us in another direction," said Gardener. "Has our killer spent some time in the navy?"

"Or is it a red herring?" said Briggs. "If you'll pardon the pun. Has he just studied ropes and knots in order to have us running all over the place?"

A silence descended, and Gardener realised they were going nowhere fast.

"What about witness statements?" Briggs asked.

A young PC brought in as support put his hand up. "I'm following up on a woman who thought she saw Leonard White getting out of a taxi outside the theatre on the Saturday afternoon. I've telephoned twice to make an appointment, but I've had no answer."

"Go round tonight, then" said Briggs. "We want the registration of the taxi, the name of the firm, the driver, where he picked him up, everything. I want someone back at the theatre to see Paul Price. We need a list of everyone who's worked there in the last thirty years. Add the hotel guest list to your witnesses and see if anyone's on both lists, or if any of them noticed the vehicle from Executive Cars. Somebody must have seen something. This bloke's luck has to give out sometime."

"You also have a white van to add to your list," added Gardener. "Seen in the city centre on Saturday afternoon. I know there must be hundreds of white vans a week in the centre of Leeds. Get as many registration plates as possible and then check them out. Go back to The Grand and once again check out the CCTV."

Gardener glanced at the ANACAPA chart before turning to face them all. "Harry Fletcher was a name that came up last time. Has anyone found him?"

Dave Rawson stepped forward – a man with the build of a rugby centre forward. He had short black hair, a small beard and moustache, neatly trimmed, and strong square teeth.

"I'm taking care of that one, sir. Back in the 1960s he was a writer, mainly detective fiction. Turned them out pretty fast, by all accounts. Then he disappeared for a while. Next thing, he was working for the watch committee in the Seventies. After that, he seems to have gone to ground again. Popped up again in the Nineties as a commissioning editor for the Playhouse, before disappearing again."

"Has he now?" said Briggs. "What do you think, Stewart?"

"He could be our man," replied Gardener. "We need to speak to him if only to eliminate him, but more importantly, if he's not our man he may know something that will lead us in the right direction."

Briggs glanced at the board again. "It's a bit coincidental that we have a writer of crime fiction from the Sixties popping in and out of the world when he feels like it, and a poet who likes killing people and leaving puzzles. What do you think the second verse means?"

"I think it's obvious we're looking for an actor," replied Gardener. "Certainly, someone connected with the theatre."

"Maybe he's a failed actor with a score to settle," said Reilly.

"Possible," Gardener continued but then paused, before addressing Colin Sharp. "An actor: Colin, found out anything about the quote on the wall and *The Phantom*?"

"Not a lot," said Sharp. "*Phantom* is basically a love story, a bit like *Beauty and the Beast*. The Phantom is a man called Erik and he's in love with a singer called Christine. He observes her from a distance, but they finally meet in a secret chamber close to the singer's dressing room.

"Erik tells her that he's brought her five cellars underground because he loves her. Because it's a silent film, it's all done with quotes on the screen, which is where we see the one from the dressing room wall. But that was only one line from the whole thing."

"What's the rest?" Reilly asked.

"'So that which is good in me, aroused by your purity, might plead for your love'. All of this leads to the famous unmasking scene."

"Why is he wearing a mask?"

"Because he was burned by acid at the beginning of the film and left for dead."

Gardener thought about what Sharp had said. "Doesn't really tell us anything, does it?"

"Other than the quote on the dressing room wall was random, in the sense that the line fitted what he wanted to say," replied Sharp.

"Yes," said Gardener, "that he's holding a grudge and he's waited some time for retribution."

"Question is, what and when?" asked Anderson.

"That's what we need to find out. Look at the last part of his bit of poetry found in the trunk. He's directing us as well. 'A shop,' where 'the next of my chosen will be a big shock.' Any luck with that one?"

"There is one in the city, specialises in theatre supplies, called... wait for it... Let's Make-up."

"You're joking?" said Reilly.

"No, I'm serious," said Dave Rawson.

"Where is it?" asked Gardener.

"One of the arcades running off New Briggate. Run by an old guy and his assistant. They call him Cuthbertson. He's been there about thirty years, knows all there is to know about theatre and stage, and just about everybody who goes in there."

"Anyone bought any aluminium powder recently?"

"Quite a lot of people. I've made a list so we can start following them up."

Gardener nodded. "You said he knows everyone who goes in there. He hasn't had any strangers in recently, asking for oddball stuff?"

"Not that he knows of. I asked his assistant, Janine Harper, but she didn't seem as if she was on the same planet."

"It could be him," said Reilly. "He runs a shop, so he'd have no trouble getting the stuff. Knows all there is to know about make-up, chances are he could apply it professionally."

"Did he have an alibi for the night of Leonard White's death?" asked Gardener.

"He claims he was at home, by himself. No wife, no kids."

"And no alibi," said Reilly.

"So, he could be our man," said Gardener. "Then again, he could be next. The riddle says, 'the next of my chosen will be a big shock'. Maybe it's nothing to do with the local watch committee. We need to check him out further, Dave."

Gardener addressed Briggs. "Do you think it's worth tailing him for a couple of days?"

"I suppose we could spare someone to watch his movements," replied Briggs. "Let me see what I can do."

"What if it's her?" asked Reilly.

"Who?"

"Janine Harper. Maybe it'll be a big shock because he's after her, not Cuthbertson."

"Why would he be?" asked Briggs.

"I'm just thinking of the *Phantom* storyline," replied Reilly, "a love story. Has he been rebuffed by this Janine piece and he's going after her?"

"It's worth a thought, Sean," said Gardener, "but it doesn't really fit. She's in her twenties, chances are that the man we're after is probably more than double her age."

Reilly shrugged, "just a thought, boss."

"And not a bad one," said Gardener, nodding to his superior, DCI Briggs. "Maybe someone on her as well?"

"Christ, Stewart, we're not made of money."

Gardener smiled and addressed the team again. "The end of the riddle. 'It's time to detect, and study the clues.' Despite being cocky, he's right. And so is DCI Briggs. He's taking us for mugs, especially if he gets away with another murder. We have to try to prevent it. Sean and I are going to pay a visit to Leonard White's former home. Apparently, it was a colleague of White's who bought it. Although he's dead, it's possible his wife is still there."

"Okay, let's be more focused," shouted Briggs. "It doesn't sound like we have much time, but you're going to have to do your best. Otherwise, the press will do their worst. The way I see it, there are three suspects." Briggs held up one hand and counted with his fingers on the other.

"Val White. She had the motive and the ability, but she has an alibi. Dig deep, someone. Harry Fletcher. We don't know enough about him either way. We can't put him in the frame and we can't rule him out, so we need to find him. Cuthbertson, who runs the stage make-up shop. He's a possible suspect, but he may also be the next victim. Someone tail him for a couple of days. We have to be seen to be doing something, despite the fact that we're getting nowhere."

Gardener glanced at the chart again, ticking off the subjects he'd covered, stopping when he reached the word ESLA.

He addressed Steve Fenton. "Anything?"

"Yes. We've got the results in. We need everyone back at the theatre with their shoes so we can check them off."

"Good. Go and ring Paul Price now and tell him I'd like everyone there tomorrow, with the shoes they were wearing on Saturday night. I'd also like to see the results at the next incident room meeting."

He glanced at them all as a group. "That just leaves the sound problem. The word that Paul Price heard spoken before Leonard White was hung."

"I know about that one, sir," said Paul Benson, another young member of the team, who produced a notebook. "It was on a cassette tape. Once we'd identified which one, I popped over to the theatre to speak to the sound technician."

Gardener glanced over the evidence bags, spotting a tape. "What did he have to say?"

"The sound tech identified it as the tape he'd been given by Leonard White about ten minutes before he went on, with the instructions that he should play it after the safety curtain had been raised."

"Where did White go then?" asked Gardener.

"To the other side of the stage to wait in the wings, only our sound technician couldn't see him. Once the curtain was up, he played the tape. At first, he thought it was blank, the wrong one maybe. Then he heard something scream out, which was a bloody sight louder than he'd anticipated. When he searched the desk for the volume level, it was too late. There was nothing else on the tape, and the body was in front of the audience."

"Did he see White at all after that?"

"No, but to be honest, I think he was in shock. He said he just stood staring at the body until Price came barging through the stage door."

"Did he recognise the word on the tape?"

"No."

"Do you?"

"The sound lads have been playing with this for ages. The recording is pretty loud, which means it's distorted," said Benson. "But they have managed to clean it up and they think it's two words, even though it's said quite fast. Someone shouts 'look out', and that's it."

Gardener glanced at the ceiling, defeated. It would be nigh on impossible to identify that, but he had to try.

"Any ideas?"

Benson spoke up again. "The sound lads think it comes from an old film. There's lots of crackling and a definite hiss, so it hasn't been recorded live. Whoever did it might have used the latest technology, but the soundtrack is very old."

"Okay," said Gardener. "Everyone take a copy of that tape. I'll have one for my dad. Any of you talking to the film historians, play it to them, see if they recognise it. I'm not expecting miracles, but you never know."

Gardener updated the board and added the word 'DVD', intending to follow up on the Inspector Burke clip.

Briggs stood up. "Before you all go, the Chief Super's been talking to a retired profiler who's offering his services for free."

"Do we need one?" asked Reilly.

"It won't hurt," replied Briggs. "And it isn't going to cost us anything. He's got a lot of experience dealing with these people. He worked on the Yorkshire Ripper case."

"Peter Sutcliffe? That's reassuring," retorted Reilly. "They never actually caught that bastard in connection with his crimes. He was apprehended on false number plates."

"We should have had the bloke who caught him working for us," shouted Thornton. "At least he clocked number plates."

The comment raised a laugh, and Gardener did his best to bring the meeting back to order. "What's his name?"

"Trevor Thorpe."

"Can't say I've heard of him."

"Well, all this is irrelevant," said Briggs. "He's offered to help, the Chief Super's accepted, so he's coming in during the next day or so to study everything we have. So, the next time we meet in this room, we'll have a guest. Can we show him some respect?"

The officers dispersed without a word. Gardener wasn't particularly happy about it, and judging by the expressions of his team as they were leaving, neither were they.

Chapter Seventeen

Martin Brown leaned forward and stared at the documents on his desk.

Running the fingers of his right hand around the inside of his collar, he realised the office was too warm. The general mess – which resembled the aftermath of a nuclear fallout – was also adding to his discomfort. The cupboard to his right was crammed full of magazines and journals. The shelves on the walls were at the point of collapse. Papers were strewn everywhere, on window ledges, pinned to the walls, left on chairs. But they *were* students; what could he expect? And they were so bloody noisy. He could hear them now in the corridor, shouting at each other all the time, even though they were standing together.

"Hold on a second, Dave." Martin rose from his seat and closed the door. He came back to the desk and picked up the phone to continue the conversation. "Are you sure?"

"Of course I'm sure, Martin. I've worked for BT for about thirty years. I've checked it out three times."

Martin struggled with the information he'd been given. "But this is William Henry Corndell we're talking about."

"So you keep saying. But who the hell is William Henry Corndell?"

"Probably one of the greatest actors of our time," replied Martin, growing more frustrated.

"Well, I've never seen any of his films."

"He's not really in films, Dave," said Martin. "He's more a classical actor who works in the theatre."

"So where have you seen him?"

"London."

"When?" Dave asked.

"Oh God, years ago."

"What in?"

"When I saw him, he was in rehearsals for *Phantom of the Opera*."

"Good, was he?" asked Dave.

Martin wasn't keen on his friend's tone. "The best, from what I saw."

"So, why didn't *he* get the part instead of Michael Crawford? And did you actually see the play itself?"

"No. I missed the opening night. Apparently, Corndell had a major accident. Fell off a piece of scenery and broke his leg."

"And after that?"

"I left London shortly afterwards. I'm not so sure what happened to him. But I'm telling you, a man of his acting prowess must have been working constantly. Which is why I'm asking, are you sure it's the same William Henry Corndell?"

"Are you?"

"I just can't believe a man of his talent isn't in constant demand. You're positive he's never had a single phone call to his landline in what, ten, fifteen years? And he's never made a call?"

"He hasn't taken a call." Dave sounded as if he was tiring of the game.

"What about a mobile?"

"He doesn't have one. I've done the most comprehensive search with the most up-to-date technology. Anyone who's anybody who has a mobile phone, I know their number, Cliff Richard, Tom Jones, Paul McCartney. All your top actors, Ben Affleck, DiCaprio I can get you just about anyone's number. Posh and Beck's, if you want. But I can't get one for William Henry Corndell because he doesn't have one!"

"Is it legal, this program of yours?"

"Of course it isn't legal. And I don't want anyone knowing about it, either."

The conversation ceased while Martin swallowed a mouthful of coffee. "I can't believe it, Dave. I really can't."

"Why do you want this bloke, Martin?"

"If you'd seen him, you'd know." Martin recalled the time he'd been in London, when Corndell had been rehearsing at Her Majesty's Theatre for the lead role. The emotion, the feeling, the way he'd delivered his lines and the expressions he'd used were as good as anyone he'd ever seen. "What about the bill? Is it paid regularly?" asked Martin.

"Like clockwork."

Martin blew out a sigh. "I don't know what to say."

"You're going to have to call him, Martin. See if he *is* your man, which I'm pretty sure he is. Maybe he'll tell you what he's been doing all these years. Maybe he's dropped out of show business. He's probably a recluse. You know what it's like, most of them can't handle the pressure."

"Not Corndell. If you'd seen him, you'd know."

"So you keep saying. But I haven't, and I'm not likely to now, if he's a recluse. Nor are you, by the sound of it. Listen, have you tried a round of the agents?"

"Yes, but he doesn't seem to have one of those, either. You're right, Dave, I'll have to give him a ring, see what he's up to and whether or not he'll do it."

"Might be too rich for university blood. You know what penny-pinching students are like."

"I'll ignore that. Anyway, thanks for what you've done, you've been a great help."

"No problem. Let me know how you get on."

"Okay, mate."

Martin put the phone down, sighing. Staring at the back wall, he allowed his thoughts to drift. He knew a natural when he saw one. Born and bred in Borehamwood, he'd lived there until he was twenty-five. Most, if not all, of his childhood had been spent at Elstree Studios. He went on to train at the RADA before lecturing in dramatic arts. His fascination with the film industry and the entertainment world were second to none, or so he thought. Eventually he moved to Leeds with his wife and two children to take a post at the university. His children, now in their late teens, were about to attend.

He'd seen and studied Corndell on and off over the years. He'd met Corndell's father, himself a fine actor who had spent many years on the stage before turning his hand to direction, where he made a multitude of films for Ealing Studios. Corndell's father had died in the 1980s, and he was pretty sure that Corndell had moved up to Yorkshire to reside in the Corndell mansion in Horsforth. But where had he been since then? There was only one way to find out.

As he reached out for the phone, his arm disturbed a file. The paper shuffled forward and a small spider scurried across the desk, running for cover. Martin jumped up and stepped back with a shiver. He wasn't keen on spiders. God help the human race if they were the larger species: even Usain Bolt couldn't outrun something with eight legs.

After Martin had calmed down, he sat and picked up the receiver, listening to the tone, hoping to find a little extra courage. He felt apprehensive. He realised he'd obtained an ex-directory number the only way you could: illegally. He dialled, listening for an age before the phone at the other end was eventually picked up.

"Hello?" The voice sounded far more nervous than Martin.

"Am I speaking to William Henry Corndell?"

"Who is this and how did you get the number?"

Bad start, thought Martin. "Mr Corndell, I'm sorry to bother you. My name is Martin Brown, and I work for the University of Leeds."

"That's one question answered."

"Am I talking to the same William Henry Corndell who once played the lead role of the Phantom in the West End?"

"Good grief, young man, you have done your homework."

Martin Brown almost laughed at the change in tone of Corndell's voice. He sounded like an eccentric country squire. "So, it is you, then?"

"It most certainly is. But I'd still like to know how you got this number, and what you're after."

"I'm sorry, Mr Corndell, but I've seen and admired your work. I've even seen a copy of the film you produced which your father directed. Ahead of its time, is all I can say."

"You flatter me, Mr Brown, but don't stop, I could get to like it. However, you still haven't answered my question. What do you want of me?"

"I'd like to book you, Mr Corndell."

"Pardon?" Corndell sounded shocked, as if what Martin was asking was not an everyday occurrence.

"I'm in charge of the entertainment at the University of Leeds, and one of the students suggested we have a night of culture. They wanted me to find a classical actor of your ability to put on a one-man show here. I was really hoping that you were still involved, and wondered whether or not you'd be interested."

"You have my undivided attention. I'm flattered you know so much about me. But there are two things I must ask. Firstly, when is it? Second, and perhaps equally as important, do you have the necessary funding?"

"I'm sure we could negotiate the price."

"Don't count on it, Mr Brown."

Martin's heart sank a little. He might be stepping out of his league, and he was beginning to think it was a bad idea. But at least he'd managed to avoid answering how he'd obtained the number. "I wondered if you would consider April 1st."

The pause on the end of the line seemed to last forever. "I'm impressed, young man. But I have to say I'm extremely busy with Hollywood at the moment, negotiating for my latest manuscript, which, of course, must take precedence. But you've obviously gone to a lot of trouble to track me down and ask me to entertain your students. And furthermore, you're asking if I'll do it on my birthday. I think it's a wonderful idea."

"You'll do it?"

"Don't sound so surprised. Isn't that what you wanted?" asked Corndell.

"Yes it is, but I never expected."

"Don't be negative, young man. Positive thinking has brought you this far. I presume you know my address, particularly as you know my ex-directory telephone number."

"As a matter of fact, I do."

"Good, then put a contract in the post to arrive no later than two days' time. I shall sign and insert the price at the same time."

"But that's just it. The price. I'm not sure we can afford you."

"The price, sir, will not be negotiable. If you want the best, then you have to be prepared to pay for it. However, my quote will not disappoint. Thank you and goodbye."

Martin was listening to the dialling tone again. He was amazed, not only to find he had booked a man whose work he admired, but the fact that the conversation had ended so abruptly. He wasted no time in making the next call.

"Hello?" answered Laura.

"Laura? It's Martin, from the university."

"Hi Martin, how are you?"

"Just great. I've got an assignment for you."

Chapter Eighteen

"You seem in a good mood tonight, Laura," Reilly said to his wife.

"I am." She helped herself to another mouthful of pasta.

"Is it the university job?"

"Yes, but I can't think why. I mean, when Martin rang me, he was ridiculously excited that he'd managed to book some obscure actor called William Henry Corndell for the uni. Like I said, I've never heard of him."

"Have you checked him out?"

"I have. Can't find any reference to him." She had recently changed direction with her career. For many years she had been a freelance photographer. Examples of her work were framed around their two-storey house in Yeadon. More recently she had gone back to the second love of her life, entertainment journalism. Most magazines carried her reviews of the local and regional plays. Every three months she travelled down to London to keep her eye on what was up and coming and would eventually be touring.

"Wallace Henry Corndell, yes, but not William."

"Who was Wallace?"

"A big film director back in the Sixties, worked for Ealing, turned out a string of comedies. Judging by the reports I've read, he was very good at his job."

"Is Corndell a relative in the same line of business?" suggested Reilly.

"Perhaps, but not as successful, otherwise I would have heard of him. Anyway, mine is not to reason why. Martin absolutely raves over the man. Said he saw him down in London when Corndell was rehearsing for *Phantom of the Opera.*"

"Well, there you are then, he must have a talent."

"But that's just it, I can't find a reference for that either. We all know Michael Crawford was the star of that show, and there have been various leading men since, but I'm sure that William Henry Corndell wasn't one of them."

Reilly finished his food, sat back in his chair. As Laura had already finished hers, he signalled the waiter once more for the dessert menu. "It must be costing the university a small fortune if they're shipping him all the way from London for one night."

"That's just it, they're not. Apparently he lives locally."

"Where?"

"About five or six miles from us, in Horsforth."

"Does he now? Well, I never knew that."

"See! You men never pay attention."

Chapter Nineteen

Gardener glanced at the clock: 7:30.

He was feeling guilty for spending the last two hours at home, leading something close to a normal life. Before leaving the station he'd phoned ahead, and Malcolm had made an early dinner of chargrilled chicken breasts and salad, with granary baguettes. All three ate together before Malcolm had taken off for a night at the small private cinema in Headingley. Gardener hoped it would lift Malcolm's spirits.

He cleared the pots, took a shower, and thought some more about the case. Most of the team had spent the day trawling through the huge pile of witness statements, consulting HOLMES. A number of cases came to light regarding blood being drained, but none of them bore any of the hallmarks of the Leonard White murder.

Despite being frustrating, it was also challenging. There was nothing Gardener loved more. The main things on his mind were the watch committee and the puzzles, the connection being Harry Fletcher. Gardener could not figure out why Fletcher would wait until now if there had been a conflict within the group. In spite of the fact that he kept fading in and out of life over the last twenty years, he had always been local. Why not take his revenge before now?

In the kitchen, Gardener placed a cup of herbal tea on the tray before him, and a can of Coke for Chris, as well as a number of chocolate bars. Gardener picked up the tray, and headed for the garage. The connecting door was open. Gardener pushed it wider with one foot, comforted by the scene before him. Chris was dressed in an oil-stained boiler suit that was at least two sizes too big. The smell of oil and petrol suffused the air. Nuts and bolts clanked as they landed in glass jars. Gardener smiled. His job was very demanding. If all he could grab was a couple of hours now and again, he'd settle for that.

Chris glanced at his father before immediately clearing a place to put the tray. "Thanks, Dad." He grabbed his Coke and a chocolate bar.

As Gardener took stock, he couldn't believe how clean and tidy the place was. Within a couple of hours, Chris had put everything in boxes, which he'd carefully labelled and placed in some sort of order. Nuts, bolts, screws and washers of all descriptions had been segregated into different glass jars, and the garage was beginning to feel more like home than a workshop, especially as Spook was stretched out on a cushion on one of the shelves, casually washing herself, totally unconcerned at what was happening around her.

"You've done a terrific job, Chris."

"I've been at it for a couple of days."

"How come?"

"Last time I saw you in here, you were searching all over for a few nuts and bolts, losing your patience."

Gardener laughed. "That's par for the course. It's part of the restoration process. You lose things, and you're allowed to swear a bit while you find them."

"Do you want me to chuck these all over the floor again?"

"Yeah, right. We don't get enough family time like this together, Chris. The way things are at the moment, I have to grab it while I can."

"It's okay," said Chris, taking a slurp of soda. "I wouldn't want your job. I don't care how good the money is."

"It's not as good as you think."

"Why do you do it, then?"

That was a good question, thought Gardener. Working all the hours God sends, chasing perverts and criminals and murderers with no thanks and no patience and no help from the public, wasn't ideal from anyone's point of view. "It's all I know. And it's personal."

"What do you mean?"

Gardener pointed to his chest. "It's in here. I suppose it's a bit like being a priest. You might wonder why he does his job, and he'd probably tell you it's not a job but a calling. That's how I feel. It's more than a job, and it has been ever since I first started."

Chris seemed deep in thought about the answer before asking, "Do you think you'll ever catch all the criminals?"

His son was full of good questions tonight.

"I doubt it. And in a way, I hope not."

"Why?"

"Because then I'll be out of a job."

They both laughed.

"At least then you can do something you really want, like fixing bikes."

Gardener finished his chocolate bar and sipped his herbal tea. "I doubt I'll ever be good enough for that. Your grandfather might be."

"Is he good?"

Gardener nodded. "He's the real brains behind this restoration. I've spent a long time tinkering with bikes because I love it, but I'm not in his league."

"I thought he was a gardener," said Chris.

"He was, but that's what he did for a living. His passion on the weekend was his motorbikes. I know he used to love his job, but there was a time when he totally refused to work weekends. He spent it with his family and his bikes."

"Did he have many?"

"Not really, no. I can only remember him having about six in life, and never usually more than one at a time. He almost gave up after he nearly got arrested."

"Granddad did?"

"Yes. God, that was funny."

"What happened?"

"He had a Triumph Speed Twin. It was his pride and joy. It was the business. I think it was a bloke called Edward Turner who was responsible for it. It had everything a bike could want.

"I can't remember what year your granddad was, but he looked after it better than he looked after me, I think. Always polishing it; stripped and rebuilt it every year. It looked like it had just come out of the showroom every time you saw it. Anyway, this one time, he'd finished his annual strip and rebuild, polished it like a new pin, and took it out for a test drive. Police stopped him near Rothwell. They'd had a report that one had been stolen from a showroom in Leeds. The description matched your granddad's."

Gardener chuckled as he remembered. "He had no identification on him whatsoever. The police impounded the bike and took him in. Me and your gran had to go down there with all the documents and sort the whole mess out. It took us an hour to get him out of there, and when we all got home, bike included, there was a letter waiting for us to say he'd forgotten to pay the television licence and if he didn't, he was going to get a visit from the police."

The pair of them erupted into raucous laughter, startling Spook, who glared at them as if they had completely lost their minds.

Chapter Twenty

Janine Harper's mood was nuclear. She couldn't believe that old bastard, Cuthbertson. He'd tricked her into doing the final stocktake for the auditors on her own. It won't take long, he'd said, and it is an emergency. A couple of hours and you'll be done, and you can still go out and enjoy yourself afterwards. He had to be fucking joking, the mood she was in.

She'd suspected all day that he'd been leading up to something. He'd been too nice: offering her a longer lunch than normal, making afternoon tea, *and buying the cakes!* He was normally as tight as a duck's arse. The only way to force a warm drink out of him was to stick your fingers down his throat.

And then came the crunch phone call, a little after four o'clock. His sister had been taken ill, rushed into a hospital somewhere – although where, he'd failed to mention. Janine didn't think he had a sister; she'd thought his only family was a test tube.

She checked her watch: it was a little after nine-thirty. She should have been with her friends now. The four of them had made plans to go out for drinks, and then on to the Italian on New Briggate. They didn't treat themselves very often. The uncertainty over Brexit had tightened their pockets.

Janine sighed loudly. She really couldn't believe she was doing it. Well, she would show Cuthbertson. Boy, would he receive a major shock when he opened the door tomorrow morning. Give him a fucking heart attack if she had her way.

She put the clipboard down and picked up her mobile phone, calling her friend Angie. No one answered. She called Sarah next, but her phone was switched off. They were obviously having a good time. She threw the mobile down on the shelf. It bounced onto the floor, where the battery disconnected and the phone slid under the Dexion shelving.

"Fucking wonderful," cried Janine. "Could things be any worse?"

In the haunting silence that followed, she suspected that perhaps things could, because the door to the shop had actually opened.

Who the hell could that be? Surely to God it wasn't a punter who thought it was late night opening. Or worse, a gang of drunken idiots. It could be anybody; maybe a tramp, they wandered all over Leeds, day and night. Perhaps he had popped in to keep warm. She'd never shift him. He might be plastered on meths. He could do anything to her. And there was no one around, because no one else worked so late. All the other shopkeepers had gone home by now, and none of them lived above the premises.

Janine's nerves tingled. She thought she had locked the shop. Her legs grew heavier, and the space inside her head started to close in. Palpitations were squeezing her chest, and she honestly thought she was going to stop breathing. *Oh Jesus, what was she going to do?*

She glanced around for a possible weapon. The shop was full of dangerous things she could use. Liquids or powders she could throw into someone's face. She'd open a bottle of acetone. Chuck that in his face, and his eyes would end up in his arse. She'd teach him to mess with her. Janine slowly reached for the bottle.

Wait a minute. What was she thinking of? Who else could it be at nine-thirty on a Friday evening? It was very obviously Cuthbertson, coming back to see if she was doing the job properly. Checking up on her.

Maybe his story had been genuine. Perhaps he did have a sister who had been taken ill. He had been to see her, and on his way home had felt guilty enough to see if Janine was still here and needed a hand. Well, whether he had or not, she would give him a piece of her mind. By the time she was finished, he would be in the bed next to his sister.

Janine marched straight through into the shop. She nearly puked when her eyes focused and fed the message to her brain.

"Oh... my... fucking... God."

Chapter Twenty-one

It was Wednesday morning in the centre of Leeds, and Alan Cuthbertson was enjoying yet another early spring day. Despite being a little overcast, the temperature was quite high. He was strolling to work, observing the masses doing the same.

The amount of people walking and eating never failed to amaze him. Everywhere he turned, someone had food in their hands; he passed a bunch of youths, cigarette in one hand, McDonald's in the other, who – judging by their appearance – had been out all night. A middle-aged couple on the other side of the road were trying to have a conversation whilst devouring a sandwich. *Don't these people ever rise early and sort out their own breakfasts? Are they really that lazy?* Staying in bed till the last minute before rolling out and into a suit and straight out of the door. It wouldn't have happened in his day.

Cuthbertson turned into the arcade, toward the shop. He almost collided with a tramp, one of many in the city centre asking for handouts, leading you to believe they weren't eating. And what happened when you gave them the money? Straight down the off licence.

"Could you spare some change, mate?"

"No!" shouted Cuthbert son. "Piss off and get a job like I have."

The tramp turned on him. A wave of fear surged through Cuthbertson's aged body. He'd heard how nasty they could be. He wished he hadn't said it now. Apart from the two of them, the arcade was empty.

"It could be you one day, son. You could be homeless, just like me."

Cuthbertson chose to ignore him, scurrying away to his shop.

At the entrance, he reached into his pocket for the keys. He tried the correct one, but it wouldn't turn the lock. Strange. Surely Janine had locked up last night? Then again, the mood she'd been in… she could be a right little madam when she wanted. He tried the Yale key. When that didn't work, he reached and turned the handle and pushed open the door.

He would have to have words with her. She was becoming very lackadaisical of late. Forgetting to lock up was the last straw. And he wasn't happy with the way she addressed customers. He would definitely nip it in the bud.

The shop was unnaturally dark as he entered. He pinched his nose, wondering what in God's name the smell was. He reached out, switched on the light, turned a little too fast. He lost his footing and hit the floor like a sack of potatoes. He was still on the ground when he glanced upwards.

The sight that greeted him saved him from falling again when he fainted.

Chapter Twenty-two

An ambulance with flashing blue lights parked in front of the arcade. Alongside that were three more squad cars and a van with dark tinted windows. Uniformed constables were standing in front of scene tape. Gardener and Reilly jumped out of their car, flashed warrant cards, walked down to the shop. At either end of the arcade, morning shoppers gathered, craning their necks to see what had happened.

The entrance to the shop was sealed with reflective scene tape. Inside, Gardener heard the voices of both Fitz and Briggs. Sitting outside on a chair, wrapped in a blanket, was a man. Gardener estimated his age around sixty. The small amount of grey hair he had left on the sides of his head above his ears was close-cropped. The man wore round, wire-rimmed spectacles. He had a bulbous nose, and his lips were thick and protruding. His complexion was the colour of flour. His teeth were chattering so hard, Gardener didn't think he would have any left in another hour.

The rest of his team was dotted around the arcade. Most of them were talking to what he suspected were the other shopkeepers. A constable in front of the shop handed the two officers their white contamination suits. Gardener dressed. He was about to enter when Briggs stepped out.

"Bit nasty in there, Stewart." He nodded towards the man on the chair. "That's Alan Cuthbertson."

"Did he find the body?" asked Gardener.

"Afraid so."

"Not touched anything, has he?"

"I doubt it. He hasn't spoken since I got here. In fact, I don't think he's spoken since he found her."

"Who found him, then?" asked Reilly.

"Bloke next door in the camera shop. Name's Battersby. He heard an almighty crash and came running to see what was up. Cuthbertson had passed out. Battersby left him to it while he rang us."

"Where is he now?"

"Back in his own shop."

"Anybody questioned him?"

"Just doing it. You'd better take a look, Stewart. I've told Scenes of Crime to hang fire until you've been in. I'm warning you now, it's much worse than the last one."

"How do you know it's the same killer?"

"There's a quote on the wall," said Briggs.

"And it's *worse* than the last one?" questioned Reilly.

"Well, you two go and have a look, I'm having a fag."

"I thought you'd given up," said Gardener.

"When you've seen what's in there, you might join me." Briggs nodded to Cuthbertson again. "No wonder that poor bastard's lost his marbles."

Gardener pushed past Briggs. Reilly followed.

Inside the shop, Gardener pinched his nose. The coppery odour of blood was ever present, along with the putrid aroma of urine and excrement. The room wasn't particularly big, but an awful lot had been crammed into the space for display purposes, such as tailor's dummies dressed in various costumes with a variety of different hairstyles. Two of the walls had shelves with latex masks and wigs, and a whole range of chemicals and powders for stage use. The only bare wall in the shop was to the left of the counter. That wall contained the message.

Which was partially hidden by the body.

The girl was naked, hanging upside down. Her legs were open, held that way by two ropes attached to ceiling beams, knotted tightly around her ankles, which – Gardener realised – bore no chafing. As his gaze wandered further down her colourless body, he didn't notice any signs of sexual abuse, but he knew a closer inspection may reveal otherwise.

Her arms had also been tied and held outwards by ropes, intricately wound around the mannequins, connected to the counter at one side, and the window ledge at the other. Her throat had been slit, allowing the blood to drain into a large bucket beneath her head. Had she been dead at that point? He'd figured she must have been, otherwise there would be blood spatter. That was something Fitz would eventually be able to tell him. The pathologist was standing quietly behind him, arranging the tools he would need.

"Notice something, Sean?"

"He's getting more adventurous," said Reilly. "But I'm noticing a lot of things. Which one are you thinking of?"

"The wall behind her has no blood spatter. Why?"

"He's done her somewhere else?"

"Possible. But how could you get a body into the arcade and into the shop without anyone seeing you?"

"He managed it in the theatre."

The SIO glanced around the shop in disgust.

Steve Fenton nodded. "I'll be outside. Give us a shout when you need me."

Gardener blew out a sigh, nodded at Fitz. "Okay." He stopped Steve Fenton leaving the shop. "Any sign of her clothes?"

"Not so far."

Gardener turned his attention to the quote:

The night passed – a night of vague horrors
– tortured dreams.

What the hell was that supposed to mean? And where had it come from? Another film?

In spite of the fact that he knew beyond any doubt she was dead, he still had to check. He felt for a pulse. No one questioned him. It was the duty of every officer – where possible – to preserve or save life. Briggs came back into the shop, muttering about the mess and the bastard who'd created it.

"Does she have a name?" asked Gardener.

"Janine Harper. Bloke next door identified her. She's worked here for years. He thinks she's about twenty-five. He's not sure where she lives."

"Any idea what time it happened, Fitz?"

Fitz sighed, removing a thermometer from her rectum. "Judging by the results, I'd say he started last night, reasonably late, so as not to be disturbed." The pathologist leaned forward and pointed. "Look at the bruising to the face. I think she resisted him. He probably punched her a few times, eventually overpowered her, and then most likely drugged her to be able to get her into that position."

"Why was she in the shop late at night by herself?" Gardener asked. "It wasn't her business."

"Ask him," said Briggs, pointing outside.

"I intend to, if he ever decides to speak." Gardener didn't say anything else, but walked around the counter and through to the back of the shop. Reilly followed. "There are signs of a struggle," suggested Gardener. His partner nodded.

A small number of bottles and boxes were scattered around the floor. The SIO glanced closely at the shelving and then down at the floor. "The nearest one's been moved, probably by force."

"Maybe she ran into here to try and escape."

"Where to?"

Reilly had no answer. "He obviously followed her."

"There's still no trace of blood spatter. So, she couldn't have been killed in here."

"That suggests she was still alive when he came into the shop," offered Reilly.

"So, what the hell did he do with her?"

"More to the point, where?" added Reilly.

Gardener turned back into the main shop, and read the quote. "What's that supposed to mean?" He stood contemplating. "I suppose it blows the theory of the watch committee." He nodded towards Janine Harper. "She certainly wasn't on it."

"Maybe not," said Reilly. "But her father might have been."

"Her father?"

"Val White gave us the names of the committee members. If my memory's right, there was a bloke called Jack Harper. If there's a connection, it doesn't blow your theory entirely."

Gardener glanced at the floor. "If that's the case, we definitely need to find Harry Fletcher now."

"What about him out there, Cuthbertson?" said Reilly. "Do you reckon he's capable of murder?"

"Could be," said Briggs.

"I'm not so sure," replied Fitz. "His shock looks pretty genuine to me. I realise you can't rule him out, but he's a bloody good actor if it is him."

"Isn't that what we're looking for, an actor?" said Gardener. "Someone with the ability to disguise himself, someone who has the means?"

"What's his motive?" asked Briggs.

"Let's find out." Gardener walked over to the front door. He spoke to the constable. "Clean him up and take him back to the station for questioning." He turned back and addressed Fitz. "Meanwhile, can you sort out the post-mortem as soon as possible? I'm particularly interested in the fact that there's no blood spatter, but there are indications of a struggle in the back room. He must have killed her in the shop. Question is, what's he used in order to stop her heartbeat? You know as well as I do if he'd done that while she was still alive, this place would be one God awful mess."

Fitz nodded. "Okay, we'll remove the body and let the SOCOs do their job."

Gardener shouted for Steve Fenton. "You know the drill. Sweep for prints. I'd like another ESLA. Be careful with the ropes. The knots look different to the last one."

He turned to Briggs. "I'll have to speak to the team. We'll need to find out where she lives, and speak to her parents."

"And anyone else that's close, if they haven't already been on the phone to report her missing," Briggs replied.

"I assume she's not married, there's no wedding band, nor a line to suggest there was one," said Gardener. "We need a written report of his information next door. And all the CCTV evidence we can lay our hands on."

"What a mess," said Briggs. "The shit's going to hit the fan with this one."

"Can you put a call into the FSS?"

Briggs nodded. "How the hell does he manage to do all this without someone seeing him?"

"He doesn't," said Gardener.

"Come again?" said Briggs.

"Plenty of people see him. He isn't worried about people seeing him because nobody knows what he really looks like. Take a look at that crowd out there." Gardener pointed through the window. "He could be in that lot, somewhere. The front row, maybe. We'd have no idea, because we don't know him. He knows that – he's playing on it. He can commit atrocities like this every day. He knows we're never going to catch him."

Gardener wanted out. He'd been here long enough. The smell had coated the insides of his nostrils.

"There's something else, boss," said Reilly. "If Jack Harper's dead and this was his daughter, that means *your* father is on the list as well."

"I know. I've thought of that already."

Another young constable appeared in the shop doorway. He waved to Gardener, but kept his eyes on the floor. "What is it?"

"The press, sir, they'd like a comment."

"I'm sure they would. I suppose we'd better tell them something. If we don't, they'll only make it up."

Gardener walked out of the shop, stripped off his paper suit and deposited it in a bin. Briggs and Reilly followed. He spotted a team of Operational Support Officers heading in his direction.

"I'd like you lot to split up and question every shopkeeper in the arcade. Find out what they know about Alan Cuthbertson and Janine Harper and the customers who come in here on a regular basis. I'd also like a couple of you out front on the streets today, question everyone you see. Find out if they were in the town last night. Did they see anyone they considered eccentric?"

He turned to Briggs. Despite his loathing of the press, he knew he would have to use them.

"I think we'd better ask the press to appeal for witnesses."

Chapter Twenty-three

"What do you think, Sean?"

"About Cuthbertson? I'll know better when we've spoken to him, boss."

They were sitting in Gardener's office ahead of the interview. As usual, Reilly was dressed in a brown leather bomber jacket and jeans. He emptied the contents of a coffee cup, and then threw it into the bin at the side of the desk.

Gardener was sitting with his hands bridged and his chin resting on them. He'd been reading the scribbled notes submitted by the officers who had interviewed the other shopkeepers in the arcade. "The comments from his colleagues are not very favourable."

"Go on," said Reilly.

"The guy who runs the camera shop next door reckons he's a loner, keeps odd hours, a little strange with his behaviour, rarely socialises. I have the impression he doesn't like Cuthbertson."

"We both know there's nothing wrong with that description, boss. He could be talking about you. But you're no killer."

"How do you know?" laughed Gardener. He really appreciated the working relationship he had with the Irishman. Had it not been for Sean Reilly, he doubted very much he would have overcome the effect of Sarah's death quite so readily. "It's not that so much, Sean. Battersby reckons he's quiet and subdued a lot of the time, as if he has things on his mind. Never discusses his private life, leaves the shop at all hours."

"Did he know why Janine Harper was working late at night on her own?" asked Reilly.

"No. Battersby noticed the lights were on, but he had no idea who was there. He doubted it would be Cuthbertson. Something about his manner doesn't add up, though," said Gardener. "I appreciate the death of his assistant would have an effect, but I thought he was too preoccupied."

"Perhaps he did it, boss. Maybe the silent treatment was a good piece of acting while he thought up an alibi for where he was yesterday."

"Maybe. According to Battersby he left the shop around four o'clock."

"Okay, so there's his opportunity. It must take a good three or four hours to apply make-up to the quality that this man needs. But we still need a motive, and he could have an alibi."

"Battersby left at six-thirty."

"Did he see Cuthbertson come back?"

"No, and he didn't see Janine Harper leaving either," replied Gardener.

"Did he say anything about their relationship?"

Gardener rifled through the notes in front of him. "No, except that they were total opposites. At times, she could be quite lively. They did have their differences, which appears to have been the usual thing, young versus old. Fresh ideas coming up against aged resistance."

A knock on the door interrupted their conversation. Colin Sharp's head appeared around the side of the door. "He's cleaned up and ready to talk now, sir."

"Thanks. We'll be there in five minutes."

"There's something else you ought to know."

"Go on," said Gardener.

"There's a lot of marks on his body."

"What kind of marks?" Reilly asked.

"Scratches, bites. Bruises."

"Has he now?" said Gardener. "Are they fresh?"

"They're recent, but I wouldn't like to say when."

Gardener gathered up the notes and returned them to the folder. "Time to go and find out what they're all about."

Chapter Twenty-four

"Is it the work of the same killer?"

The question was from Johnny Stevens, an experienced journalist with *The Yorkshire Post*. Alan Briggs knew he had served his time on some of the worst cases in the county, the Yorkshire Ripper to name but one. He was a bloodhound, well paid. Delivered results. A meeting with the press was the last thing Alan Briggs wanted right now. The day started terribly with the discovery of Janine Harper's body, and became worse when he was summoned to a meeting with his superior – who shouted loud enough to wake the dead. Now it hit an all-time low because Gardener was otherwise engaged.

Not that Gardener would have cared. Offering him a press meeting was like serving up garlic bread to Dracula. As much as he admired Gardener's dedication to the job and the reason for his hatred of the press, he would have much preferred to interview Alan Cuthbertson.

"There are similarities between the two murders. We are taking into consideration the theatrical and geographical links."

"Oh come on, Briggs."

"Hey!" The DCI raised his hand, stopped the reporter there. "Mister Briggs to you, if you don't mind."

"Okay, Mr Briggs," Stevens repeated the name with distaste. "Who has he killed this time?"

"You know very well I'm not at liberty to say."

"Is it a child?" shouted another reporter.

"No, it is not a child."

"Has he killed another thespian, Mr Briggs?"

Briggs took his time in answering because he knew what would come next. But he couldn't hold out forever. "No."

Johnny Stevens was on his feet again. "The public have a right to know what's going on, Mr Briggs. *We* have a duty to tell *them*, and *you* have one to tell *us*."

"I agree that the public have a right to know, son, and as soon as we have something concrete to tell them, we will. But this meeting is about utilising the newspapers to appeal for witnesses. We want the public of Leeds to keep their eyes open, report anything unusual."

Another reporter jumped down his throat. The questions were coming thick and fast. "Do you have any leads?"

"We have discovered one or two points worthy of further investigation." Briggs was pleased with himself for that one.

"Have you identified the man?"

"We are at present interviewing someone." Briggs held up his hand. "But let me make it absolutely clear, he is only helping us with our inquiries, he is not a suspect."

Another reporter stood up. He was about to throw a question when Briggs himself rose from his chair.

"I'm afraid I'll have to stop you there, gentlemen. We do have a very important investigation on our hands. Thank you for your time."

Briggs left the room, closed the door behind him, relieved that it was over. He was still furious that they were no further on; two murders within a week, both in the same part of town. There were similarities, neither of which had turned up any evidence. The next meeting in the incident room would be one to remember.

Chapter Twenty-five

Gardener studied Alan Cuthbertson.

The expression of fear on the shop owner's face had Gardener concerned. Was he frightened about the situation he was in; felt he was being fitted up for something he hadn't done? Or was it guilt because he *had* committed murder, and the police had figured him out a lot sooner than he'd anticipated?

They had taken his clothes and supplied him with a plain black T-shirt, dark blue jogging bottoms, and black plimsoles – standard issue custody clothing. Cuthbertson's pallor was deathly white. He constantly twitched. He also rubbed his hands together a lot whilst inspecting his fingernails every few seconds.

"Am I under arrest?" he asked.

"Not yet," replied Gardener. "You're helping with our enquiries."

"Do I need a solicitor?"

"Do *you* think you need one?"

"I haven't done anything wrong!" he shouted.

"Bit of a shock for you, seeing that" said Reilly.

"Shock!" repeated Cuthbertson. "I was bloody traumatised. It's not every day you open your shop and find your assistant hanging upside down with her insides in a bucket."

"Not so shocked that you didn't take everything in, by the sound of it," said Reilly.

Cuthbertson fixed Reilly with a stare. "What are you suggesting?"

"How would you describe your relationship?" asked Gardener.

"What's that supposed to mean?" retorted Cuthbertson. His eyes were like slits and his expression had hardened. "I've heard about you lot and your strong-arm tactics. Well, you won't get me to admit to something I haven't done."

"We don't want you to. But we would like an answer to the question I've just asked."

"Oh, God." He placed his arms on the desk and supported his head with his hands. "What a bloody mess."

Gardener didn't feel the need to repeat the question. He chose instead to simply stare at the suspect.

Cuthbertson sighed. "My relationship." He lifted his head and rubbed his hands together. "Well. It was pretty much like any other. She was a good worker. Usually on time, never really took time off sick."

"Had she caused you any problems recently?" asked Gardener.

"I think she's had something on her mind. Last couple of days she'd been late, and her attitude with customers wasn't what I would have expected of her. More than once I had to smile and make an apology."

"Did she say what it was?"

"No, but she was certainly withdrawn. I did ask of course, but she just blamed it on women's problems. Maybe it was boyfriend trouble."

"Do you know the boyfriend?" asked Reilly.

"Yes, met him a couple of times. He'd picked her up from the shop. He seemed all right, but then don't they all when you only see them for a couple of minutes?"

"Do you know anything else about him? His name? Where he lives? His job?"

"Carl Simpson, lives over Esholt way; don't know where exactly. Plays in a band, as far as I know. He's a drummer, likes to make a bit of noise. Not the sort of band I'd want to see, nor you two by the look of you."

"Were there any other problems?" asked Gardener.

"Nothing she let on about."

"So, you worked well together?"

"Yes, I just said so, didn't I?"

"How long had she worked for you?"

"About five years. The shop had been growing steadily busier, and I advertised for an assistant. She was the best of the bunch."

"Did she ever talk about her home life? About her relationship with her parents?" asked Gardener.

"A little. She had a younger sister who was still at college. Her father's dead. Her mother takes in ironing."

News of her father's death struck a raw nerve with Gardener. Was it Jack Harper of the watch committee? If it was, then they needed to find Fletcher for all sorts of reasons. "Did you know her father?"

"No. He died before Janine came to work for me."

"She ever mention his name?"

"I can't remember. Look, where the hell are you going with all this? It's not helping find the killer, is it?" asked Cuthbertson.

"We have to build a picture of what Janine was like," said Gardener. "You've already told us she wasn't herself of late. We need to know why. Was it family problems? Boyfriend trouble? Had someone threatened her? Did she have money problems? Any debt? Do you know anything about her social life?"

"I'm her employer. The kind of questions you're asking me should be directed at her mother. She knows her better than I do."

"In that case," said Reilly, "let's talk about you."

"Me?"

"Yes, you. Tell us something about yourself?"

"There's not much to tell."

"I wish I had a pound for every time I'd heard that, don't you, boss? I'll tell you what, we'll make this easy for you. We'll ask questions, you answer. How long have you had your business?"

"Thirty years. I haven't been in the arcade for thirty years because it wasn't there then. I started off in a little village, Burley in Wharfedale back in the Eighties. That's where I live, you see."

"Business was good then?"

"Not to start with. But I've always been interested in theatre and stage, and I had a lucky break thirty years ago. I won twenty-five thousand pounds on the football pools. It was a lot of money back then. So, I decided to pack in work and open the shop."

"I see," said Gardener. "So, because you'd won all that money, it didn't really matter whether or not the business got off to a slow start, you had enough capital to see you through."

"That's about the size of it. Look, can I get a drink or something?"

Gardener left the table. Outside the interview room door, he asked for two coffees – fresh ones, not the crap from the machine, and a bottle of water. He came back to the table and sat down. "Okay, so you had the shop at Burley. When did you decide to move to Leeds?"

"Ten years ago. Business was expanding and I was beginning to attract lucrative custom from London. A lot of my business is mail order."

"I'm pleased you mentioned that. We would like to see records, everything you've sold, both over the counter and mail order for at least the last five years."

"That isn't a problem. Anyway, I moved into Leeds, on Briggate. Five years ago, I decided to take one of the arcade shops because it was considered a more prime position. And I took Janine on."

A uniformed officer returned with the drinks. He left them on the table and walked out. "What about your customers? How well do you know them?"

"I know a few, repeat business from people who are touring."

"What about new customers? Have you had any in the shop recently that you haven't seen before?"

"Quite a few."

"Any strange ones?" asked Reilly. "An eccentric? Someone who stands out a little more than usual?"

"Can't say that I've noticed. Most of the people who come in are pleasant. You get the odd few that think they're above everyone else, people who think that just because they're in a local production, they're film stars."

"Anyone come to mind?"

"Not off the top of my head, no." He sipped his coffee.

"I'd like a list of all your clients, Mr Cuthbertson. Names and addresses."

"I don't know if I have the addresses of all of them."

"We'll settle for everyone that you do have," replied Gardener. "Now, let's come back to something you said earlier. You'd always been interested in theatre and stage. Films as well?"

"Yes, films as well."

"What's your favourite?" asked Gardener.

"Pardon?"

"Your favourite film, what is it?"

"I... er... I'm not sure. Something black and white I imagine, an Ealing comedy."

"Why?"

"What do you mean, why?"

"Simple enough question, Mr Cuthbertson. Why do you like films from that era, Ealing comedies in particular?"

"Because they knew how to make films then. Good, wholesome films with people who could act. Not just the comedies, but the kitchen-sink drama as well. Films that dealt with real people in real situations. Not the garbage you get now, science fiction, horror, sex. There's enough horror in the real world without having TV and cinema ram it down your throat. You only have to look at my shop to see that. And here you are accusing me when I haven't done anything."

"No one is accusing you. If anything, we're trying to eliminate you from our enquiries, and the only way we can do that is to be very thorough. Wouldn't you agree?" asked Gardener.

"Absolutely."

"Wouldn't want to go to prison for something you haven't done, would you, now?" said Reilly. "Especially for a crime like this. You know what they do to people in prison who have killed women?"

"Look, if you're trying to frighten me..."

"We're not," replied Gardener. "We're trying to find out why a young girl has been butchered on your premises, and there are times when our job is not very nice, but we still have to do it. If you're innocent, you have nothing to worry about. Now, can we please get back to the matter in hand?"

Cuthbertson took another sip of coffee.

"Ealing comedies," said Reilly.

A silence descended upon the room. When it was obvious that Reilly wasn't going to elaborate, Cuthbertson spoke up. "What about them?"

"Does the name Wallace Henry Corndell mean anything to you?"

Cuthbertson took his time before answering. "No, should it?"

"William, maybe?"

"No. I've never heard of him, either."

"What about Inspector Burke?" Gardener asked.

"Who the bloody hell's he?" asked Cuthbertson. "Another one of your lot?"

"For a man who likes his films, you don't know much about them," said Reilly.

"I never said I was into films, not in the way you mean. Theatre and stage is more my thing."

"I see," said Reilly. "Well that figures, given the type of shop you run. Like dressing up, do you? Putting on the make-up, that kind of thing?"

Cuthbertson narrowed his eyes. "I've done a bit, why do you ask?"

"What other interests do you have?" asked Gardener.

Cuthbertson stalled before answering, as if he was trying to work out where they were heading. "I like to read."

"What sort of books?"

"Biographical. Mostly non-fiction."

Reilly leaned forward and folded his arms across the top of the table. "For long weary months I have awaited this hour."

"Pardon?" asked Cuthbertson. Turning to Gardener, he asked, "Is he all right?"

"Do you not recognise it? And you being a thespian, shame on you."

"I never said I was a thespian. Look, is it me, or is it hot in here?" Cuthbertson loosened his shirt collar and ran his hands around his neck.

Gardener wondered why he'd done that. He'd seemed okay until Reilly had mentioned the quote. Why had that unbalanced him? He leaned forward. "The night passed – a night of vague horrors. Tortured dreams."

"Look, what the hell are you two talking about? Is there something in the coffee? If I'm not under arrest, why am I still here?"

"I've told you already, you're helping with our enquiries. We just wondered how well you knew your films, and whether or not you recognised the two quotes."

"Oh, I see." Cuthbertson folded his arms. "You think I did it, and now you're using the quote on the wall next to Janine's body. Trying to catch me out." He leaned forward himself now, a smug smile crossing his features. "I'm afraid you'll have to do better than that, gentleman. I've already told you, I have nothing to hide."

"I wouldn't say that, judging by the state of your body," said Reilly.

"What?"

"How did you come by the marks?" asked Gardener.

"I don't know what you're talking about."

"Take your shirt off," demanded Reilly. "Maybe that will refresh your memory."

"Look, okay, I admit to having one or two bruises, but they're not what you think."

"How do you know what we're thinking?" asked Gardener.

"You two think I killed Janine, and the bruises on my body are proof. That's what you're thinking."

"Wouldn't you?" said Reilly. "On the night a young girl was butchered in your shop, you'd left at four o'clock and were not seen again until the next morning. But when you do make an appearance, you look like you've survived a terrorist attack."

"It's not as bad as you're making out."

"Show us," said Reilly.

"Gentlemen..."

"Show us now!" Gardener demanded. Although Cuthbertson appeared unwilling, he did finally peel off his shirt.

Gardener grimaced. His back bore the marks of a cat of nine tails: long, stripe shaped cuts. Most of the bruising was purple, yellow in the middle. What Gardener couldn't understand was why Cuthbertson had not shown any outward signs of discomfort. But having said that, the man had not sat back in his seat.

"So, where were you last night, and how did you get those?" asked Reilly.

Cuthbertson replaced his shirt and returned to his seat.

"Well?" persisted Reilly.

"It's not what you think."

"You keep trying to tell us what *we're* thinking, instead of what's going through *your* head," pressed Gardener.

Cuthbertson rubbed his hands down his face and sighed heavily. "I never killed Janine Harper. She was my assistant, my friend."

"Last night!" Reilly reminded him. "Where were you?"

"Ruffin Street," he replied, quietly.

"Say again," said Reilly.

Cuthbertson brought his head up a little fast, his manner aggressive. "You're enjoying this, aren't you? I said, Ruffin Street."

"I thought you did."

Gardener tried to picture the area. He knew where the street was, but he wasn't quite sure what Cuthbertson was trying to say. "What's on Ruffin Street, Mr Cuthbertson?"

"I'd have thought you'd know, being a policeman."

"I'm aware that it's an area of ill repute, but I don't frequent the place myself. So, you'll have to do a little better than that. We need your alibi."

"I ... I was..." He stopped talking, licked his lips.

Gardener waited.

"I was at Madame Two-swords. Happy now?"

Gardener turned to Reilly. "Where the hell is Madame Tussauds in Ruffin Street?"

Reilly's smile widened. "Trust me, boss, you wouldn't want to know. But I'll tell you this and I'll tell you no more, it's not a waxwork museum."

"What is it?"

"Madame Two-swords, and the spelling is two as in the number, and swords as in the sharp bladed implements that knights used to use, is a house of ill repute for people who like to be fulfilled sexually in a very strange way."

Gardener glanced at Cuthbertson, who was staring at the floor. He passed over a pen and paper. "Write the number down. We'll check. Were you there the night Leonard White was murdered?"

"Yes, I was."

Gardener couldn't believe what he was hearing. "What? Do you go for that kind of punishment every night?"

"No."

"How often?"

"I'm there most nights, but not for anything physical. A lot of them like to dress up and wear make-up. I can supply all their needs. Sometimes I help them put it on."

Gardener shook his head.

Cuthbertson continued. "But I can promise you, I never murdered Janine, and I didn't do Leonard White, either."

Gardener realised there was little more he could ask Cuthbertson at the moment until he could confirm his alibis. He informed the man he was free to go for the time being.

Chapter Twenty-six

"We need to nail this bloke, and fast! Otherwise we're all going down." Briggs was agitated. The incident room was full, but you could have heard a fly fart in the next world. "I've had the press and the Commissioner on my back, and neither of them are in the mood for negative answers."

"It isn't our fault," said Reilly, glancing at the stranger sitting quietly in the corner of the room.

"Well, everybody seems to think it is," retorted Briggs. "We're paid to protect the public, and we're failing. We've had two murders on our patch, and the press have already made the connection. In fact, they know as much as we do because we can't do our jobs properly."

Briggs threw his folder on the desk and studied the photographs on the easel. "So, can anyone tell me anything new?"

Sharp inched forward. "I've spoken to the taxi driver who picked up Leonard White on the night he was killed. Or should I say, the man impersonating Leonard White."

"And what did he have to say?" asked Briggs.

"Very little. He wasn't called in advance, he simply happened to be driving by the theatre at the time and was flagged down."

"Where did he take him?"

"The station."

"The station?" questioned Briggs. "It's only a five-minute walk, for Christ's sakes."

"He was an actor," said Gardener. "Famous or not, he's not likely to walk through the town centre."

"Okay," said Briggs, "fair point. What happened when he dropped him off? Did he see where he went?"

"No. White shoved a ten pound note in his hand and then walked into the station without waiting for change."

"Don't suppose he's still got the note, has he?"

"He didn't say."

"Well, check it out, for God's sake! People keep souvenirs for all sorts of reasons."

Gardener interrupted. "What good would it do us? We wouldn't be able to lift any prints worth having."

"We don't know that," said Briggs, turning to address Colin Sharp again. "Did White say anything while he was in the taxi?"

"Apparently not. He got in, told him to go to the station, and then got out after paying. The driver tried to engage him in conversation because he recognised him, but White wasn't having any of it. He simply ignored him."

"Brilliant. Did you question anyone at the station? Ticket booth operators, railway porters, cleaners, tramps?"

"I did, but no one saw anything unusual."

"They must have done, for Christ's sakes, he wasn't exactly dressed for travelling on trains. Didn't White buy a ticket to anywhere?" demanded Briggs.

"I did talk to the person who was selling tickets all night. I showed him a photo because he didn't know who Leonard White was, but no one of that description bought a ticket."

"Well, he can't have just disappeared in the middle of a fucking station! He was a well-known actor."

"He may not have left the station as Leonard White," said Gardener.

Briggs hadn't thought of that and quickly moved on. "Anything on CCTV?"

"We're still checking," said Sharp.

"Keep at it. And while we're on the subject of transport, what about white vans?"

Anderson spoke up. "We've drawn a blank so far. Not many companies hire out seven and a half ton trucks, those that have can account for them, and the customers."

"How does he do it?" shouted Briggs. "Not only does he *walk* around Leeds, but he drives around in big white vans that no one remembers seeing, both of which finally disappear into thin air. Thank Christ somebody has their eyes open. Eyewitness reports indicate a very strange person seen in Leeds on the night Janine was murdered. We've interviewed a couple of them and managed to sort out an artist impression."

Briggs passed around the sketches from his folder.

"You'd have to be blind not to notice *him* walking round. He looks like Dracula," said Anderson.

"This is precisely why we can't catch him," said Gardener. "The first murder saw him impersonating Leonard White. His second sees him as someone totally different. He can commit as many as he likes if we can't figure out what *he* looks like."

"I agree, but there might be a link between the people he's impersonating. It might be something to do with films, maybe they're all from the same film, or a series of films made by the same director. Or maybe portrayed by the same actor. Have we got a list of the films White made? Did he star in anything with a vampire that looks like the impression?"

"I've made a start on that one," said Dave Rawson. "I called his agents and they've agreed to draw up a list."

"Get his wife back on the phone," said Briggs, "she'll have a list as well."

Gardener quickly took over, glancing at Colin Sharp. "Colin, the quote on the wall next to Janine Harper, anything?"

"Same film, sir, *Phantom of the Opera*."

Gardener stared at Briggs, "that might answer one of your questions, films with the same actor or director. *Phantom of the Opera* is favoured here." He addressed the rest of them. "Two quotes from the same film, *Phantom*, so what's happening here? Is he obsessed with *The Phantom*? Was it a case of unrequited love: he stalked Janine Harper but got nothing in return? It's definitely a lead worth following."

"You wouldn't say it was the same film judging by the disguise he used in Leeds on the night she was killed," said Briggs, nodding toward Reilly.

"The CCTV from the arcade is interesting enough, but it doesn't show us anything more than we already know." Reilly switched on the recording and they all watched as the vampire character matching the witness statements entered the shop at nine forty-two, and left well after midnight. "No one else was in the arcade, so he was allowed to come and go unchallenged," he said.

"Correct me if I'm wrong,' said Anderson, 'but the character he used there was not from *The Phantom*."

"You're not wrong," said Colin Sharp, "I've watched it all the way through now and there is no character like that in the film."

"Something else to go on," said Gardener, "it's not the same film so are we back to films all starring the same actor, or made by the same director?"

"How did you get on with Cuthbertson?" Briggs asked Gardener, changing the subject.

"It's not him," said Gardener. "He's very strange, but he has a cast-iron alibi."

Gardener briefed them about the interview and the things he'd uncovered.

"We still have no idea if there's a link between Cuthbertson and White?" said Briggs. "Was Janine killed, when it should have been Cuthbertson?"

"It's a possibility," said Gardener. "Which could rule out the watch committee connection. But I think there's a real urgency now to find Harry Fletcher."

"Two murders carried out with relative ease," said Briggs. "We're struggling because we don't know what he looks like. Look around the room. You're all out there doing your job, but not one of you has come up with anything concrete. I'm not knocking any of you, I know how hard it is, but if he murders someone else, and the chances are he will, we're all going to be back out there, looking for another job. It's not funny. We need a positive lead." Briggs rubbed his forehead. "What about Scenes of Crime?"

"We found Janine Harper's mobile phone in the back of the shop, under the Dexion shelving. No idea why it was there. Maybe she was trying to call us, and in the struggle it was knocked under there. Anyway, we've checked it for prints and can only find hers. We've also gone through the contacts and all the messages, so we have a lead on the boyfriend."

"Good work," said Briggs. "Bring him in, let's talk to him."

"And we found a list," offered Fenton. "It looks like an order for make-up, but it's not easy to make out. It was screwed up in a bin, and it looks like it's had coffee on it. The only thing I can really see is the name Corndell."

"Anyone know that name?" asked Briggs.

"I do," said Reilly. Before the Irishman had a chance to elaborate, Thornton came through the door and apologised for his lateness. He was also out of breath.

"Everything okay, Frank?" asked Briggs.

"Yes." He turned in Gardener's direction and had the common courtesy to offer his apologies to his superior officer. "Anyway, I've uncovered something interesting. The knots used to hold Janine's legs were different to the first murder. He used a double loop bowline."

"Which is what?" asked Gardener.

Thornton explained the technicalities of the knot. "Apparently, it was used at sea for lowering injured men from boats, one leg through each loop." Thornton sat down, sipping the coffee he'd brought in with him, staring at the stranger in their midst.

Gardener took over. "So, once again we have a link to the navy, or the fishing industry. The first time, he used a sailor's eye splice. This time he's used a double loop bowline. So, someone needs to check these out. Is our killer a fisherman? Or does he simply have a good knowledge of knots and he's using that fact to throw us?" He glanced at Thornton. "Well done, Frank. Can you keep going with that one? Find out as much as you can about the rope itself."

"Right. Reilly–" started Briggs.

"Excuse me, sir?" The voice belonged to the youngest member of the team, Patrick Edwards. He was fresh-faced, nineteen years old, and had an earring in one ear that no one was pleased about.

Briggs glanced at him, but didn't offer a question.

Edwards took it as his cue. "I've got something on a missing limo. Took a call about ten minutes ago from a company in Bradford who hire them out for all sorts of reasons. One of them has gone missing. It was hired out for the whole of last week and should have been returned on Monday. It hasn't."

"What? And it's taken them till now to report it missing? Okay, as soon as we're out of here get yourself over there, lad, and get every scrap of information you can." Briggs turned his attention to the Irishman.

Reilly stood up. "The list that Scenes of Crime found ties in with what the boss and I have in mind. We have a lead on Corndell, and we're going to see him this afternoon."

Briggs was quick to notice a confused expression on Gardener's face. "Does your partner know about it, Reilly?"

"Of course he does. William Henry Corndell is his name."

"And where does he fit in?"

"He's an actor. Lives in a big house near Horsforth."

"What makes you think he has anything to do with it?"

"I'm not saying he has, but something Laura said tells me he might be able to help, if nothing else. Apparently, there's a bloke out at the university who books all the entertainment. He reckons this William Henry Corndell is the best there is. Worked the stage in the West End, films as well. Anyway, he's playing a one-man show at the uni, and Laura's covering it. And if you want another reason, Steve Fenton's just given it to us with the list they found in the shop."

"Fair enough, it's a lead."

Gardener asked a question of the CSM, Steve Fenton. "Any luck with that piece of film starring the infamous Inspector Burke?"

"Yes and no. The tech lads have finished with it. They tell me it's not an old piece of film. It was made to look that way with modern technology. It was filmed recently, but that's all they can tell us."

"What brand of disc?"

"TDK."

"Can you get anything from the batch number?" Gardener figured he was searching for a needle in a haystack, but he had to try.

"Not the kind of info you wanted. I spoke to TDK this afternoon. The only thing they can tell us from the batch number is that it was manufactured about fifteen years ago, and not necessarily in the UK."

Gardener sighed, disappointed. "What about the tape you took from the theatre?"

"Same with that, it was also TDK," said Fenton. "But no one uses cassette tapes so they wouldn't speculate at all on that one. We're pretty sure the words shouted are 'look out', but no idea if it's been recorded live or comes from a film."

Gardener updated the ANACAPA chart, even though there was little new evidence.

Briggs addressed them all. "I think it's time to introduce you to the new man in the corner. I've noticed the looks you're all giving him." The man stood up and offered a smile.

"Trevor Thorpe," said Briggs. "The profiler."

Chapter Twenty-seven

As the officer in charge, Gardener walked over and shook hands with Thorpe, introducing himself and using the opportunity for a quick but close inspection. He was slightly shorter than Gardener and similar in weight. His rugged exterior conveyed a tough life. The left eye was a little bigger than the right, and he was quite clearly blind in it. A scar on his forehead ran down past the eyebrow, below the eye. His brown hair was closely cropped with flecks of grey running through it. The texture of his face resembled a piece of old leather. Thorpe was dressed in a well-worn tweed jacket and a pair of brown corduroys, and brown casual slip-on shoes.

Gardener returned to his seat. As he did so, he asked the question, "So, Mr Thorpe, I'm sure DCI Briggs has briefed you about everything that's happened. Do you have anything to add to what you've seen so far?"

"Can I thank you all first for, er, inviting me?" Thorpe walked around the room with his hands behind his back, like a schoolmaster. When he spoke it was very slowly, while he stared at the ceiling.

"There was a lot of, er, work accomplished here, a lot of articulate planning. Couple it with the clues, and you can see straight away that this man is very intelligent. He cares about what he does. It's an art form. He plans everything down to the last detail. He has medical knowledge."

Gardener thought Thorpe sounded like a politician. "Why, in your opinion, is he doing it?"

Thorpe went back to his seat and sat, his legs astride, resting his arms on the back, choosing to face his audience, rather than the ceiling. "Because he can." He lifted one hand matter-of-factly. "I think he likes playing sadistic games. He'll have played them all his life. When he was younger it would have been animals, children younger than himself. In fact, anything that was defenceless."

Gardener was beginning to feel irritated by the man's demeanour. Perhaps that was his manner. He had to accept that the man was here of his own free will. He was not being paid. Maybe Gardener simply didn't like what he saw.

Thorpe stood up, started to pace, staring at the ceiling again. Gardener felt like he was being lectured.

"Murder usually stems from a deadly fantasy, a need to exert power over the victim, to inflict pain and fear, which can then be played for real. He almost certainly has a grudge, and he is exerting his power. I think you'll find that's because he was repressed when he was younger. He had a domineering mother who allowed him no freedom. No chance to express his emotions.

"And that is what we are seeing here. He's, er, no different to most serial killers. Because they kill so casually, without emotion, they're almost impossible to catch. Just as difficult to understand. As far as he's concerned, killing is an art form, no different to eating a meal." He returned to his seat and pulled a handkerchief from his jacket pocket and mopped his brow.

"Everything all right, Trevor?" asked Briggs.

"Er, yes, may I have a drink of water, please? I, er, need to take a tablet."

Briggs asked Patrick Edwards to do the honours. After the tablet, Thorpe continued. "Now, where was I? Oh yes, most of them live, er, outwardly normal lives and have a very high IQ. We can see that by the games he's playing, and the puzzles he's leaving."

"Why does he drain the blood?" asked Reilly.

Thorpe took to his feet again. "Well, you see, there's another interesting point. Blood may be very sacred to him. Have you checked to see if either of these people who have been killed have any blood-related diseases? Particularly in the case of the girl. Was she promiscuous? Was she HIV positive? Maybe he thinks that blood is very precious, and these people..." – Thorpe turned and reached out with his arms – "...are not treating their bodies like a temple, as he does."

"What makes you say that?" asked Gardener.

"Everything we've seen so far. The man is articulate. He's careful, precise. You have no leads because he leaves you no clues with which to catch him. Here is a man who takes life very seriously."

Gardener's mobile interrupted their meeting. After a concerned conversation, he flipped it off and glanced at Briggs. "It's Fitz. He wants us over at the morgue straight away."

"Why? What's wrong?" asked Briggs.

"He wouldn't tell us over the phone," replied Gardener, "but he said we're not going to like it."

Chapter Twenty-eight

The three of them made it to the morgue in record time. Fitz was in his office. The desk was impeccably tidy, as if all the paperwork had been positioned using a set square. The files on the shelf behind him were arranged neatly in alphabetical order, with the writing facing the same way. Gardener couldn't identify the piece of classical music that Fitz was listening to, but assumed it to be an opera.

"You didn't waste much time," said Fitz, glancing at Gardener.

"It sounded urgent."

Fitz rose from his chair, adjusted his glasses. "There's never an urgency when you're dealing with the dead."

"Well, there is in our case," said Briggs.

"Follow me." Fitz left the office, collecting a green gown and a fresh pair of gloves from a cupboard. He walked over to Janine Harper's corpse and removed the cover. Her fragile body lacked colour, emphasising the severity of the bruising on her face. Only now, she had a Y-shaped incision where Fitz had done his job.

"What have you found?" asked Briggs.

"Something that needs further investigation," replied Fitz. "There are traces of a drug called ephedrine in her bloodstream."

"What's that?" asked Gardener.

"It's an alkaloid drug normally used to relieve the symptoms of asthma."

"Did she have a history of asthma?" asked Briggs.

"Yes, according to her records. I also found alcohol in her system, sherry to be precise, along with traces of nuts."

"What type of nuts?"

"Nothing specific, a bit of a mixture."

"Which leads us where?" asked Gardener.

"I think, and I stress *think*, that what he's done is ground the nuts into a fine powder and mixed them with the sherry, which, when using the correct quantities, creates a venomous cocktail with the drug ephedrine. I'll come back to that in a second, but just take a look at this." Fitz lifted the head. "De-epithelialisation."

"What the hell is that?" asked Reilly.

Fitz drew out Janine's tongue. It was red raw, inflamed. "He's very carefully removed the top layer of skin from her tongue."

Briggs stared at the ceiling and sighed. "Did he do that when she was alive?"

"There wouldn't be much point when she was dead," replied Fitz.

"Oh Jesus," said Briggs.

"Someone must have heard the screams," said Reilly.

"How?" Gardener asked. "It's not as if someone's going to stand around while you pull out their tongue and then slice off the top layer of skin, is it?"

"I wondered about that," said Fitz.

"Is that what the ephedrine was all about? He's drugged her so he could perform delicate surgery?" asked Gardener.

"I don't think so. There are traces of a very mild sedative in her bloodstream as well. For what it's worth, I think he entered the shop and used the element of surprise to take advantage. They've had a bit of a fight, which he won by exerting his strength. You can see that by the bruising." Fitz pointed to the top of her left arm. "If you focus just here, there's a pin-prick where he's injected the sedative. That made her drowsy, more co-operative.

"I suspect he's then taken his time to set up precisely how he wants her, and waited for the sedative to wear off before carrying out the second part of his plan, which was removing the top layer of skin from her tongue. And he also appears to have scraped her fingernails clean. In fact, they're immaculate. I'd say that's because he doesn't want what's underneath being used against him."

"Like Trevor Thorpe said, he's very precise," said Briggs.

"So, where does this drug come in?" said Gardener. "The one that's made from sherry and nuts?"

Fitz sighed. "He had another purpose in mind. You see, ephedrine is a relief for asthma sufferers, but it can have diabolical side effects if you raise someone's sense of fear to the limit and then administer lethal doses of the cocktail he's mixed up. Combined with adrenaline, it eventually causes a stroke. But before you die, the agony would be immeasurable."

"Is that what she died of?" asked Briggs. "A stroke?"

"In the end, yes, but one drawn on through careful calculation."

"Why is he going to such lengths?" asked Briggs.

"Because he can," replied Gardener. "It's like your profiler said, he's exerting his power. But I think it's more than that, I think he's making a point. We just don't know what it is."

"Any recorded case, Fitz?" asked Reilly.

"Not that I'm aware of. But better use of the police computers and the internet may provide us with clues. It's a very clinical and precise way of killing someone. It's almost as if he's perfected the technique."

"You think he's used the method before?" asked Gardener.

"It's worth keeping an open mind," said Fitz.

"Stewart, Sean," said Briggs. "Pull out all the stops and find this bloke!"

"We'll have one of the lads draw up a list of all thespians living in the area, while Sean and I go and interview the one living in Horsforth."

"Before you go rushing anywhere," said Fitz, "I haven't finished."

"What else has he done?" asked Briggs, as if he couldn't believe there would be anything else.

Fitz walked over to the stainless-steel counter at the back of the room. "I found this inserted in her anus."

"What is it?" asked Gardener.

"It's a glass tube," said Fitz. "There are no signs of sexual abuse. And the tube wasn't inserted into her anus for sexual reasons." Fitz picked up the glass vial, held it out in front of him. "The next puzzle is in here."

Seeing as the pathologist was the only one wearing gloves, no one else volunteered. After Fitz had removed the paper and unrolled it, they could see another verse had been printed on the same style paper as before.

Another one gone … how many more?
Pity you couldn't save this little whore

I've left puzzles and clues, but you haven't got very far
Here's another: follow The Scarlet Car

I implore you again, to study your needs
Another is all set to fall, down and out, in Leeds.

Chapter Twenty-nine

As Reilly pulled the car to a halt outside the wrought iron gates, Gardener jumped out and surveyed what could only be described as a kingdom. He gazed upwards, wondering whether or not Corndell was simply security conscious or totally paranoid. The gates were electronically controlled, which opened onto a gravel drive surrounded by pine trees, all under the watchful eye of CCTV cameras. He couldn't see the house, but he could guess its size.

Reilly stepped up beside Gardener. "Remind you of anyone?"

Gardener glanced at his partner. "Derek Summers?"

"One and the same. Let's hope these entertainment types are not all tarred with the same brush."

Gardener shuddered as he recalled the havoc a group of paedophiles led by Summers had caused him and his partner three months previously: he'd been beaten within an inch of his life, his son had been kidnapped, his father had gone through hell, and he'd lost the only woman who'd meant anything to him after his late wife Sarah. But through it all, his friend and partner Sean Reilly had stood by his side, fighting all the way.

"God forbid, Sean. I don't think I could deal with another one."

"I'm not sure which is worse. Summers was bad enough, I'll grant you, but whoever is torturing and killing people the way this bloke does is on another level."

Gardener stood with his hands in his pockets. The bright March morning with its clear blue sky added to the postcard view before him. "This is one hell of a place. I can't wait for a proper look."

"You'd better press the intercom, then."

Gardener did as advised and waited, but no one answered. "Do you think he's out?"

"I doubt it, boss, it probably takes him a week to get round it all."

Gardener laughed as the intercom buzzed. "Yes?" asked the voice.

"Mr Corndell?" questioned Gardener.

"May I inquire who's asking?"

Gardener glanced at Reilly, and then at the intercom. "Major Crime Team, Mr Corndell. Detective Inspector Gardener and Detective Sergeant Reilly, we'd like to ask you a few questions."

"But you have no appointment. I don't see people without appointments."

Gardener pressed his authority. "We don't need one. We are the police."

The reply – when it came – sounded forced. "You'd better come in, then." The gates opened. Both detectives returned to the car and drove into the grounds.

The house was a three-storey Victorian mansion with gothic turrets on either side. Built with grey Yorkshire stone and a grey slate roof, the building had dark oak frames and leaded windows, with two black arched front doors. The gardens were well landscaped, the perimeter covered in poplar trees. As they drew closer, the poplars were replaced by bay trees. To the right of the building was a double garage. Opposite the front door was a large fountain.

Reilly pulled the car to a halt and switched off the engine. "Even Derek Summers would have had trouble keeping up with this one."

"It's not bad for someone we've never heard of," said Gardener. "How does he manage to make such a good living if he's not in the limelight?"

"Perhaps it's time we went and found out."

Both men left the car and approached the house. Gardener rang the bell. Eventually, the door opened.

Chapter Thirty

An agitated Corndell glared at the detectives. They peered back with confused expressions. He didn't like the one on the right, wearing the brown bomber jacket and jeans. He was hard and Corndell suspected there would be trouble, most likely a personality clash. The other one was well groomed, smartly dressed in a blue shirt, black slacks and a grey striped suit jacket. Corndell warmed to him, especially the grey leather hat. "Come in," he said invitingly.

The two men stepped over the threshold. Corndell shut the door and leaned against the wall, returning to a conversation on his mobile. "I'm sorry?" He paused before resuming. "Perhaps you'd be kind enough to tell Rupert Julian that if he's not happy with my script, we can always bring in Wallace Worsley to direct." He rolled his eyes, covering the phone with his hand. "Please excuse me. Problems with Hollywood."

When he returned to his phone, he noticed that the taller and better-dressed of the two detectives was studying the film posters decorating most of his dark, oak-panelled hall. "I can promise you, George, we shall not be having this conversation again. Either Rupert Julian stands down or I take my script elsewhere."

Having said his piece, he cut the connection, gripped his walking stick, and shuffled towards them. "I do apologise, gentlemen."

"Not at all, Mr Corndell. I was admiring your posters."

"Wonderful. Are you into films, Mister...?"

"Gardener," he replied. "And my partner, DS Sean Reilly. I'm afraid I don't get the time, but my father does. He's the biggest film buff I know."

"Really," replied Corndell, wondering where he was heading.

"Oh yes, never away from the cinema."

"Any particular era, Mr Gardener?"

"He likes pretty much anything, the older films in particular, black and white, something with a story. I'm sure he'd like a look at these."

"A man after my own heart. It's taken years, Mr Gardener, and a lot of patience," replied Corndell. "You see that poster there." He pointed, and Gardener followed the line of his cane. "That's an original for Boris Karloff's

Frankenstein, made in 1931. There are only four left in the world, and one recently sold for a $198,000."

"Jesus Christ!" said Reilly. "For a poster?"

Corndell laughed. "Language, Mr Reilly." He glanced back at Gardener. "Do you know something? Karloff was still an unknown at forty-four when he made that film, and it was his eighty-first. What do you think to that?" The detective glanced at him with an uncertain expression. "The things I could tell you about the film world, Mr Gardener. But I'm sure that isn't why you came here."

"On the contrary," said Gardener. "It is *one* of the reasons."

"Dear me," said Corndell. "Where are my manners? I haven't offered you a drink. Please, come through."

He led them into the kitchen, where he made drinks and small talk before finally taking them through to the conservatory. He asked Gardener if he would be kind enough to carry the tray.

They all sat down. Corndell picked up the conversation. "Films play a big part in my life, Mr Gardener, so how can I help you?"

"Have you starred in many?" asked Gardener.

"None," replied Corndell.

"Oh," said Gardener. "I thought you were an actor."

"I am," replied Corndell, sipping his tea. "But I prefer to act on a stage rather than behind a camera. Not that there's anything wrong with acting for a camera, but I think there's more skill involved in theatre. I'm also a scriptwriter, and I regularly have my work accepted in Hollywood."

"That must be rewarding," said Gardener. "Are you responsible for any of the modern-day material gracing our screens at the moment?"

"Not at all, Mr Gardener. My work is deeper and more meaningful than the stuff you see in the cinema today. There is more emotion to my material, more acting skill required. I write with the old masters in mind, those that didn't have the privilege of working with sound. Now, that was acting."

"So, if you don't write film scripts for Hollywood, what *do* you write?"

"I do write film scripts, as you call it," replied Corndell, sipping his tea and becoming more unsettled. He didn't like being questioned. "But I also supply the Hollywood agencies with a lot of theatrical material, regularly seen all over America."

"Have you starred in any of your own material?" asked Gardener.

"Only once, in London. It was a play shown at Her Majesty's Theatre before *The Phantom of the Opera*."

"Was it a success?"

"Mr Gardener, all my work is successful. I also took the leading role in *The Phantom*."

"I thought Michael Crawford was in that," said Reilly.

"He came after me, Mr Reilly." Corndell smiled. "Unfortunately, I broke my leg and was unable to continue... hence the cane. I don't have to use it all the time, but I have my off-days when the stiffness is a little too much."

"Apart from your love of theatre and your scriptwriting, I can see you also collect film memorabilia," said Gardener.

"Oh, yes, all the time. It's a life's work trying to track down the lost films of the silent era. I have my own cinema."

"Really?" he asked Corndell. "Where?"

"Here, in the house."

"Your knowledge of films might just come in useful," said Reilly.

"You'll forgive me for asking," Corndell said, "but I find it strange that you two gentlemen should come out here to my house and talk to me about films. I'm sure that there's something else on your minds."

"There is," said Gardener. "We're investigating a couple of extremely unpleasant deaths in Leeds recently."

"Are you talking about the young girl who was killed in the shop in the arcade?"

"Did you know her?" asked Gardener.

"No, but I read about it in the papers." He leaned even further forward. "You don't think it was me, do you?"

"Was it?" asked Reilly.

Corndell stood up, his left eye twitching rapidly. "Am I under arrest?"

Gardener left his seat as well. "Not at all. We've come to you because we believe you may be able to help us. With your knowledge of film and theatre, you might be a real asset."

"Of course," said Corndell, sitting back down, using the arms of the chair as a guide.

"Would you take a look at these, see if you recognise them?" asked Gardener, passing over a piece of paper containing the quotes they had found next to the bodies.

Corndell studied the paper before passing it back to Gardener. "I can't say I do, but they're very dated."

"Why do you say that?"

"Look at the phrasing, Mr Gardener. People don't talk like that now."

"So, they're not from anything you've seen?" asked Gardener.

"I wouldn't say that," replied Corndell, sipping more tea. "I have seen literally thousands of films, and not just the well-known ones. My collection goes as far back as 1900. And in my experience, that could well be the era from which they originate, the Golden Age of Hollywood, the silent films. As I mentioned earlier, there is more acting skill involved in a silent film, your gestures are usually exaggerated. If you look at those quotes, that was how the dialogue was presented to audiences."

"So, the person we're looking for may be old, or he might live his life in that time period?" asked Gardener.

"Possibly both, maybe neither," replied Corndell. "May I ask why you think he's an actor?"

"It's speculation at the moment, but the people he's killed so far have both been connected to the entertainment world."

"So, you think he might be a failed actor? Someone with a grudge?"

"Not entirely, but we have reason to believe that he's very good at disguising himself. The eyewitness reports we've collated describe him as looking like two completely different people."

"Maybe it *was* two different people."

"Unlikely. The modus operandi was very similar, and then we have the quotes, quite apart from the fact that he was actually the spitting image of one of the people he killed."

Corndell was about to take a drink, but decided to hold his cup before it reached his lips. "You don't mean that nice Leonard White?"

"You knew Leonard White?" asked Gardener.

"Yes, I did. Not that I worked with him, but he actually starred in one of my father's films many years ago, just as he was starting out."

"Which one?" Reilly asked.

"*Tales From A Village Pub*, 1957. It was a compendium of short stories. I saw him on and off over the years after that."

"But you hadn't seen him recently?" asked Gardener.

"No. But I must say, I rather wanted to go and see him at the Grand Theatre the night he was killed. He was only there for the one night, and I would have loved to have heard him talk, perhaps even had the chance to talk to him myself."

"Where were you that night?" asked Reilly.

"I was here, at home."

"Alone?" questioned Reilly.

Corndell knew that one was coming. "I'm always on my own, Mr Reilly. I am in constant demand with my work and I rarely, if ever, get the chance to leave the house these days."

"Didn't you buy the house from Leonard White?" asked Gardener.

"My father did, many years ago."

"How well did you know him?"

"My father?" Corndell grinned. "Sorry... just my little joke. Well, I wouldn't say I knew him all that well. I have seen most, if not all, of the films he made at Hammer. You have to remember, we travelled in different circles. When my father bought this house I was still in London, and remained there until after he'd retired. It was quite sad, really, because he never had the chance to appreciate it. He died four months after buying it. I came up to Leeds after his death, and stayed to look after my mother."

"Is your mother still alive?" asked Gardener.

"I'm afraid not, she died of cancer many years ago." Corndell finished his tea and continued with another question. "If he's that good with his disguise, how will you catch him? You won't know what he looks like."

"Very true," replied Gardener. "That's something else we wanted to ask you about, make-up techniques."

"That's an art in itself, Mr Gardener."

"Are you involved much with make-up?"

"Very little. Over the years of course, with my theatre work, I have applied my own. As I said, my life is scriptwriting these days."

"Not completely," said Reilly.

"Sorry?"

"It's not all writing, is it, Mr Corndell?" retorted Gardener. "I believe you've recently accepted a live performance at the University of Leeds."

"You're very well informed."

"It pays to be," replied Gardener.

"It's true, then?" asked Reilly.

"Yes, it is. The gentleman who books the entertainment called me a few days previously. May I ask how you knew?"

"My wife's a theatre critic. She'll be there. I'm sure she'll give you a good review."

"She won't need to, Mr Reilly, my work speaks for itself."

"Will it involve make-up?" continued Reilly.

"It most certainly will."

"Where do you buy it?"

"Quite a few places, the internet mostly. But unfortunately for me, I have recently visited the shop in Leeds where the young girl was killed," replied Corndell.

"Why unfortunate?" asked Reilly.

"Because despite what you and Mr Gardener say, Mr Reilly, I still feel as if I'm a suspect."

"Quite the opposite," replied Gardener. "If you were a suspect, we'd have had you at the station by now. No, my colleague wants to know more about make-up. For our man to be so practised in the art of disguise, he would need quite a lot of different products. We wondered if you'd know what they were and whether or not the shop in Leeds would sell them. Or would you need to be somewhere far more specialised?"

"Oh, I see." Corndell nodded. "Well, without knowing the extent to which your man is disguising himself, it's difficult to say. However, if he can pass closely for Leonard White, he must be good."

"Why would someone use aluminium powder?" inquired Gardener.

"Colouring his hair, particularly white or grey. What about the second murder, did he look like Leonard White then?"

He noticed Gardener glance at Reilly before replying. The detective reached into his pocket and produced an artist impression of the vampire. "From the eyewitness reports we have, we think his disguise was this one."

"Oh my good God!" shouted Corndell.

"Do you recognise the character?"

"No, but to create an effect like that, you'd need quite a few things. I would imagine flexible collodion for one, which is a plastic skin adhesive. It provides a coating for make-up construction. And then there's rigid collodion, a liquid used to make scars and pock marks. When you put that stuff on, it draws and puckers the skin. For something like this he obviously used a wig, and then there's the costume..."

"All of which you can buy at the shop in Leeds?"

"I would imagine so," he replied. "As I mentioned, I have used the place on occasion, but I don't think I've spent a lot of money there, or taken too much notice of their costumes. You really do have your work cut out, gentlemen."

A silence followed before Reilly spoke. "Is it true that thespians are a tad superstitious?"

"I'm sorry?" replied Corndell.

"Superstitious," repeated Reilly. "I've heard a lot of strange stories about actors, particularly those in the theatre."

"Well, of course there are a number of superstitions connected with the theatre."

"And what are yours?"

"Since you ask, I don't particularly like live flowers being delivered before a performance. They have a very short life and I believe it reflects the life of the play. I'm not particularly keen about whistling on stage, it's bad luck and can lead to accidents. And under no circumstances do I like someone wishing me good luck."

"And away from the stage?" Reilly persisted.

"I'm not sure I follow you."

"I couldn't help noticing when we drove up to the house that it's surrounded by poplar trees. As you draw closer you have bay trees, or laurels if you like. And then, as sure as God's my witness, if you haven't got houseleek placed in the roof."

"You're... very observant, Mr Reilly."

"It's my job."

"To answer your question, you're quite correct about the trees. If you're that knowledgeable, perhaps you know that laurel trees guard the doors of great men's houses."

"I certainly do, but I also know that the bay tree is said to keep away witches, devils, and bad luck, and that a house guarded by such a tree should never be struck by lightning."

"I can't say I know anything about that, Mr Reilly," replied Corndell. "And I'm certainly not aware of houseleek, as you call it."

"Are you not? So, you haven't placed it there as a protection against lightning?"

"I can't have done, can I? Which begs the question, which one of us is really superstitious?"

Reilly made no reply.

"Tell me, Mr Reilly, where did you learn about myths and superstitions?"

"I'm Irish, Mr Corndell. We invented most of them."

"Oh, does that mean they're not true, then?"

"You tell me," retorted Reilly. "You're the superstitious one. There's no shortage of the colour red around here. Your hall has a tiled floor which contains red, and then there are red velvet drapes leading into each of the rooms, and they all seem to have something red in them."

"Red is my favourite colour, Mr Reilly, mostly because it's the colour of Aries, but also because it's associated with good luck, health, and joy, and hence the living body as opposed to the corpse."

"And you're not superstitious? I'll bet you know as well as I do about the references in folklore to the use of threads, ribbons, wool, or pieces of flannel which prevent a variety of ailments," continued Reilly. "And isn't red thread used as a protection against witchcraft?"

"Is there anything else I can help you gentlemen with?"

"And it has nothing to do with it being the colour of blood?" asked Reilly.

"Why would it?" replied Corndell.

"Just curious, Mr Corndell. It was you who made the comment about the living body and not the corpse, was it not? I thought maybe you had a kind of superstition about blood being pure and all that."

"I really haven't the faintest idea what you're talking about."

At that precise moment, Gardener's mobile chimed. He reached into his jacket pocket and then excused himself into the kitchen, where he took the call.

Reilly asked Corndell if he could use the bathroom.

After the phone call and the toilet break, the two detectives returned to the conservatory.

"I'm afraid we'll have to leave you, Mr Corndell." Gardener turned to Reilly. "That was the station. Apparently, Albert Fettle wants to see us, urgently."

"It's no problem, Mr Gardener, I'll show you both out."

As Gardener reached the door, he turned to face Corndell. "Just one more question."

"Which is?" asked Corndell.

"What's your favourite film?"

"Excuse me?"

"Your favourite film. You must have one, a film buff of your calibre."

"I certainly do. *A Blind Bargain*," replied Corndell, still wondering why the question had been asked in the first place.

"Can't say as I know that one," replied the detective.

"You won't, Mr Gardener. Before your time."

"I'll have to look out for it. What about *The Scarlet Car*?"

"I'm afraid you have me there, Mr Gardener. But if you have the time, I'd be more than happy to look it up for you," replied Corndell.

"Another time, maybe. Anyway, thank you, you've been most helpful. I'll leave you a card, and perhaps we could call back if we need you again." Gardener tipped his hat.

"Don't hesitate," said Corndell.

Chapter Thirty-one

The atmosphere at the theatre was still grave when Paul Price met them at the stage door. "Do you have any idea when I can reopen?" he asked, testily.

"Shouldn't be too long, Mr Price," replied Gardener. "We do have a few more people to interview."

Price's expression showed his irritation. "So, you're not here to tell me it's business as usual?"

"No, we're here to see Mr Fettle."

"You do realise how much this is costing me, don't you?"

"Not as much as Leonard White," replied Gardener.

"Have you made any headway catching the lunatic responsible?"

"It is a murder investigation." Gardener turned to glance down the street. "And I would rather not discuss it on the doorstep, if you don't mind."

Paul Price stepped to one side, allowing them down the stairs to where Fettle kept himself hidden. "Two policemen to see you, Fettle. Though I can't think why."

"I asked 'em," replied Fettle, once again invisible to the naked eye. When it became obvious that no one was going to speak until Price left, he grunted and did so, adding that he could be found in his office if needed.

"He's like a bear with a sore head. You've really upset him," said Fettle, when he finally appeared.

"He's the least of our worries," replied Reilly.

"You've not found him yet, then? Anyway, best come in and have a pot of tea."

"Tea is the last thing we need, Mr Fettle," replied Gardener.

"I'm sure it is, but it'll do for starters." Fettle drew them in and poured the tea from a recently boiled kettle. He then threw a book on the table, opened to a page which contained the photograph of a man Gardener had asked him about on a previous visit.

"Inspector Burke of Scotland Yard," Fettle proudly announced. "You asked me if I knew him last time you were here."

When Gardener realised he had been holding his breath, he still didn't speak, but turned to the front cover of the book. It was an old issue of *Film Review*. "Where did you get this?"

"I've had 'em years. Been in that cupboard yonder." Fettle pointed, but neither man bothered to see where.

"So, which film does the photograph come from?" asked Gardener.

"*London After Midnight*," replied Fettle.

"And what do you know about the film other than Inspector Burke?"

Fettle sat down and sipped his tea. "It's a bit of a classic, maybe the most famous of all the lost films."

Gardener suddenly thought back to what Corndell had told him about collecting lost films, wondering if he had it. More to the point, what hadn't Corndell told them? Had it been a cryptic clue, like those found with the bodies? He realised he was ahead of himself. Perhaps a lack of evidence on the case had forced him into thinking irrationally. "Go on."

"It's commonly known as the Holy Grail of archivists and film collectors throughout the world." Fettle picked up a scrap of paper. "The last known record of the film existing was in the 1950s. According to what I've found out, an MGM vault inventory from 1955 shows the print being stored in Vault 7. In the 1960s there was a fire in Vault 7, destroying the last surviving print."

Reilly whistled through his teeth.

"What makes it so rare and collectible?" asked Gardener, intrigued.

"Quite a lot of things, I should imagine. It was at the top of MGM's hit parade for 1927-28."

"Twenty-seven?" interrupted Gardener.

"Oh aye, it's going back a bit."

"It was a silent film, then?" asked Reilly.

"Aye," replied Fettle. "I mean, it was one of them films that broke records. Eerie sets, and Chaney's vampire make-up was incredible."

"Who's?" asked Gardener.

"Lon Chaney."

"Vampire make-up?"

"Aye." Fettle flicked over a couple of pages and Gardener grew intensely cold. He pulled out the picture he had of the vampire suspect in Leeds on the night Janine was killed. They were alike to the last detail.

"Who is Lon Chaney?" asked Gardener.

"You're kidding me," replied Fettle. "Only the greatest actor that ever lived."

"Well, I've never heard of him."

"You won't have, will you? He was well before your time."

"Can you recall any of his other films?"

"The two most well-known were *Phantom of the Opera* and *The Hunchback of Notre Dame*."

"Did he star in something called *A Blind Bargain*?"

"I think he did," replied Fettle.

Gardener realised he was still standing. He sat down, grabbed his mug and took a mouthful of tea. "So, what do you know about Lon Chaney?"

"He was a genius. In the early 1920s, there was a well-known saying around Hollywood, 'Don't step on that spider, it might be Lon Chaney'. His make-up was that good, he was known as 'The Man of a Thousand Faces'. Both his parents were deaf, so the only way he could talk to 'em was through mime, which is where he picked up his ability to act. He was brilliant, man. His make–up, well, you've never seen nowt like it. He did it all himself."

Fettle pointed to the page. "That film was just the business and he did all his own make-up. In fact, I remember reading somewhere that the film was so chilling, it inspired a murder. Some bloke in London claimed that after seeing it, he had visions of Chaney's vampire character. It terrified him so much, that he went into an epileptic fit and killed an Irish housemaid."

"I thought you said he played Inspector Burke."

"He did," replied Fettle. "He also played the vampire. Two parts. Just look at the make-up involved."

Gardener turned to Reilly. "Well, even if we don't know who's doing it, we know who he's emulating."

"I wouldn't say that entirely," replied Reilly. "Remembering where we've just been."

"What do you remember about *A Blind Bargain*?" he asked Fettle.

"Not much, I never saw that one, either."

Fettle left the table and lunged over to the cupboard in the corner. He tossed a few books around, creating a fair amount of dust, before returning with another dog-eared copy of *Film Review*.

"Here we are. Another lost film, second only to *London After Midnight*. In fact, he played two parts again, the Mad Scientist and the Ape Man."

"What was the film about?" asked Gardener.

"Summat about a doctor who's experimenting on people. Apparently, the half-man half-ape is the result of one of his earlier experiments."

"I take it all his films were silent films."

"All except one, I think," replied Fettle.

"In which case, the words came up on the screen if the actors spoke to each other."

"Aye," replied Fettle.

"You've no idea if a film script for these films still exists, have you?"

"You must be kidding," said Fettle, finishing his tea. "Although I did hear talk once that there was a book about the reconstruction of the film."

"*A Blind Bargain?*" asked Gardener.

"Aye," said Fettle.

"Any idea who wrote it?"

"Haven't a clue, sunshine."

Gardener turned to Reilly. "Sean, make a note, see if we can find the book."

"You reckon he's using quotes from Chaney's films?" asked Reilly.

"It's looking that way," replied Gardener.

"What quotes?" asked Fettle.

"I'm sorry, Mr Fettle, we've kept them from the public. You remember that day you took us into the cellars and we found a puzzle?"

"Oh aye."

"They're not the only ones he's been leaving. We've found one-line quotes next to the bodies."

"And you think they're from the films?"

"Possibly," replied Gardener.

"And if you could get film scripts you'd know for sure."

"Maybe."

"Do you have a copy of the quotes?"

Gardener passed over the evidence bag with the paper he'd shown to Corndell. After a couple of minutes of studying it, Fettle shook his head. "No, can't help you there."

"Do you know anyone who can?"

"No, afraid not. You see, most of Chaney's films are missing, and I doubt there's any records of the scripts lying around, they're just too old."

"Do you know if any of the films are available today?"

"Only way to find out is to use the internet. I dare say you might pick up *The Phantom of the Opera*, or *The Hunchback of Notre Dame*."

"I'll check that out," said Reilly. "I'll also ask Laura what she knows, or maybe who she knows. Her friend at the university might help."

"Maybe Corndell could," suggested Gardener.

"Who's Corndell?" asked Fettle.

"William Henry Corndell. Do you know him?"

"Should I?" asked Fettle.

"I would have thought so," replied Gardener, "given his pedigree."

"Pedigree? What pedigree?" asked Fettle, taking a mouthful of fresh tea.

Gardener and Reilly told Fettle what they knew about Corndell. Fettle consulted all his *Film Reviews* but nothing materialised. "There's plenty about Wallace Henry Corndell. He was a pretty prominent director."

"Did he ever make a film called *Tales From a Village Pub*, starring Leonard White?" asked Gardener.

"Aye, he did, but Leonard White wasn't the star of the film."

"But he was in it?" asked Reilly.

"Aye. But there's no mention of a Corndell."

Gardener stared at Fettle. "Got another question for you. Do you know anyone connected to the London theatre scene?"

"What do you want to know?" asked Fettle.

"I want to know about William Henry Corndell. He came up here from London. Apparently he's big in the world of theatre, writes a lot of material, and he once played the role of the Phantom before Michael Crawford."

"I didn't know there was anyone before Crawford," said Fettle.

"Corndell seems to think there was," said Reilly.

"Can you find out for me?" asked Gardener.

"Aye, I can. In fact, a mate of mine used to work backstage at Her Majesty's. I'll see if I can track him down, he'll know."

"Thanks. And while we're on the subject of people, do you know anyone called Harry Fletcher?"

Fettle grew silent before answering. "The name rings a bell. I think he was a writer, worked for the Playhouse."

"Do you know where he is now?"

"Can't say as I do, I haven't seen or heard from him in ages."

"When did you last see him?" asked Gardener.

"Oh Christ, must have been ten, fifteen years ago, when he was at the Playhouse."

"Any idea where he lived back then?" asked Gardener.

With his eyes screwed shut and his mouth agape as he thought, Fettle resembled a frog. "Sorry, Mr Gardener, I didn't know him that well."

"Do you know anybody who does?"

"You could talk to the people at the Playhouse, but I don't think he's still there."

"He isn't, and the people who are don't know him, either."

"They've probably changed staff since then."

Gardener was still frustrated despite having acquired more information about the case. Someone would have to check out Lon Chaney and Corndell, all of which would take time, and there was still no real evidence as to the murderer's identity. Which meant he could strike again, and the press would really have a field day.

As he was about to give up, Gardener had another thought. "Did Lon Chaney make a film called *The Scarlet Car*?"

Fettle consulted more of the *Film Review* books. A few more minutes passed before he eventually answered. "Aye, he did."

"When was that?" asked Gardener.

"1917."

"Christ," replied Reilly. "What was that about?"

"Doesn't say," replied Fettle. "But you've gotta remember, Chaney made bloody hundreds of films. Most of 'em were little shorts, three or four reels. They weren't all feature films, so there isn't much information about 'em."

"What about something called *Whispering Creek*?"

Fettle seemed pleased to be useful. "As in *The Tragedy of Whispering Creek*? That's even further back, 1914."

"What's that about?" Reilly asked Gardener.

"That was the name of Corndell's house."

"Seems to me that this Corndell bloke has a bit of an obsession with Chaney," said Fettle.

"That's what worries me. On the face of it, so does the killer. He's very good with make-up. He leaves clues, which may or may not be from the films, but I suspect they are. Even in the clues, there's a reference to one of Chaney's films," said Gardener.

He rose to leave. "Okay, Mr Fettle, thanks for the information, you've been a great help. If you could look into what we've asked, I'd appreciate it."

"No problem. I'll give you a ring when I've done."

Gardener and Reilly climbed the stairs to the stage door. Before leaving, Gardener stopped, turned, and walked back down to Fettle.

"What have you forgotten now?"

"I don't suppose the names Rupert Julian or Wallace Worsley mean anything to you, do they?"

Fettle consulted the books again.

"I don't think you'll find them in there," said Gardener.

"I think I will," said Fettle. "They don't sound like actors with modern names, do they?"

"Directors, from what I can gather."

"Aye, you're right there," replied Fettle after scanning a few more pages. "What do you want to know?"

"The kind of stuff they're directing at the moment?"

Fettle glanced up from the book and laughed. "You're joking, aren't you? They're both dead, man. Years ago."

Chapter Thirty-two

Despite the information they had so far received, Gardener sensed an air of trepidation descending upon the incident room. His colleagues were beginning to show signs of wear, as they always did when an investigation yielded nothing but dead ends.

On the face of it, the meeting with William Henry Corndell had proved intriguing to say the least. His knowledge of his trade may well prove valuable. He knew enough about the films and the theatre to provide a smattering of information, although Gardener had been far from satisfied, and would like to have heard more.

However, he had provided a link worth pursuing. A connection between silent films and the man they were trying to find. But was the killer really emulating a film star? If that was the case, had Fettle provided the answer in Lon Chaney? Was Corndell himself obsessed with Lon Chaney, and had simply chosen not to mention it? What about his lost films collection? What did he have in there, and did he have any of Chaney's?

Gardener also suspected that there was a lot more to the house than met the eye, and Sean Reilly had already revealed to him that each and every one of the rooms upstairs were locked. Why was that? Surely there was little need to lock any door in your house if you lived on your own and never left. Did he have a house full of valuable items, or was he hiding something?

Although the meeting with Fettle had confirmed the link to Lon Chaney, it revealed nothing further about Corndell. Gardener was satisfied that they *were* searching for a man with an incredible knowledge of the film world, and very likely the actor Lon Chaney, for whatever reason. But the fact that Fettle had never heard of William Henry Corndell – given his pedigree – was interesting.

So, was Corndell who he said he was? Who he led people to believe he was? Based on a first meeting with little evidence, had they actually been talking to the maniac responsible for the two most violent murders they had ever seen? Or was Gardener on the wrong track? They had so far drawn a blank with every lead. Had he allowed himself to concentrate on someone who was perhaps mad but harmless? One way or another, he would have to incite his team into producing results before another murder was committed.

Briggs opened the door and entered the room, breaking Gardener's train of thought. He threw a folder down on the table and immediately launched into the meeting. "Right. Let's recap on what we already know. I'll go first. I've had a lengthy meeting with Janine Harper's mother, and the Commissioner. Neither one is pleased about what's happened, but we have discovered that Jack Harper was her father. The same Jack Harper that served on the watch committee with Leonard White and Harry Fletcher."

Briggs paused. "Which leaves us with one link. Your father, Stewart. So, if it's okay with you, I'd like to have a word with him. While you might know him better than I do, I'm concerned about your involvement becoming personal."

"It isn't personal," replied Gardener.

"Maybe not," said Briggs. "But I warn you, Stewart, if the killer finds Harry Fletcher before we do, then you know as well as I do where this is going. What we need to know is why. Perhaps the only people who can tell us are your father, or Harry Fletcher."

Gardener took over, glancing at Dave Rawson. "You spoke to Val White, Dave. Did she give you a list of her late husband's films? Does she have an alibi for the night Janine was murdered?"

"Yes on both accounts. The list of White's films is pretty long, and I've used a couple of the support officers to try and track them down, or at least people who knew White, to see if we can find any further connection."

"Okay, and what about Val White?"

"She'd been to his funeral that day, and was at a bereavement held in his honour on the night time."

"So, that rules her out. What about Janine's boyfriend?" Gardener asked. "Did anyone speak to him about his movements?"

Thornton raised his hand. "I did, sir – with Anderson. Apparently, they'd had a row and he hadn't seen or heard from her."

"What was the row about?"

"He said it was personal," replied Anderson.

"How personal?"

Anderson shifted about uncomfortably. "It was something to do with sex. I don't particularly want to go any further."

"I don't want you to, either," replied Gardener. "Okay, so they had a row. When was that, exactly?"

"About a week before," said Thornton.

"And they never saw each other after?"

"No. He wanted to give her some time to cool off. That and the fact that he wasn't sure whether or not he actually wanted to see her again."

"Anything strike you about his nature that may lead you to think he had homicidal tendencies?" asked Gardener.

"No," replied Anderson. "If he has, his sexual tendencies are outweighing them at the moment."

"He was out shagging another bird that night," said Thornton.

"And she's confirmed, I suppose," said Gardener.

"Oh, definitely. Three times, apparently."

"Which rules *him* out and leaves *us* where?" asked Briggs. "I'll tell you where, back to square one. Two murders, no witnesses, no killer, no clues."

"Steve?" said Gardener. "Any luck with forensics? Any prints from anywhere?"

"Not yet."

"Any results from the ESLA?"

"We haven't done everyone, but so far we have no foot or shoe prints on there that we can't identify."

"In that case, check this out." Gardener produced a polythene bag containing the paper with the quotations, which only he and Corndell had handled.

"What's that?" asked Briggs.

"It's a piece of paper with the quotes on. When Sean and I went to see William Henry Corndell today, I let him handle it. I'm the only other person who has."

"Well done," said Briggs. "How did you get on with him?"

"He's intelligent, and he knows a lot about his trade. But I think he has a secretive side," said Gardener.

"Don't we all?" asked Briggs.

"I'm still not sure whether or not the whole interview was an act."

"What are you trying to say?" asked Briggs.

"We need to take a closer look. He's locked up inside a huge mansion that looks like a shrine to the film world. It's full of posters and very probably props."

"And locked rooms," added Reilly.

"What do you mean, locked rooms? Have you been searching his house without a warrant, Reilly?"

"It wasn't my fault, I couldn't find the toilet."

"Oh, Jesus," said Briggs, running his hands down his face. "Why is it that everything he does has disaster written all over it?"

"With all due respect, sir," said Gardener, "you'd have to see him to know what we're talking about. He's superstitious, although he denies it. Eccentric. He hates being challenged. Self-conscious. He was dressed all in black with a red tie. Not that that's a problem, but you'd think he could match a few more colours together."

"None of which proves he's mad," retorted Briggs.

"Maybe you're right. When all is said and done, he did provide what I think will be a valuable clue."

"Go on," said Briggs.

"He suspected the quotes came from the silent film era, the Golden Age of Hollywood, as he calls it. When films were silent, with no synchronized sound, they used title cards to communicate what was being said. He feels these quotes are written in the same style as those cards."

"Did he recognise them?"

"He said he didn't."

"But you think otherwise?" Briggs asked.

Gardener nodded. "We went to see Fettle afterwards, the old guy who looks after The Grand in Leeds. He told us about Lon Chaney, an actor in the silent films who was a master of disguise. He played the part of Inspector Burke of Scotland Yard, and the part of the vampire here." Gardener held up the artist impression. "In a film entitled, *London After Midnight*."

"I remember him," said Briggs. "He also made that film about the Hunchback."

"And *The Phantom of the Opera*. Fettle also mentioned a film called *A Blind Bargain,* another of Chaney's, about a mad scientist. Both that one and *London* are what you call 'lost films'. Corndell told us he collects lost films, and that his favourite was *A Blind Bargain*, and he provided us with a lot of information about make-up. What bothers me most is a conversation he was having on his mobile phone when we arrived, supposedly with Hollywood. He was discussing the choice of director for his work. He wasn't happy about it, and said he would make changes if they didn't like his script."

"The problem is?" asked Briggs.

"When I asked Fettle to verify the directors Corndell mentioned, Fettle said both of them had been dead for years."

The silence that followed was claustrophobic. Gardener sensed the clocks ticking and the wheels turning. Had they found their man? He faced Trevor Thorpe, the profiler. "Trevor, any thoughts?"

Thorpe was dressed as they'd seen him previously, in a tweed jacket and brown cords. Once again, he left his chair and glanced at the ceiling as he walked.

"Well, Mr Gardener, a very interesting character. Someone I would perhaps like to meet. Did he appear very confident when challenged?"

Reilly nodded. "Pretty much."

"What was his house like? Clean and tidy?"

"Yes," replied Gardener.

Thorpe returned to his chair and sat down, exactly as he had last time, legs straddling the chair and arms across the back. "Did he have a display of curtains in the house?"

"As far as I remember," replied Gardener, confused.

"Did you check the knots in the cords?"

"No, why?" asked Reilly.

"Just curious," replied Thorpe. "Our man likes to tie knots, does he not? And the colour red was prominent, you say?"

"A little more than usual, yes," replied Reilly.

"And he appeared... confident, you say?" Thorpe asked, spreading his arms out in front of him.

"Most of the time," replied Gardener.

Thorpe stood up and stared Gardener in the eye. "They're all coincidences, Mr Gardener. We need to find out more. Is he married? Was he married? I think the man we're looking for is not a loner."

He turned to stare at Reilly. "Security conscious... I doubt very much he will be. He's spent so long being repressed, that he now wants to be free! He will not lock himself away. He'll be out most nights, mixing and mingling, because he craves company. He wants to express those locked-in emotions. He wants to feel wanted! Loved!"

He sat back down on his chair. "No, Mr Gardener, I don't think Corndell is your man. You're seeing what you want to see because it fits in with what you think. You need to widen your thought patterns." Thorpe said nothing else, and when it was obvious he'd finished, Briggs took over.

"Okay, how do you want to proceed, Stewart?"

Gardener turned to face the team. "Colin, I'd still like William Henry Corndell checked out. See what you can find. Where did he live in London, and what was he up to? Find out everything you can about him after he moved here. Check his credit and his bills. Fettle has a contact who worked for Her Majesty's Theatre for years. According to Corndell, he played the part of the Phantom before Michael Crawford, so Fettle's checking that for us.

"Thornton, Anderson, you two check out Lon Chaney. Find out every film he's been in and what they're about. I also want you to see if you can locate anything on a film called *The Scarlet Car.*"

Gardener pointed to the copy on the board. "Look at the last two lines. He's telling us he's about to kill another in Leeds. What does he mean by 'down and out'? Is it an area none of us frequent? A seedy part perhaps? That puts Alan Cuthbertson back in the picture. He regularly visits places of ill repute. Or does he mean something entirely different? A tramp maybe?"

Gardener thought back to Derek Summers and the Christmas murders. At the time he met someone called Bob Crisp, a disbarred lawyer who'd turned tramp and lived underground in fear of his life. Since that investigation had been closed, he hadn't seen the man. But he'd had no reason to. A pet hate of Gardener's was anything unclean. He shuddered as he thought of the time he'd been beaten senseless because he'd dressed like a tramp, only to regain consciousness in the company of the man he had been searching for. But at the same time, he also realised what a friend Bob Crisp had turned out to be. Question is, where is he now?

"I want the rest of you to continue trying to find Harry Fletcher, chase up the leads we already have. Explore new avenues."

Chapter Thirty-three

The following morning, Gardener showed Alan Briggs through to the kitchen. Malcolm was sitting at the table drinking his second cup of tea. The meeting was meant to be informal. Despite Briggs's reservations, Gardener thought it best if they spoke to his father at home and with him present.

"Now then, Malcolm," said Briggs. "How are you keeping?"

"I'm fine, Alan. You?"

"Can't complain. Is there any more tea in that pot, Stewart?"

"Coming up, sir."

Briggs pulled out a chair and sat opposite Malcolm. "I'm only here to ask you a few questions about Leonard White and the watch committee, if you don't mind? It's a sensitive issue, and by rights Stewart shouldn't be with us, but he thought you might feel a bit better if he was."

Gardener placed a cup of tea in front of Briggs and took a seat at the table. He noticed the strain in his father's eyes, the drawn expression on his face. Since White's death, he hadn't been sleeping well. The fact that Jack Harper's daughter had also been killed had brought the whole issue closer to home.

"What can you tell us about the watch committee?" asked Briggs.

"There isn't much to tell, Alan. We used to vet the films when they came to Leeds. We had the power to censor what we felt was unacceptable."

"And did you?"

"In a few cases."

"Any in particular you can remember?"

"Not off the top of my head. I remember we considered a couple that were soft porn gone a little too far. We suggested cuts and the directors agreed."

"So, you had to get the directors' permission?"

"Not really, no. We just thought it polite to involve them."

"Did the directors approve without opposition?"

"Mostly. They knew we had the power to ban the film, if they didn't," replied Malcolm, sipping his tea.

"Where did you do all this, Dad?"

"The Town Hall in the early days. Then, as time moved on, so did we." Malcolm paused. "I think we moved over to a warehouse, near the Playhouse."

"Can you remember where?"

"Not the exact address, but it was at the back of the Playhouse."

Gardener nodded. "I know where you mean, don't think it's in use now."

Briggs resumed his questioning. "You knew Leonard White pretty well, didn't you?"

"There were people who knew him better."

"The day he was murdered at The Grand, you went to see him. Is there anything you can think of now that was unusual about his behaviour?"

"Only the tea. I told Stewart he was legendary for halting productions because he wanted a regular supply of tea. When a tray of tea came for us both at The Grand, he never touched a drop."

"Did he pass you yours?"

"No."

"Did he move the tray?"

"Not that I can recall. In fact, to be honest, he was applying the finishing touches of his make–up, but he was wearing those surgical gloves."

"Finishing touches? What time were you with him?" asked Briggs.

"About two o'clock, as I remember."

"And you didn't find it strange that he was applying the finishing touches of his make-up at two o'clock in the afternoon, when he wasn't due on stage until seven-thirty in the evening?"

The expression on Malcolm's face changed. "Now you mention it, it did seem a little odd, but I didn't think anything about it at the time."

"What about his voice? Can you remember if it sounded any different?" asked Briggs.

"It was a little higher. But voices change."

"The colour of his eyes?"

"Can't say as I noticed," said Malcolm. "But you have to remember it was a good twenty plus years since I'd seen him, and I had no reason to believe it was someone else."

"Fair point," said Briggs.

Gardener interrupted. "Dad, can you think of anything that brought the committee into disrepute? Were there any arguments about anything in particular? Were any of the members ever threatened?"

Malcolm sat back in the chair. "I've had a lot of time to think about it, Stewart, and I have remembered something, way back."

"Go on."

"I'm trying to think. It's such a long time ago, but I'm pretty sure that one film did have to be banned."

"Why?" Briggs asked.

"I can't remember," said Malcolm.

"Was it pornographic?"

"I don't think so, I'd have remembered that," laughed Malcolm. "Harry Fletcher would know. He used to keep a diary, with him being a writer. If there were any films he particularly liked, he made a note of the closing credits. He also kept meticulous notes of the films where we had recommended cuts."

"How well did you know Harry Fletcher?" asked Briggs.

"About as well as I knew the rest of them. We socialised quite often, went out for meals as a group and discussed the films."

"Had you ever met him, or heard from him before the watch committee formed?"

"A couple of times, mostly at the cinema. I'd read a couple of his books."

"Did you meet up with Harry Fletcher more than the others?" pursued Briggs.

"Not particularly."

"What was he like?"

Malcolm paused. "When I think about it, typical writer. A bit strange."

"In what way?" Briggs asked.

163

"What I mean by strange is, he was very quiet, a bit of a loner. You wouldn't see him for weeks. There were occasions when he missed the watch committee meetings and then offered little explanation as to where he'd been. He'd just tell us he was working on a new book and had to meet deadlines. He was very inquisitive, obsessive. He was always asking questions without ever really telling you why."

"What kind of questions?" Gardener asked.

"I really can't remember, Stewart, it was too long ago. I suppose he'd ask us questions when he was writing a new book, to help with his research. He was a people watcher as well, but most writers are."

"What were his books about?" asked Briggs.

"As far as I can remember, thrillers and murder mysteries. One of the two I read was similar to Agatha Christie, only not as good." Malcolm took a sip of tea and then asked, "Why are you asking me all these questions about Fletcher?"

"We can't find him," said Briggs. "We've checked the electoral register and he's not on that. We can't find any bank records apart from a couple that were closed down years ago. We've even spoken to the people at the Playhouse, and the only address they had for him was a flat somewhere in Leeds. But he's moved on since then."

"He didn't live in a flat when I knew him."

"Where did he live?" asked Gardener.

Malcolm cupped his hands under his chin. "Burley in Wharfedale. I remember it well, he had a little cottage, set back from the main street. It had a conservatory and a small study where he used to write. I can't quite remember the address, but I could take you there."

"We need to check it out," said Gardener. "What about a telephone number?"

"I might be able to help." Malcolm stood up and left the room.

Briggs turned to Gardener. "He's doing well. I can see it's taken its toll, but he's handling it great."

"Yes," replied Gardener. "I'm pleased, he's been so down of late."

"He must have a lot on his mind, Stewart. He knows as well as we do that the connection is most likely the watch committee, and if we find Harry Fletcher dead, then he's next. But he hasn't given us much to go on."

"I'm sure if we give him enough time, he'll remember more. He's brilliant with films."

"Okay," said Briggs. "We'll change the subject, and then come back to it."

Malcolm returned to the room with a phone number. Gardener left the table and rang it. The line was dead, so he called the station, asking them to follow it up and supply an address. Then he sat back down. "No luck. I've asked the station to check it out."

"Stewart was just saying how much you enjoy films, Malcolm. Do you go and see many?"

"I love films, Alan. Always have. I go a couple of times a week. Chris joins me at least once."

"What sort of films?"

"All sorts of films. What I like about films is that they take you away from reality, show you someone else's problems for a couple of hours." Malcolm chuckled. "And they usually have happy endings. I love the black-and-whites mostly. They didn't rely on special effects, just bloody good stories. They knew how to make them, then."

"Are you into horror?" asked Briggs.

"I've seen a few," replied Malcolm.

"Remember an actor called Lon Chaney?"

"Who doesn't?"

Gardener was especially grateful to Alan Briggs for the way he was handling the interview.

"What was so good about Chaney, Malcolm?"

"He was the best, pure magic to watch. They called him 'The Man of a Thousand Faces'."

165

"Why was that?"

"Make-up expert. There wasn't anything he couldn't do. He did it all himself, and he used to carry a little black bag around. I did hear that the make-up case is in the Natural History Museum in Los Angeles. But the thing is, nobody knew how he did things. He used to endure such pain and torment just to get the part right. He wore a seventy-pound hump for *The Hunchback of Notre Dame*, and for *The Phantom of the Opera* he was said to have pushed discs up under his cheekbones to create the effect."

Briggs' expression grew distasteful. "Going a bit far, isn't it?"

"That was Chaney for you," replied Malcolm. "He was a perfectionist. That's probably why he was the highest paid actor in Hollywood."

Briggs then slid the quotes towards Malcolm. "Do you recognise these?"

Malcolm studied them, but shook his head. "No, but if you don't mind I'll write them down and check it out. Do you think they're from Chaney's films?"

"Possibly," replied Gardener.

"Even if they are, Son, and even if the killer is an expert with make-up just like Chaney was, it still doesn't tell you why he's doing it, or who he is."

"True," offered Briggs. "But if we know that's where he's heading, we may find something in Chaney's past that will give us a clue. Was Fletcher ever into that kind of thing? You know, make-up and acting?"

"No. Not in the time that I knew him. He was a bookworm. Why? You don't think he's your man, do you?"

"That's why we need to find him, Malcolm. If he isn't the killer, he could be the next victim. If he is..." Briggs left the sentence unfinished, leaving Gardener aware of the implications. He knew his father well enough to know that he, too, would have worked out the answer. "Have you heard of a director called Wallace Henry Corndell?" Briggs asked.

"Yes. That's who Leonard White sold his house to."

"What about William Henry Corndell?"

Malcolm paused before answering. "There's no director of that name."

"Not a director, Dad, an actor," said Gardener.

"I don't recognise him as an actor, either. What's he been in?"

"Mostly theatre work," replied Gardener. "But I get the feeling he's living off his dad's reputation, and I can't find reference to anything he's been in. He reckons he was in *Phantom* in the West End before Michael Crawford."

"I thought Crawford was the first," replied Malcolm.

"So did I."

"And you suspect he's lying? Do you think *he's* the killer?"

"Well if he is, it'll take some proving," replied Gardener. "We have very little evidence against him."

Malcolm snapped his fingers loudly. "That film that was banned by the watch committee. I know why I can't remember much about it, I wasn't there."

"Why?" asked Gardener, suddenly feeling awkward, as if he should know the answer himself.

"I was in hospital, don't you remember? I was landscaping for Leonard White at the time, the property in Horsforth, Corndell's huge place. I landscaped the grounds for him when the drains gave way and collapsed. I fell in and broke both my legs."

Gardener did remember. His application for the police force had been accepted, but his start date was delayed so as he could help his father to recuperate. "Can you remember why the ground gave way?"

"From what I heard, the house had a series of tunnels running underneath it."

"Anything confirmed about the tunnels, why they were there?" asked Briggs.

"I've no idea," said Malcolm. "Harry Fletcher came to see me in hospital. He had his book with him and he told me about a film they'd had to ban. Apparently, it was the most horrific thing they had ever seen."

"Can you remember anything else about it?" asked Briggs.

"No. It was such a long time ago. But I'm sure the records will be kept somewhere."

"Even from thirty years ago?" asked Briggs.

"It's a long shot, but it's worth a try."

"Makes sense," said Gardener, "if the director had his film banned. But surely it wouldn't have caused that much trouble. Wouldn't he have simply edited it?"

"I don't think he did," said Malcolm. "There was more to it than that. I'm sure Harry said there was bad blood."

"Maybe we're on to something, Stewart," said Briggs. "See if you can trace the records, and while we're at it, let's tighten up our search for Fletcher. If he still has the diary, that may be one reason why we can't find him. It might hold the biggest clue we have."

"Let *me* trace the records," offered Malcolm. "I'd have a better idea where to look than you. Besides, my name may still carry a little bit of weight."

"If you're sure?" asked Gardener.

"I'd like to do it. Who knows, it may help to catch the lunatic before he does any more damage." Malcolm rose from the table and left the kitchen in search of a notebook and pen.

"Are you okay with that, sir?"

"If we could spare someone to shadow him, it might serve two purposes."

"Protect him, and at the same time, lead us to the killer."

"Works on TV, doesn't it?"

Gardener laughed.

Malcolm returned to the kitchen. "There's someone outside waiting to see you."

"Me?" said Gardener. "Who is it?"

"You'd best go and see."

Gardener was puzzled. He wasn't expecting anyone. However, he was delighted to find that Jeff Harrison had finally returned with his Bonneville chassis frame.

Chapter Thirty-four

Martin Brown had tried to call Corndell three times already, and it wasn't even eleven o'clock. Each call had remained unanswered. In fact, he'd been unable to reach Corndell since his first. He was concerned, and had been since the return of the contract, which had been promptly signed, sealed, and delivered the day after he'd sent it. Corndell had made clear his conditions. Under no circumstances should any of his demands be disobeyed, or he would refuse to perform.

Martin sighed and sat back in his seat, perusing the paperwork. He studied the contract, hoping to Christ the university could maintain the standards required.

In the hall, a bunch of noisy students had gathered outside his door. He returned his attention to Corndell's first demand – the election of a supervisor to oversee the whole project from the beginning. The man would arrive on March 31st and set up the stage. Martin hadn't yet seen him, but to be honest he'd hardly had a chance to leave the office.

Corndell's man would handpick his own crew to help with whatever construction was required. Once the stage and the sound system had been designed to Corndell's satisfaction, the hall had to be closed and locked, and no one allowed access except Corndell's supervisor; only *he* would be present to greet Corndell when he arrived around noon on the day of performance.

Anyone found whistling on the set will be fired; particularly if the tune was Three Blind Mice. No live flowers should be present, or delivered beforehand. No interviews would be granted either before or after the performance. The first customer to buy a ticket and enter the hall should not be a woman.

Corndell had also requested that the dressing room walls be painted with pastel colours and furnished with a dressing table, a mirror, adequate lighting, and a comfortable stool. A meal consisting of a green, crisp salad, accompanied by Chinese green tea, should be delivered to the room no later than four o'clock. Corndell would dine alone.

The biggest surprise – and only bonus – was that Corndell had agreed to put on the show for free.

Martin couldn't work that one out. But then again, he couldn't really work any of it out. He sighed loudly, wondering if anyone in the world would even see Corndell, including himself. He still couldn't help feeling that the person who said he was Corndell wasn't, that it was some two-bit actor masquerading as a more superior one. He threw the signed contract back on the desk and left his office, in search of said supervisor.

* * *

When Martin entered the theatre hall, he was taken aback. The gothic stage set was magnificent, with red velvet drapes and impressive backdrops containing huge still-frame photographs from very early Universal horror films. There was no doubt that one of them was the Notre Dame Cathedral. A round platform – similar to the one where The Hunchback had been tied and whipped in the village square – had been erected centre stage. In Martin's opinion, there were heavy overtones of Lon Chaney.

Four strobe lights were equally positioned around the base of the podium, and the fog machines were currently being tested. Between all the photos, the design of the crumbling brickwork with its arched windows and gothic turrets impressed Martin. All of them had been coated with cobweb spray and enhanced by carefully concealed lighting.

A mixture of smells assaulted Martin's nostrils, some of which he could place: mint, and possibly avocado, which reminded Martin of a shampoo his wife had recently bought. There were others, but he had no idea what. The effect was sensational. The students were going to love it. Perhaps Corndell really did know what he was doing. Judging by the set, the show would be nothing short of spectacular.

Martin suddenly jumped as the haunting sound of Mike Oldfield's *Tubular Bells* reverberated through the sound system. Although he couldn't see the speakers, they had a sound quality to die for. He wondered if the music had been chosen for the show. He couldn't see how it fitted in.

Martin breathed a sigh of relief when, at last, he saw someone on the stage, who Martin hoped was Corndell's electorate.

The music stopped before the man made his approach. Martin was surprised by his appearance. The man was seventy if he was a day. He wore a grey boiler suit and carried a small bag of tools in his left hand. He had a flat cap and a pair of pince-nez perched over the bridge of his nose, and a thick grey moustache. His eyes were a little watery, and so black and so deep they resembled two olives on a bed of cream. Martin struggled to believe that the old man was Corndell's supervisor.

"Can I help you, son?" asked the old man, with a Bow bells accent. His voice was a choking rasp, as if he smoked sixty cigarettes a day.

"I was looking for William Henry Corndell, I don't suppose he's here?" asked Martin.

"Cor blimey, mate, you ain't asking much, are you? He's a very busy man, our William."

"You know him, then?" questioned Martin.

The old man jumped back and nearly dropped the bag of tools. "Know him? Well, of course I know him. What do you think I am, a doughnut?"

Martin was beginning to wonder. No one still talked like that down in London, did they? Not unless they lived in Albert Square. "Are you his stage supervisor?"

"I am." The old man jumped down off the stage – pretty sprightly for his age – and extended his right hand. "Jake Bollard."

Martin was about to shake when he noticed the old guy wearing surgeon's gloves. But that wasn't what stopped him. It was the name.

"Pardon?"

"Bollard, Jake Bollard."

He did shake, so as not to cause offence. "Nice to meet you, Mr Bollard." Martin struggled to remain straight faced. What kind of a name was Jake Bollard?

"And you are?"

"Martin Brown, I'm in charge of entertainment. I wanted to see how things were going, and if the team were looking after you."

"Champion, mate." Bollard turned and admired his handiwork.

"Where are they?"

"Gone for a tea break. They've worked like ten men. I thought they deserved it."

"Fair enough. It's looking good." Martin didn't know what else to say.

"It has to. He's a bit of a stickler, is old William." Bollard turned and let out a rasping laugh, slapping Martin on the shoulder. "He'll bloody well have me if he hears me calling him old."

Martin laughed as well, despite not finding the comment – or the slap – very funny. "Where is he, then?"

Bollard's expression switched as quickly as his manner. "Don't you read contracts, son? You won't see him today."

"Why not?" Martin asked.

"He's never in the theatre the day before. Never has been, it's one of his little quirks."

"I see. How long have you worked for him?"

"As long as he's been doing it," replied Bollard, dropping the bag of tools and sitting on the edge of the stage.

"He's reliable, then?" asked Martin. "It's just that I find it a little strange that he isn't here overlooking everything, a man of his calibre."

"He doesn't need to be, does he? That's why I'm here. I know exactly what he wants and where he wants it. Things have to be done in a certain order, and William will not enter the building until they have."

Martin was becoming more concerned. "What kind of things?"

Bollard stood up and waved Martin towards him. "Come with me, son."

Martin accepted a helping hand on to the stage. The smell caught his nostrils first, and as he glanced upwards, he saw the garlic bulbs. They were mostly hanging by threads, but from the floor you couldn't see them.

"What are those for?" asked Martin.

"To keep the spirits at bay," replied Bollard. His wild-eyed expression conveyed his belief in the statement he had made.

"Spirits?"

"Oh, yes, my son." Before Martin knew what was happening, Bollard had climbed up on to the podium and positioned himself as if *he* was going to do the show. His arms were open and his gaze high. *Tubular Bells* regurgitated its way around the sound system again. Quite how, Martin had no idea; he hadn't seen anyone operate anything.

"You see," shouted Bollard, glancing back down towards Martin. "There are those that believe the nature of William's plays invoke spirits from beyond. He uses well-known quotes from some of the old masters, which have the power to summon."

Martin stepped back as Bollard's voice suddenly boomed out through the sound system. He must have had a hidden microphone:

> *O' winged serpent, I summon thee to me*
> *Come forth through the clouds for all to see.*

The music reached a crescendo, the density of the fog deepened, and Martin started to cough, but Bollard continued unabated, his timing perfect.

> *Seek out the sinners and toll the bell*
> *Boil them alive in the fires of Hell.*

The stage grew silent, but not before a huge crashing sound. The strobe lights were extinguished, the smoke machines stopped, and the darkness became so total that Martin started to wonder what had really happened, and which side of the dividing line between good and evil he was now on.

"Mr Bollard?" said Martin. "I really think you ought to climb down, it's not safe for a man of your age."

The lights came back on and Bollard was directly in front of Martin, startling him. "What do you mean, my age?"

"How did you do that?" Martin glanced around. Nothing on the stage was out of place, and whatever had caused the crash must have come from the sound system.

"It's in my blood, my son. Been doing it all my life, so don't you worry about me." Bollard reached down into his bag of tools and brought out a small bottle. He opened the top and took a quick swig of the not quite clear liquid.

"I don't think you should be drinking when you're in charge of such expensive equipment, Mr Bollard."

"Drinking!" said Bollard. "Drinking. What do you think this is?"

"Well, I'm not sure, but it looks like alcohol."

"Give over, son. Try it." He passed the bottle over.

Martin sniffed. Whatever it was immediately coated the inside of his nostrils, and he sneezed violently. His eyes stung, and he could hardly see for the excessive water.

"Jesus Christ! What is that?"

"Garlic vinegar, mate. Me and William, see, we swear by it. Protection, my old son. The protective qualities of garlic were valued during the plague epidemics in the seventeenth century. Thieves who plundered the homes of the sick drank this to safeguard them from infection. Sure you don't want a drink?" He offered the bottle again.

"No, thank you, Mr Bollard. I'd really like to make tomorrow night's performance."

Bollard put the top back on and placed it in the bag of tools. "Yes, I know what you mean. Anyway, I've loads to do, so if you don't mind, I'll let you get back to your work." He walked away without saying another word.

Chapter Thirty-five

Gardener was sitting in the office, reflecting. He had spent most of the previous day with his father, trying to trace any records the local watch committee may have left behind; and a banned film would surely leave a stain. They were still operating, but out of a government office in the centre of Leeds with private screenings at various places. None of the current members recognised Malcolm, although one of them remembered hearing his name mentioned more than once.

After a lengthy conversation, they had discovered that no records older than ten years were available. They were also told that they might have better luck with one of the local historians, or maybe the film museum in Bradford.

Having driven over there, Gardener had treated his father to a pub lunch and, afterwards, had tried the museum. All records had been stored on discs and could be accessed by computer but they, too, proved fruitless. There was no mention of a banned film, despite Malcolm's persistence that it had caused a stir at the time.

What little time they had left before people were starting to wind down for the evening was spent trying to trace Harry Fletcher. Two people had remembered him, though they had no idea of his whereabouts now; one of them, however, had seen him recently. He simply couldn't remember where. Frustrated and tired, they drove home.

Gardener had spent the evening trawling the internet in an effort to shed further light on the banned film. Malcolm had no details and no title, so he'd given up a little after ten o'clock.

He had downloaded a short history of Lon Chaney and a bibliography, but neither of them proved useful. One site had contained an appraisal of Chaney by none other than William Henry Corndell. But try as he might, no further information about Corndell himself was forthcoming. The only connection for the quotes at the scenes of the murders came back to what Colin Sharp had told them: they came from the film *Phantom of the Opera*. Nothing in the film's storyline gave any indication of what they were dealing with.

Gardener was left with questions and no answers. Why was there no reference to Corndell in the West End musical *Phantom*? Or Hollywood? More importantly, who really *was* the man who lived in a world full of dead people but thought they were still alive? Maybe he would find out when he joined Laura and Sean for Corndell's university performance tonight.

Sean Reilly came into the office and placed a coffee and a cup of tea on the desk; he was carrying a packet of Bourbon creams in his mouth, which he also dropped on to the desk.

"Is that from the machine?" asked Gardener.

"It's free," replied Reilly.

"But it's from the machine," insisted Gardener.

Reilly passed over the biscuits. "Have one of those, it'll take the taste away."

"It's not the taste I'm worried about, it's the after-effects. Colin Sharp claimed this stuff has turned his water green."

"He's only saying that to get attention. He thinks we might actually treat him as an equal."

Gardener laughed, taking a biscuit. "So, how did you get on yesterday?"

"Some pretty interesting stuff," said Reilly. "Initially, the planning department knew nothing about any tunnels under the house or the grounds. But one of their senior guys who's been there years had a story to tell. Apparently, the house had originally been built in 1840 by a man called Jacob Wilson, a pretty wealthy industrialist by all accounts, into everything. Anyway, he owned a mine, and he had the house built near it. One of the problems he had was transporting the coal, so he devised a network of tunnels under the ground which led to the railway station."

"Which one?" Gardener asked.

"Horsforth."

Gardener leaned forward on his desk. "We had a witness who said that Leonard White had entered the station in Leeds. No one has a record of him buying a ticket. No one saw him leave, and no one knew where he went to."

"Sounds about right."

"Do you think there's a tunnel under the station in Leeds which goes to Horsforth as well?"

"Still looking into that one, but I did find out about one of those nature walks that goes from Leeds station and eventually finishes up there. Which would be a hell of a walk to do at night. We're appealing for witnesses."

"Okay. It may not be much of a lead, but it's something. Let's see if Briggs will put a couple of the junior officers on to it. In the meantime, you and I should go and see Corndell again, see if we can have a better look around the house."

"I'm all for that," replied Reilly.

A knock on the door diverted Gardener's attention. Steve Fenton opened it and walked in, immediately helping himself to a biscuit. Before the door closed, Frank Thornton and Bob Anderson entered as well, each carrying a folder in one hand and a coffee in the other. They, too, helped themselves to biscuits.

"What the feck's going on here, then, open biscuit day?" Reilly exclaimed.

"Give it a rest, Reilly. You probably pinched them anyway," said Thornton.

"That's hardly the point now, is it?"

"Depends whose office you raided," said Anderson.

"Yours."

Gardener was amused by the banter of his colleagues, the first since the investigation had started, as far as he could remember. "Okay, Steve, what do you have for us on the prints?"

Fenton reached out for another biscuit, but Reilly was quicker and held them close to his chest. "Information first, son."

Fenton turned to Gardener. "Nothing, sir. Yours are on there. And Corndell's, I assume, because his are not on file."

"Okay, it was worth a try. Give him a biscuit, Sean."

"Feck off! That's no good to us."

"Frank? Bob? What have you got?"

"There's a lot of information about Chaney, but I don't suppose any of it's new," said Thornton. "I've copied some stuff and put it in the folder. Basically, it's a rags to riches story about a bloke who was born to deaf and dumb parents. His ability to act came from miming for his parents. He went to Hollywood, but it was quite a few years before he made it big."

Thornton seemed embarrassed by the fact that he'd found very little.

"He did make a film called *The Scarlet Car,* but I think the killer has used it purely as a red herring. It *was* filmed in 1917, and information is a bit bloody thin on the ground. I think the film rhymed with what he wanted to say, and the only reason was to point us in Chaney's direction."

"Despite being an icon, very little was known about Chaney," said Anderson. "Apparently, it's believed he once gave an interview and the only thing he said was, 'My whole career has been devoted to keeping people from knowing me', and with that he got up and left."

"You're joking," said Gardener.

"Apparently not. He was very secretive. As I said, there was no bigger film star, but very little was known about him."

"A bit like our friend Willy," said Reilly.

"At least Chaney had a traceable career," replied Gardener. "Anything on Harry Fletcher?"

"I spoke to a bloke who used to work with him at the Playhouse. Apparently, he left there and went to work in one of the Broadway theatres in New York. Anyway, he didn't stay too long, and the last time the man saw him was a couple of years ago. He was back living in Leeds but didn't say where, and he was quite excited about a new project, but didn't say what."

"What is it with these thespian types?" said Gardener. "They're always shrouded in bloody mystery. Keep trying. He must be somewhere. If you've found one person who knows and remembers him, there may be others. We need to find them."

"Before it's too late," added Reilly.

"Assuming he isn't the killer," replied Gardener. "Trace the flights, there must be records."

"But it's two years ago," said Thornton.

"I know that, but we need a break before someone else gets murdered. Trace the flights, talk to the taxi drivers, someone must have picked him up. Maybe recognized and remembered where he took him. If it was a hotel, they'll have records. There will be a trail. It's a matter of finding it. We can't leave any stones unturned."

Colin Sharp interrupted the conversation as he knocked and walked in. He also had a coffee in his hand, and managed to spot the biscuits straight away. "Hey, my favourites."

"And everybody else's, by the look of it," moaned Reilly.

Gardener glanced at Sharp. "Okay, what do you have?"
"Not a lot."

"If one more person says that today…" said Gardener.

Sharp sat down in the only available chair and opened his folder. "I checked out with BT first. You might find this interesting. In the last ten years, Corndell's only had one phone call to his landline, and hasn't made any."

"What?"

"He's made no calls, and received only one."

"Who was that from?"

"Martin Brown," said Sharp.

Gardener glanced at his partner. "Isn't that Laura's friend at the university?"

Reilly nodded. "What about his mobile?"

"He doesn't have one," said Sharp.

"He does," said Gardener. "He was using it when we visited."

"Sorry, sir, according to my records, he doesn't have one."

180

Gardener was confused, but didn't see the sense in arguing. Sharp was a very dedicated member of staff who chased up leads with a determination he'd never seen before. "Okay, patronize me. Check a little deeper, will you? How does he pay for his BT line?"

"All his transactions are done electronically. He never goes into the bank or pays a bill in person."

"Which bank is he with?" asked Gardener.

"An independent in London."

"Why London?" asked Gardener, astonished.

"I assume it's because he came from London originally."

"But surely you would change banks if you moved so far away," pressed Gardener.

"Unless you wanted to hide something," said Reilly. "What about an income?"

"He doesn't have one," replied Sharp. "But then again, he doesn't need one. His parents left him over three million pounds, and the house."

"How did his parents die?" asked Gardener.

Colin Sharp sorted through his notes. "His father had a heart attack."

"Brought on by what, I wonder," said Gardener.

"Who, more like," said Reilly.

"I don't think it was anything to do with Corndell. He was still down in London when it all happened."

"Doesn't mean much," said Reilly. "He could still have had a hand in it."

"Well... he could, but it doesn't seem feasible at the moment."

"What about his mother?" Gardener asked.

"Died in 1985. Cancer."

"Okay," said Gardener. That tied in with what Corndell had told them. "Anything else?"

"The only thing left for me to do is follow up the London lead, find out everything I can about his life down there. If anything's going to give, that's where it will come from."

"In that case, go down tomorrow. That privately owned bank must have a previous address. His father was famous enough, try the film studios, the West End. That reminds me, Sean, check with Fettle and see whether or not his mate has any information."

"Do you two really think Corndell is our man?" Thornton asked Gardener.

"He's at the top of the list for now."

"Then why don't we bring him in?" asked Anderson.

"No evidence," said Reilly. An air of defeat circulated the room.

"Another murder should do that," said Anderson.

"Only if we can tie him in," said Gardener.

"Does he have alibis for the previous two?" asked Steve Fenton.

"No, but you can't prove or disprove what he's said because he was home alone. And let's face it, even if he wasn't, who's to know with the two disguises he's used? Quite frankly, another murder would put us bottom of the popularity stakes, and Briggs would come down so heavy on us we'd have to reach up to tie our shoelaces."

Gardener sighed as another knock on the door came and Patrick Edwards poked his head around the frame. "Anything on that missing limo, Patrick?"

"Not a lot," replied Edwards. "Still hasn't turned up. It was paid for in cash by a man called Robert Sandell, and we've now found out all the documents produced were false."

"Wonderful," replied Gardener. "Okay, I have something else for you. I want you to check all the rental companies and find out whether or not a William Henry Corndell has hired any vehicles recently using electronic transfers from a London bank as payment. Colin will give you the name of the bank."

"Okay, sir," replied Edwards, still standing his ground. "Sir, that number you wanted us to check, Burley in Wharfedale?"

"Oh, yes."

"It's not in service anymore. When the owner sold the property and moved on, the new owner had it changed."

Gardener glanced at the sheet of paper that Edwards had passed over. The address – a side street off the main street, seemed familiar. "Who lives there now?"

"Someone called Cuthbertson... Alan Cuthbertson."

Chapter Thirty-six

Midday had come and gone, and with early afternoon approaching, Harry Fletcher had to try to organise the next day's supplies for the soup kitchen. He'd been at work since six o'clock and he was bushed, having prepared and served all the breakfasts, and afterwards, helping to rearrange the furniture in the room of the big house for that night's local council meeting. But five minutes with a cup of tea and his diary wouldn't hurt.

Mary Phillips, one of three volunteers, was cleaning the kitchen. She'd said it was fine by her if he took a break, seeing as he started two hours before anyone else. Kathy and Sarah, the other volunteers, had left early due to doctor's appointments.

Harry took a sip of the now lukewarm tea. He dipped a custard cream and popped it into his mouth, savouring the taste because it was the only thing he had eaten all day.

Since leaving New York, Harry had changed his life completely, starting with his name. Here, he was known as

Henry Fowkes, the name he was known by on Broadway. He had a very strict diet, eating virtually nothing during the day, but finishing the evening with a decent meal. Two hours prior to supper he used his time wisely, writing in his study. After his meal, he would then spend a further two hours writing, before retiring to bed early with either a good book or his portable television.

Since returning to Britain he had enjoyed himself, but his current project was coming to an end, and he felt that he should speak to his friend Stan very soon about the whole thing. He had hoped he'd see Stan today, but he hadn't yet shown his face.

Harry liked Stan. The first time the man had walked into the homeless shelter – which had only been three months ago – Harry had known he was the one. Stan was perfect for the part without a word being spoken. For all Harry had known, Stan could have been a deaf mute. But he wasn't, and they had started speaking, and the more they had talked, the more he'd seen his project opening up into a bestseller. Americans loved stories about eccentric Englishmen.

Stan's first appearance had been towards the back end of January when the weather had turned bitter. Hunched into a topcoat with the flaps of his deerstalker down, he'd crept quietly through the door, glancing everywhere, as if he was searching for someone but he wasn't sure who.

He wore woollen mittens with his fingers poking through, and always had a pipe clamped firmly between his teeth, perfecting a Sherlock Holmes that Conan Doyle would have been proud of. There was no tobacco in the pipe; whether it was because he was trying to give up or he couldn't afford it, Harry had never determined, and it didn't seem that important anyway.

Stan had chosen a quiet corner in which to sit, and as Harry approached, he'd tipped his cap and then hesitated, as if he shouldn't really be there. Harry had laid a hand on his shoulder because he felt sure that Stan would have left the table and the shelter had he not made the gesture. Harry had made tea and sandwiches and sat with his newfound friend while he consumed them. Stan's mannerisms had reminded Harry of a typical, old English gentleman, as though he had suddenly materialised out of nowhere from that Victorian era.

Stan's strange phobias and superstitions also suited the part. Harry would never forget the day of the big storm.

Stan didn't like storms. That had proved interesting. Harry had closed all the doors and windows, and had insisted that Stan stay at the table and finish his meal. He would never forget the fear in the man's eyes, and *his* insistence that all doors and windows should be opened at once to allow any lightning bolts to pass straight through. With white knuckles he had gripped the table, refusing to eat. When the storm had finally passed, Harry had paid a taxi driver to take Stan to wherever he felt he needed to be.

But for all that, he enjoyed Stan's company. All he had to do now was persuade him to give up his life here. What life? Harry knew he was homeless, but homeless people lived somewhere, even if it *was* only a makeshift shelter at the back of the shops on Albion Street. Harry had toured the city in search of Stan, and none of the vagrants had had any information. No one knew him; neither had they heard of him. He'd checked the other shelters, but Stan had not frequented those either. Having finally found the taxi driver and asked him where he had taken the man who resembled Sherlock Holmes, the answer had been the train station in Leeds.

Harry was puzzled by that one. That was another thing about Stan: he loved his puzzles.

"Hello Henry," said a voice behind him.

Harry turned and saw the man he had been thinking about. Stan was staring down at him, dressed in his usual garb.

Poor Stan must have had a tough life. Harry estimated his age as mid-sixties, and because he had odd eyes, his expression was one of constant torture. Not only were they different colours, one was lower than the other, and bore the marks of a nasty scar. Harry had brought it up in an earlier conversation but Stan had refused to talk about it. His skin was extremely wrinkled and leathery to touch, like the hide of a bull. But for all that, he was well nourished. Although he ate little at the shelter, the man had to be eating somewhere.

"Stan, my man, how's it hanging?"

"Oh Henry, I'm not at all sure I shall ever catch on to your use of language."

"You should have done by now, what with living on the streets."

Stan removed his pipe from his lips before speaking. "One cannot change one's upbringing, Henry. A terrible place the streets may be, but because one lives there doesn't mean one should lower one's standards and adopt the ways of others who do."

"I've not seen you for days, where have you been?"

"Keeping low, Henry, pondering over the rising violence within the city, and wondering where a man's to go for safety in times of crisis."

Harry wasn't keen on the tone of conversation today. But Stan could be like that. One time he would be all cheerful and full of himself, talking of a life that Harry wasn't sure he had actually lived or simply wanted to. It was saddening to hear. Other times he was very philosophical, taking the world's problems to heart. Today was going to be one of those days. Perhaps it really would be best for him to tackle Stan about a change.

"Come and sit down, Stan. I'll make a fresh cuppa, and then I'd like us to talk."

Stan did as he was asked, returning the pipe to his mouth. Glancing at the floor, he suddenly asked Harry a question.

"What's with the rope?"

Harry stooped and picked it up. It was about twelve inches in length and had a large knot in the middle. "Oh, it's nothing, just something I'm checking out for a new project."

"What kind of a knot is that?" Stan pointed.

"I've no idea, that's what I'm trying to figure out. Anyway," said Harry, "let's not worry about that now, you and me have other things to discuss."

When the tea was made, Harry placed a cup in front of his friend. "I've brought your favourites as well. Fig rolls."

"Praise the Lord that I should ever have found a friend like you, Henry."

"What's troubling you, Stan?"

"Is this to be the subject of our conversation, what is bothering me?"

"Amongst other things, yes."

Stan placed his pipe on the table and sighed and rolled his eyes upwards.

Harry thought again that he was so perfect for his play. It was simply a question of whether or not he could adapt to another life, and utilise what was very obviously a natural talent. It was one thing to convey expressions and mannerisms in everyday life, but to display them on a stage in front of a crowd of people was another matter entirely.

"I know things, Henry."

"What kind of things, Stan? Come on, drink your tea and have a fig roll."

"You don't understand, Henry. Tea and fig rolls will not help alleviate the problems of the world." Stan's tone worried Harry. Despite knowing what he could be like, he had never seen him acting as weird as today. Another indication that he should make his move.

"Has something happened?"

The old man gripped Harry's hands with a speed that startled him. "Do you not read the newspapers, Henry?"

"Which ones? What are you talking about?"

187

"There's a murderer on the loose. He has to be stopped."

"You don't want to worry yourself about that. I'm sure the police will catch him before long."

"I hear things on the street. The police have no idea who they're looking for. They have no idea where he'll strike next. The city of Leeds is no safe place."

"When you say you know things," said Harry, "do you mean you know things about the killer which could put you in danger?"

Stan remained silent for so long it really unnerved Harry. During the ensuing silence, his thoughts were sporadic. Was Stan's life in danger? Did he know the killer, or something about him? "Where exactly do you stay at night, Stan?"

Stan's glare created a feeling of depression within Harry. Their conversation was not going to plan. "The streets are unsafe."

"Would you like to stay here tonight?"

"Is it any safer here than anywhere else?"

"Well, I'm here. There'll be plenty of other people here tonight, we have a council meeting."

"I'm not sure, Henry. You are too good a friend to me, I have no desire to place you in the danger I myself may be facing."

"Nonsense, you're worried, and I'd like to help. And there's something else we can talk about tonight."

Stan picked up the empty pipe and puffed on it, as if it contained tobacco. "What?"

"My work here is nearly done, Stan."

"Are you leaving?" Stan's eyes widened and his grip grew tighter, and it was only then that Harry realised his hands were still coupled to those of his friend. "You can't leave! Where will I go, who will I talk to?"

"Well, that's just it, Stan. Where I'm going, you can come, too."

"What?" His friend seemed horrified by the suggestion. Yet only seconds ago, he had feared for his life on the streets.

"I'm going back to New York. I want you to come with me."

"To New York? Are you out of your mind? I can't go to New York, it's less safe than here." Stan stood up and abruptly let go of Harry's hands. "Besides, I don't know anyone in New York. What if they don't like me? Or I can't make friends? What shall I do then?"

"Stan, stop worrying and calm down. You'll be with me."

"Doing what, for heaven's sake?"

"That's what I want to talk to you about," replied Harry.

Stan made for the door, knocking over a chair in the process. "I can't. I just can't." He turned to Harry. "Don't you realise, Henry, here is all I know? I may not have much of a life, I may be in danger, but I know here. We drive on the right side of the road. We don't eat pancakes smothered in syrup for breakfast. We drink Earl Grey tea, not coffee in Styrofoam cups..."

Harry thought he had stopped but the barrage continued. "We are civilised human beings." He pointed a crooked finger at Harry. "We don't carry guns."

Harry sensed the man was physically distraught and suspected the situation was about to spiral out of control when Mary Phillips came into the room. Her appearance momentarily calmed Stan down.

"Is everything all right, Mr Fowkes?" asked Mary.

"It's fine, Mary, Stan's just a little worried about something. But I've asked him to come and stay here tonight, haven't I, Stan?"

His friend hesitated before replying. "If you're sure I'm not intruding."

"Don't be soft, man." Harry turned to Mary. "Can you make up a spare bed for me?"

"Of course I can." She turned to Stan. "You'll be more than welcome, love."

He tipped his deerstalker. "If you're sure it's no bother."

"None at all," said Harry.

He tipped his hat once again and bowed. "I must be on my way."

"Where are you going?" asked Harry.

"There are things I need to attend to, but I shall return. And only if you are sure." It was a point he kept making.

"I've said so. You stay here tonight, we'll have a meal and a talk, and I'm sure everything will seem much better in the morning."

"You're very kind." He stepped back into the hallway. "Till tonight, Harry." His friend was gone in an instant.

"That's odd, Mr Fowkes," said Mary.

"What is?" asked Harry, clearing away the pots into the kitchen.

"He just called you Harry."

Chapter Thirty-seven

Despite Reilly having made a little more effort with his attire, he was still dressed in denims. Laura wore an expensive two-piece suit in emerald green with matching jewellery. Gardener, however, had once again used his son as a guide. He was wearing a plain black jacket tailored by Pinstripe, a midnight blue Lee Cooper shirt, and a pair of bleached black Koman original vintage jeans imported from the United States. He wasn't convinced, but Chris told him they were in. More than half the students must have thought so, because they had glanced in his direction as if he played a part in the events about to unfold.

The stage had been prepared to create the perfect ambience to an evening which he suspected would be full of surprises; the fact that Corndell could actually act, for one. Two blackout curtains had been used to maintain the secrecy of what lay behind. There were speakers either side, positioned top to bottom. A fog machine belched out a fine mist at carefully timed intervals, and the lighting created an eerie silhouette of a sinister figure, rising up and down on the surface of the curtain. The background music was Mike Oldfield's *Tubular Bells*. The idea was clever, but Gardener was unable to concentrate fully because of what had been said at the meeting earlier in the day.

He turned to Sean, noticing that Laura was deep in conversation with the person next to her. "Did you manage to find Cuthbertson, Sean?"

"No. Called him three or four times, and then took a car round his place. Neighbour said she hadn't seen him for a couple of days, which was unusual, because if he ever went anywhere for long, he normally left her a key to look after the place."

"Has she gone round to see if he's okay, or still there?"

"Only once. She was out in the garden and heard his phone ringing. If he *was* in, he never answered. After that I drove round to Ruffin Street to Madame Two-swords. They haven't seen him for a couple of days either."

"I don't like the sound of this. You don't think he's done anything stupid?"

"Like topping himself and leaving a suicide note to say that we're responsible because we wouldn't leave him alone? It's a possibility."

"I wasn't actually thinking of that. More along the lines of fleeing the country. Have you tried the shop?"

"Yes, still closed. I don't think he's left the country, boss. I'm sure the neighbour would have seen him bundling a suitcase into a taxi. She didn't strike me as the type to miss anything. We should probably check the airports anyway."

"Like we really need this right now," said Gardener. He changed the subject. "Anything on the rental companies?"

"Not yet, but that's a big job, so it is."

Gardener leaned further forward, noting that Laura was still talking. "Do you think she'll miss us for a few minutes?"

"What do you have in mind?"

"I thought we might pay a visit to our friend's dressing room, seeing as we're all in the same building at the same time. We may not get another chance."

"It's a good idea, but I think you'd achieve more if you went alone," said Reilly. "I don't think he'll talk anyway, but if he sees both of us, we'll have no chance. What do you think he'll say now that he didn't before?"

"Nothing, but I'd just like him to know we're here. And while I'm at it, I'd like a word with Martin Brown. I want to know what time Corndell arrived, and how."

"I'll talk to Martin," said Reilly.

"Okay." He watched as Sean leaned towards Laura and had a quick word in her ear. She glanced around, and then pointed to a man on the far side of the stage talking to one of the students, which he took to be Martin Brown.

Gardener and Reilly left their seats, shuffled to the end of the row, and down to the stage where Martin Brown's conversation was coming to an end. He smiled and politely nodded as the student walked off.

Down as close to the stage as he was going to be, Gardener felt it was much warmer, and wondered whether or not it was an effect of the lights.

"Can I help you gentlemen?" asked Martin.

"Maybe," said Gardener, flashing his warrant card. "We'd just like to ask you a few questions."

"Has something happened?"

"We're interested in Corndell."

Martin Brown wasn't at all what Gardener had expected. Standing a little over six feet, he had mousy coloured hair in a style more erratic than most of his students. Perhaps he hadn't combed it today. He wore a beige shirt left hanging out of his denim jeans, and a pair of loosely fastened brown loafers. Despite being born and bred in London, there was only a trace of an accent. He was slim, and had one of those postures that could easily be mistaken for a man who preferred other men.

"You could have picked a better time, he's on stage," he replied, glancing at his watch. "He is due on in ten minutes, and I have to announce him."

"It won't take long. How and when did he arrive here today?"

"I really haven't the faintest idea."

"I thought you ran the entertainment around here," said Reilly.

"I do."

"So, how come you don't know what's going on?"

"Because I have a lot more to do than keep my eye on who comes and goes and at what time."

"You must have some idea," said Gardener, eager to return to the point.

"I believe it was around four o'clock. I wasn't here myself. Naturally, I would assume he arrived by taxi."

"I wouldn't assume anything with this man," said Reilly.

"What are you trying to imply?" asked Brown.

"Nothing," said Gardener. "We're just making sure you answer the questions correctly and to the best of your knowledge, not with what you think you know."

Martin Brown glanced at his watch again, seemingly more agitated.

"So, did he arrive by taxi, or didn't he?" pressed Gardener.

"Just a minute." He walked over and consulted another colleague. On his return, he had better news. "Yes, he did arrive by taxi; just after four o'clock."

"From where? And do you know which taxi firm?" asked Gardener.

"Look, is this really necessary? I do have a show to present."

"We wouldn't be asking if it wasn't," said Reilly.

"Aren't you Laura's husband?"

"Now that *is* an unnecessary question," replied Reilly. "But for the record, yes. So, can you tell us where he was brought from?"

"No, I can't. I assume, rightly or wrongly and quite frankly I don't care, his home in Horsforth."

"I'd like to go backstage and have a word with him," said Gardener. That statement took Martin Brown one step closer to madness, or so his expression conveyed. "Are you kidding me? The man is about to go on stage and present a show. Have you any idea of the kind of pressure he will be under?"

"Not as much as me," replied Gardener.

"I don't think it would be wise."

"I'm not really interested in your opinion, Mr Brown. And whether or not you like it, I *am* going behind that curtain and I *am* going to have a word with your client."

"Are you here on official business?"

"In what capacity?" Gardener asked.

"Police capacity. Has Mr Corndell done anything wrong?"

"Not to my knowledge."

"Then, I don't see any reason why it can't wait until after his show. And before you ask, I have to tell you his contract specifically states that no one will be granted interviews either before or after the show."

"I don't want an interview, I simply want to wish him all the best," Gardener answered.

"Haven't quite gone the correct way about it, then, have we? As I mentioned, his contract stated no interviews, no guests. He was very particular about the contract being followed to the letter."

Gardener noticed the crowd growing restless. The background music changed again, to another heavily orchestrated piece he didn't recognise. "Do you have that contract to hand?" he asked.

"It's in my office."

"I want a copy before I leave. And now, I'm going backstage for a quick word, after which, you can introduce him." Gardener turned to his partner. "Sean, you stay here and see that Mr Brown is kept amused."

Gardener tipped his hat and walked off. He entered the stage through the side curtain, suddenly caught off balance by the atmosphere.

The set was incredible, a mock cathedral with red velvet drapes and huge backdrops and images from horror films. In between the photos, the crumbling brickwork had arched windows and turrets, bearing the hallmark of a million spiders spinning their webs. And he could smell garlic.

But none of what he saw had prepared him for the centrepiece. In the middle of the stage stood a huge podium surrounded by strobe lights, which were currently being switched on and off one by one. A fog machine added to the effect. A number of stagehands were asking the person on the podium if everything was okay, and he knew from the replies that it could only be one person behind the breathtaking make-up.

Even Gardener – who was by no means a film buff – knew that Corndell had recreated the character Quasimodo from *The Hunchback of Notre Dame*.

The attention to detail was fascinating, hypnotic. His nose was shaped like a tetrahedron, a sort of four-sided triangular pyramid, with a mouth arched like a horseshoe. Corndell's left eye was pushed upwards, and his eyebrow had bristles like those of a carrot. The right eye was buried behind a tumour. He had irregular teeth like the battlements of a fortress, and a horny lip over which the teeth protruded like a walrus tusk. His head was covered with red bristles, and between his shoulders he had a hell of a hump. How he had balanced it, Gardener had no idea. His legs were so strangely positioned that they only touched at the knees, as if they had been broken in order to achieve the effect.

He wore a dark grey three-quarter smock that must have been laid on a warehouse floor for the last ten years, and a tight pair of black leggings for which Gardener was sure Corndell had used padding. No one on earth could have legs like that. The whole effect was neatly finished with Corndell trussed up and held firm to the podium by chains that appeared to be real, but were surely not.

Suddenly, as if in slow motion, Corndell turned his head, spotting Gardener. Despite the intense amount of make-up, Gardener detected an expression of pure rage on Corndell's face. His remaining eye widened and nearly popped out of its socket.

"Would you please remove that man from this stage? Now!" he whispered, but still managed to make it sound like he was shouting.

"Now, now, Mr Corndell, that's no way to treat an old friend."

"If you were my friend, Mr Gardener, you wouldn't be here. I will not give you any further instructions other than either leave the stage now, or the whole show is cancelled."

"If that's what you want," replied Gardener.

Martin Brown appeared at Gardener's side. "Can I ask you what the hell you think you're doing?"

"I told you. I came to see an old friend."

"You don't look like a friend from where I'm standing. Now you either leave or I'll call the police and have you removed officially!"

"Okay." Gardener raised his hands. As he was about to leave, he turned. "Oh, Corndell, by the way..."

The Hunchback glanced in his direction but didn't speak.

"Good luck," shouted Gardener. He didn't wait for a reply.

As he passed the curtain in front of the stage, he could hear the commotion he had caused. Corndell was quite clearly distressed and Martin Brown was doing his best to reassure him that everything was fine and that they really had to continue with tonight's performance. Gardener doubted very much that it would be cancelled now, what with Corndell already chained up, but it may well be delayed.

One thing was certain: Corndell's excellent use of make-up had only confirmed his suspicions about who their killer *could* be. Gardener joined Reilly back in his seat, removing his hat.

"How did it go?" asked the Irishman.

"Let's see, shall we."

"You didn't upset him, did you?" asked Reilly, smirking.

"Would I?"

The main hall lights dimmed and the background music died. The lighting creating the eerie vampire effect on the black curtains diminished and eventually they were lifted, leaving the red velvet drapes and a silhouette of the Hunchback. The entire stage lighting petered out, leaving the whole theatre in darkness.

The tension was electric. People spoke in hushed whispers, and he could see that most of them struggled to contain their excitement. The drapes opened, followed by the hiss of fog machines and a blast of the white mist. The speakers roared into life, and despite the fact that he'd been ready for something to happen, the sound still startled him and half the audience. He did not recognise the piece of music, but figured it would feature in one of the film versions of the character Corndell was playing.

At that moment, Gardener was beginning to believe there was a possibility that Corndell really could act; perhaps he *had* been a big name in the theatre, had done all the things he'd professed. The effect was certainly dazzling.

All four strobe lights lit up, each one of the beams directed at Corndell. Even with his head bowed and the chains in place, he still managed to send a ripple of fear around the audience.

The music grew in volume and intensity, and as it reached a crescendo, died instantly. In that moment, Corndell raised his head and screamed, breaking the chains, launching them across the stage. He raised his hands, which were now free, and glared directly into the audience, more so towards Gardener. Or so it felt.

Until that point, the show was as professional as any he'd seen. What came next blew those thoughts completely.

Whether it was Corndell's fault or the podium on which he was standing, Gardener didn't know, but the whole thing completely overbalanced and Corndell fell forwards. He hit the stage with a thud and rolled over, crashing into one of the monitors at the front. Despite the sound created by the pandemonium, the word "Bollocks!" was very prominent. But for that, no one would really have known whether the slip was part of the show or not.

Corndell was quickly on his feet, and the whole audience erupted into raucous laughter. Students rolled about in the aisles and laughed and pointed at the pathetic figure on the stage.

Gardener stifled a smile, but that was wiped from his face when Corndell pointed outwards and shouted, "Fucking police!"

He stormed off the stage to his right. The laughter died, replaced by questions.

Gardener and Reilly were quickly out of their seats, heading towards the front, leaving Laura open-mouthed. They reached the front row. Martin Brown was already on the stage, glancing around. As they stepped up, he turned on them. "Are you satisfied?"

"About what?" Gardener asked.

"That you've managed to ruin the whole evening."

"How do you make that out, Mr Brown?" asked Gardener.

"You upset him. He was all for cancelling the show, but it was me who persuaded him otherwise. I could see he wasn't happy. But I'll tell you this much," – he pointed a finger in Gardener's direction – "I will be placing a formal complaint about your behaviour here this evening."

"We're just doing our job," said Reilly.

"You told me you were not on official business. As far as I'm concerned, you came here deliberately to upset him, for what reason I have no idea. What the hell has that man done to warrant you hounding him?"

"Where is he now?" asked Gardener.

"I have no idea, but wherever he is, I don't suppose he'll want to see you."

"That's irrelevant." Gardener pushed past Martin Brown, but was unsure in which direction to go. He turned back again. "Where are the dressing rooms?"

"That way."

"Don't point," said Gardener. "Show me!"

Martin Brown reluctantly did so, glancing back at the students who had paid good money for the show and were now lost as to what was going on.

At the end of the corridor, they found the door to Corndell's dressing room open and empty. To the side, the door that led out on to the street was also open, the cold night air creeping in. Gardener stepped outside but he couldn't see anyone.

Martin Brown was in the dressing room when he came back. "He must have gone. Are you satisfied?"

"Not really." He turned to his partner. "Sean, let's take your car."

"Where are you going?" asked Martin Brown.

Gardener didn't answer but simply left the building. When they reached his sergeant's car and jumped in, Reilly turned and asked, "Horsforth?"

"I don't think he could have got that far just yet. Drive around the streets. See if we can see anything of him. After all, the way *he* looks, he won't be hard to spot, will he?"

* * *

Fifteen minutes of driving yielded nothing. Gardener was mystified. Corndell couldn't possibly have disappeared so quickly, unless of course he'd managed to flag down a taxi immediately. Or had his own transport.

They eventually pulled up outside the house at Horsforth. Gardener jumped out of the car and in the background, through the trees, he noticed lights burning on the bottom floor. Then a bedroom light went on. "He must be here, Sean."

Reilly stood close to the gate and the intercom. He reached into his inside jacket pocket and drew out a miniature digital voice recorder, and then pressed the button on the wall.

The intercom flicked into life with Corndell's unmistakable voice. "I do not wish to talk to anyone."

The intercom cut off and the bedroom light went out. Reilly pressed the intercom once more, but nothing happened.

Chapter Thirty-eight

Gardener was in the office for eight o'clock. The heating hadn't yet kicked in, and the room was chilly. Reilly hadn't arrived, and the overpowering silence was something he could do without. He crossed the room, switched on the small radio perched on the window ledge, and immediately re-tuned to Radio 2, listening briefly to a news broadcast about the economy. As he turned towards his desk, Maurice Roberts, the night shift duty sergeant, tapped on his door and entered. He was holding a clipboard.

"Morning, sir."

"Morning," replied Gardener, about to take a seat.

"A message came in for you last night, about nine o'clock."

Gardener remained standing. "Who from?"

Roberts consulted his notes. "A man called Henry Fowkes."

"Can't say as I know him. What did he want?" Gardener's emotions started to race. Although Roberts hadn't said as much, his manner and his posture were associated with bad news. He wasn't his normal cheerful self, and the expression in his eyes was not simple fatigue.

"He runs the St John's Hospice."

"Where's that?" asked Gardener.

"In the town, sir, a couple of streets from Mark Lane. You know, where St John's Church is."

"What did he want?" asked Gardener.

"He was a bit concerned about one of his... clients, is how he put it."

Gardener wondered where the conversation was going. "Concerned, how?"

Reilly's presence in the office lifted Gardener's tension a little.

"He didn't go into details, sir," replied Roberts. "But a man he's come to regard as a friend was acting very strangely yesterday, worried about the state of the city and the violence. He was particularly concerned about a killer whom we can't catch. According to his friend, we had no idea who we're looking for, and he feared for his own safety."

"Did he give any names?"

"No, sir. I had the impression that Fowkes thought he was a doctor – patient confidentiality, and all that. Anyway, he left a contact number."

Gardener glanced at his partner and then Roberts. "Did he say anything else?"

"No, but the way he was talking, I think he had a lot more on his mind. He wants to speak to you."

Roberts placed the number on the desk and then left the office.

"Any chance we have a lead on Harry Fletcher there, boss?" asked Reilly.

"It's possible. Shall we ring the number or drive straight over there?"

"We may as well drive–" Reilly's answer was cut short as duty sergeant Roberts launched himself back into the room.

"Sir?"

"What is it?"

"We've just taken a call from St John's Hospice, there's another body. I think the killer may have struck again, only this time, it's much worse."

"Worse! What could be worse than last time?" asked Gardener, moving around the desk.

"The woman's hysterical, but she did manage to blurt out the name Henry Fowkes. She kept saying 'poor Henry'."

"Let's move," Gardener said to Reilly.

Chapter Thirty-nine

Everyone arrived simultaneously: Gardener and Reilly, forensics, Fitz, and even Briggs. Gardener jumped out of the car and immediately started barking orders, which included sealing off the building with scene tape, constables to be placed front and rear, and no one allowed in or out until he said so.

He glanced around. It was surprisingly quiet. Considering it was a homeless shelter, he would have expected to see more people. The building was Victorian, three-storey, in a good state of repair with guttering, window frames and front door, all new.

Entering the building, Gardener heard hushed female voices in another room. To his left was a group of vagrants. He turned around. Glancing down the path, he shouted to one of the officers, "Come in here." He faced the tramps. "I'm afraid you gentlemen will have to leave."

"What about our breakfast?"

The two policemen entered the building. Gardener gave them their instruction before walking away. In the kitchen he found the three women, each in tears, comforting each other. A strawberry blonde was leaning over a draining board, repeating the phrase, "poor Henry". A large pot stood on the cooker and, above that, the one thing he could have done without.

Scrawled on the wall, written in blood, was the new message.

Gardener's whole world closed in around him. The kitchen was suddenly reduced to the size of a shoebox; sounds were blocked out, people disappeared, and he sensed a rush of adrenaline like he'd never experienced before. His whole body felt full of pins and needles. He was cold, but at the same time he was sweating.

Briggs' loud voice brought him out of his momentary stupor. "I don't suppose anybody recognises *that*?"

"I do, sir," said Colin Sharp, "it's from the *Phantom* film."

Gardener read the message again:

So far so good, for a house with a curse on it.

Drawn on the wall underneath the message was an arrow, pointing to the cooking pot. Gardener dreaded to think what was inside. He turned to the three women. "Has anyone touched the pot?"

The strawberry blonde nodded. "I did."

He realised the stress she was under, but he needed to know the answers to his questions. "What exactly did you do?"

She took her time in replying. "I lifted the lid."

"Other than the pot, have you touched anything else?" he asked her.

She shook her head, as if to confirm she hadn't.

"Can you tell me your exact movements from the time you came through the door?"

She was obviously very upset, and Gardener sensed she was perhaps closer to the man they called Henry Fowkes than the others. He waited patiently while she described her movements. She'd been the first to arrive. Let herself in, hung up her coat, and came straight through to the kitchen, where she'd remained, joined by the other two as they arrived.

Fitz came into the room. Gardener produced a pair of gloves. After slipping into them, he approached the cooking pot and lifted the lid. The strawberry blonde turned her head and let out a stifled sob. The pan was three quarters full with warm water – tinged pink. A severed head stared back at him. Gardener wondered if the blood had been drained prior to death – and where.

Because the water wasn't boiling, the skin had not blistered, and the face would be recognisable to anyone who knew him. The eyes were open and the depth of shock disturbed Gardener; if they could speak, he was quite certain he would not want to hear what they had to say.

"Is this the head of Henry Fowkes?" he asked the strawberry blonde.

Although she didn't answer, one of the others confirmed it.

"Has either of you been anywhere else in the house?"

They said they hadn't.

"So, none of you have any idea where his body is?" Gardener asked.

Once again, they confirmed they did not.

Frank Thornton and Bob Anderson were also in the room. Gardener addressed them. "Can one of you take these ladies out of here and see if you can arrange for a strong drink? Meanwhile, call the station and have them send round a couple of female councillors."

Gardener wasn't very pleased that they had probably contaminated the crime scene, but there was little he could do about it now.

Briggs had moved a little closer. "What's that in the bottom of the pan?"

Gardener followed his line of vision, and only then did he notice what Briggs was talking about. He glanced around the kitchen, found a pair of tongs and lifted out the object: a sealed test tube with a note inside.

Briggs turned away in frustration. "This bastard's been busy." He threw his arms in the air. "And I suppose no one saw him again. And even if they did, we're not likely to know who the fuck he was this time."

"We don't know that, yet," said Gardener, removing the stopper and the note from the tube.

The silence in the room became intolerable as each man patiently waited for Gardener to unfold what would more than likely be another puzzle, which would send them off to God knew where in order to find God knew what. Hopefully it would be the remainder of the corpse.

He read the message out aloud:

Here's the man you've been looking for,
So continue your search, out through the door.
Poor old Harry has met his doom,
If you want the rest, it's in his room.

"Does this mean we've found Harry Fletcher, who might be called Henry Fowkes?" Briggs asked.

"Possibly," said Gardener, passing the note to Briggs. "At least it would explain why we couldn't find him." Before leaving the kitchen, a uniformed officer deposited some scene suits and each officer donned one. They walked slowly through the house to find the three women whom Thornton had taken away. They were all sitting in a lounge. "Which one is Henry's room?"

One of them women stood up. "I'll show you."

"It's okay," said Gardener. "Just tell us." After the information, Gardener, Reilly, and Briggs traipsed up the stairs to a second storey landing.

Briggs glared in Gardener's direction. "Before we go in here and see what he's left for us, I want it made abundantly clear right now that I don't care if we have to turn the entire city upside down or how many men it takes, I want this lunatic caught."

Gardener glanced at Reilly and then Briggs. He understood his superior officer's frustration, for he felt it himself. Choosing not to reply, he turned and opened the door.

Nothing on earth could have prepared them for the carnage.

The smell hit them first, and each man took an involuntary step back, assaulted by a vile, cloying odour, which immediately coated the insides of their nostrils. Gardener doubted that the remains of a skip full of tightly packed corpses sealed up for the entire summer period would have topped it.

His cast-iron reserve almost slipped and forced him to show his emotions. He had seen what The Roundhay Ripper had left behind, had attended all manner of suicides, observed the victims of car crashes, lived through the experience of the Christmas murders; and he was pretty confident that his partner had seen his fair share of atrocities during his time in the Royal Ulster Constabulary. But here, in what was beginning to resemble a Charnel House in a Yorkshire city, in a man's private study, they were now observing perhaps the most inhuman degradation that any of them had ever witnessed.

Briggs remained speechless, as did Fitz, Anderson and the SOCOs – who by now had joined them. Even Reilly inhaled a sharp breath.

In the middle of the room was the naked corpse of Henry Fowkes. To all intents, he was levitating. In a spectacular illusion, his whole body had been suspended in mock crucifixion, but there seemed to be nothing holding him in place. The entire room was awash with blood. By far the biggest and most disturbing stain was on the ceiling. He had obviously been decapitated here, in his study. Large globules that had been ready to fall to the floor had finally given up and congealed. Splash patterns doused the walls and the carpet and his PC.

"Jesus Christ!" said Briggs, peering a little closer. "What's holding him up?"

Gardener glanced to the sides of the room and immediately understood. A series of pulleys were screwed to the walls, and as he strained his eyes he could make out the tines of catgut, or fishing wire. It had been wound round so tight, that the limbs it held were bulging and must have been close to being severed.

In his right hand, a sheet of A4 paper had been fastened. It had the same scroll pattern as the ones they had seen at each crime scene, and no doubt contained another cryptic message. On the floor directly below Henry's body was a pile of discarded clothes, amongst them, a deerstalker and a pipe.

However, despite everything, the killer had really played an ace, because the most disturbing scene was that the corpse was not headless, raising the question of all questions: whose head was on top of Henry Fowkes' neck?

"I really don't believe this fella anymore," said Briggs. "If Henry Fowkes' head is in a cooking pot in the middle of the kitchen, who does that belong to? And where is the rest of that fella?"

Gardener's scene suit rustled as he brought his hands to his head and ran them down his face, exhaling a loud sigh. "We need to see what's on that paper."

Briggs turned to Fenton. "You lads seal the room off and do what you have to do, as quickly as you can. He's right, we need to see what's on the paper." He turned to Gardener. "We have to do something, Stewart. The press get wind of this, and we'll all be out of a job. And quite frankly, I can't see any way of preventing them from hearing about it."

"Well, let's start by going downstairs and interviewing."

Chapter Forty

The blonde appeared more composed. She took a sip of tea, and then introduced herself as Mary Phillips.

"How long have you worked here, Mary?" asked Gardener.

"Four years," she replied.

"What do you do?"

"A dog's body, really." Her gaze was devoid of emotion. "I suppose that's a bit harsh. I help out with a bit of cooking and a bit of cleaning, nothing special."

"How long have you known Henry Fowkes?"

"He started work here two years ago." She took another sip of tea, and Gardener suspected he was going to glean little more information from her than standard replies to his questions. But he'd settle for that. For now.

"Did he live here?"

"Yes, his room was up the stairs, and he pretty much had the run of the house in return for all he did for us."

"Which was what?"

"He ran the place, Mr Gardener. He was up early in the mornings, cooking all the breakfasts. Once that was over, we'd all have a cup of tea and then we'd straighten the place round. He used to see to all the deliveries."

"Did he have any family that you know of?"

"No."

"Any idea how he spent his spare time?"

It was a while before she answered, and Gardener wondered whether or not she'd actually heard him, or had simply forgotten the question.

"Come to think of it, no."

"When did you last see him?"

"Yesterday teatime, about five o'clock. We'd set out the room for the council meeting."

"Do you know what that was about?" asked Gardener.

"Henry wanted to try to raise extra funding to keep the place open. We rely on charity, you see. He thought if he could get the council involved we might be able to keep going indefinitely. Anyway, they came for an inspection."

"They? Do you know how many?"

"Afraid not."

Gardener stood and left the room. When he found Bob Anderson, he asked him to contact the council for a list of all the names of the people who had attended the previous night's meeting. When he returned, he continued to question Mary Phillips. "You don't happen to know where he worked before here?"

"I've no idea, but I did hear him mention America once or twice. But he was a very private man, never said much about his personal life."

Gardener's heart was beginning to sink slowly towards his shoes. "Did he say where in America?"

"If he did, I never caught it."

"What's America got to do with anything, Stewart?" asked Briggs.

"Something Thornton and Anderson had found out. A number of years ago, Harry Fletcher left Leeds to go and work on Broadway. He came back a couple of years ago, but no one's seen him since."

"Who's Harry Fletcher?" asked Mary Phillips.

"That's what we'd like to know. Tell me, Mary, do you happen to know if Henry was his real name? I don't suppose he was ever called by any other name, was he?"

Mary's expression darkened. "Now you mention it, yes. Only yesterday."

"Go on," said Gardener, growing concerned when she had stopped.

"Well, I found it a bit strange. We had a bloke come into the shelter a few weeks back. Started talking to Henry, and they were getting on right well. Anyway, yesterday Stan, that was his name, Stan. Anyway, he was in yesterday and he was in a right state with himself, and Henry asked me to make a bed up for him. He wanted Stan to stay the night."

"And did he?" asked Gardener.

"I don't think so."

"You don't know?" asked Reilly.

"Well, I've not checked his bed." She rose to her feet.

"It's okay, Mary, love, you stay where you are," said Briggs. "You tell us the room and I'll check." She did as she was asked and then sat back down.

"Carry on, Mary," prompted Gardener. "A strange incident."

"Oh, yes. When Stan was leaving, he called Henry by the name of Harry. I just thought it was a mistake, but maybe it wasn't." Tears welled in her eyes and she brought a handkerchief to her face.

Briggs returned. "The bed hasn't been slept in."

"I know this is hard for you, Mary, but we have to carry on. You said that Stan left, have you any idea where he went?"

"No, he just said he had business to see to and that he would come back later."

"But you never saw him come back?"

"No."

"How well did you know Stan?"

"I didn't. In fact, until yesterday, we'd never really spoken. I'd only nodded to him. He seemed pleasant enough."

"Any idea where he came from?"

"No. He was a down and out, but I've no idea which places he went to, and Henry never said."

"Couldn't give us a description, could you, love?" asked Reilly.

"Shouldn't be a problem. He'd certainly stand out in a crowd. I'd say he was in his sixties, and he had odd eyes, they were different colours and one was lower than the other. He had an awful scar as well, just under the right eye. He'd not looked after his skin, poor love, but then who could? When you're living rough, moisturiser's not top of your list, is it? Lots of wrinkles, and it looked leathery. But for all that, he didn't look hungry."

Gardener really didn't like where the description was heading. "How did he dress?"

"Well, there's another funny thing. He reminded me and Henry of Sherlock Holmes. He had a deerstalker, and he used to smoke a pipe, well, not smoke it exactly, just stick it in his mouth as if he used to smoke and had given up."

She gave out another sob. "Do you know, I can't believe anyone would do something so awful." Her voice rose an octave. "He had his head cut off, and where's the body, for God's sake? Who would cut off a head and take the body?"

Gardener hadn't the heart to tell her what they'd found upstairs, but he figured she'd find out soon enough. "I appreciate you didn't know Stan very well, but in the time you did see him, was there anything unusual about his behaviour?"

"Again, not really. He was a nice enough chap, talkative. Had some funny ideas about the world and where it was heading; none too keen on insects, as I remember, or things that flew around: moths and butterflies. He was frightened of storms. We had one once, a right humdinger. I remember seeing him sitting at the table, his knuckles were as white as his face."

"At least that's something," said Gardener. "Anything else?"

"To be honest, Mr Gardener, I didn't really know him, and Henry didn't talk about him that much, either."

Gardener sighed inwardly. For someone who could cause so much damage, information was pretty thin on the ground. "Can you think of any strange things happening over the past week or so?"

Mary Phillips paused and then said, "Nothing that I know of." And then she cried into her handkerchief again.

Gardener thought it best to terminate the interview. She was stressed enough as it was. "Okay, Mary. You've been a great help. I'll leave you a card. If you remember anything, no matter how trivial you think it is, ring me. Day or night, I'll get the message."

Mary took the card and he told her she was allowed to leave. Before she actually left the room, Gardener called over. "Miss Phillips?"

Mary turned. "Yes?"

"Just one more question if you don't mind. I know you've worked with Henry for two years, and you've said he was a private man. But, can I ask, did you spend any time alone with him? In his quarters, or anywhere else for that matter?"

"What are you suggesting, Mr Gardener?"

"Nothing. I simply want to ascertain how well you got on. At some point, I'm going to have to go over his room and collect all his personal belongings. I'd like you to try to remember and make an inventory. I need to know if there's anything missing, anything personal."

As quick as a flash her eyes widened. "Do you think there is?"

"I really don't know. I wondered if you knew him well enough to do that for us." Gardener smiled.

Mary Phillips paused before answering. "I'll try, Mr Gardener."

After she had closed the door, Briggs glanced at Gardener. "What was all that about?"

"Just a hunch," said Gardener.

He turned his back and paced the room. "So, there we are. Once again, we've been given a perfect description of someone who doesn't exist. Someone who doesn't look like that every day."

A knock on the door interrupted Gardener's chain of thought. He answered, and Steve Fenton passed over the note they'd found upstairs. Gardener read it and then passed it to Briggs:

> *Three dead, and I bet you're vexed.*
> *I'm sure by now you'll know who's next.*
> *But how will you stop what you can't see?*
> *Let's face it Gardener, you'll never catch me.*

A penetrating silence had enveloped the room, allowing Gardener his personal thoughts.

He turned, resting his back against the door, struggling to come to terms with everything. The killer's intelligence took him well beyond the norm. He was quite right in what he was saying, how could he catch a man he couldn't see? Any eyewitness reports were useless, which was why the killer had been allowed to come and go as he pleased. It didn't matter if he was seen or not, no one could possibly identify him. So, who was it?

There were two possibilities, but no way of proving either. Cuthbertson could well be their man. He had the ability to disguise himself, and regularly applied make-up over at Madame Two-swords. His only saving graces were his alibis, and the fact that he was genuinely shocked by the death of his assistant Janine Harper.

Which left William Henry Corndell, a man they knew little or nothing about: a mystery man. And Gardener was willing to bet he could disguise himself a whole lot better than Cuthbertson ever could. However, he was a suspect without a motive; he had no alibi they could confirm, aside from last night. If anyone could give him an alibi for last night, it was Gardener himself. Where did that leave him?

Technically speaking, the note was incorrect: it said three dead, but there were in fact now four. So, who was he and how did he tie in to everything? Were the murders still tied to the watch committee? Did that mean there was a fifth member that no one had so far talked about? There couldn't be, his father would have known.

And what of his father's safety? There was no question now that his father would be next, that the murders were revenge for something that happened years ago with the committee and, quite clearly, had to involve the banned film. The one that no one could remember – the one that had no traceable records. Did the killer have anything to do with that? Was he so computer literate that he could hack into the necessary archives and wipe clean any information that could lead them to his door?

Gardener turned to Briggs. "The more I think about it, sir, the more convinced I am that William Henry Corndell has something to do with it. I know it's not much, but I've never come across anyone who can create a disguise like the man we're looking for. And if you'd seen Corndell last night, you'd realise it puts him well in the frame."

"But that's the problem, isn't it, Stewart? Last night. He has an alibi, you saw him at the theatre."

"He wasn't there all night. We know that for a fact."

"Didn't you turn up and find him at home?" asked Briggs.

"We turned up at his house," replied Reilly. "Doesn't mean he was there."

"I thought you spoke to him on the intercom," persisted Briggs.

"Not really," said Gardener. "He said he didn't want to talk to anyone and refused to answer any further calls. We need to talk to him again, even search the property if we have to."

"On what grounds?" Briggs asked.

"On a number of grounds," replied Gardener. "His home is littered with references to the film world, the Golden Era as he puts it. He has a cinema in the house. The day we called to see him he was talking on a mobile phone, when there are no records of him having one. To say that he's a great actor seems to be a serious overstatement. If he's so in touch with Hollywood, why is it that he's only taken one phone call to his landline in the last fifteen years? Why is it I can't find any reference to any of his material?"

"None of these things make him a killer. An eccentric, maybe, but not a killer," retorted Briggs.

"So, why keep all the rooms in your house locked if you're the only one that lives there?" Reilly asked. "What is he hiding?"

Gardener continued, "Last night was all the proof I needed. He lives in the past. We know for a fact that we're looking for someone who has an obsession with the old film star Lon Chaney. Last night's performance was a homage to Chaney."

"What about the other film, the one the watch committee banned? Can we tie him to that?" asked Briggs.

"Not at the moment. We don't even know what it is," replied Gardener. "I'm sure it's only a matter of time. And last time we spoke to him, his conversation on the mobile referred to two Hollywood directors, both of whom have been dead for years. Sir, we really do have to interview this man a second time. However circumstantial it all looks, we need to speak to him again."

Briggs sighed and glanced at the note he held in his hand. "You do realise I'm in an awkward position, Stewart."

"In what way?" Gardener asked.

"Whoever the killer is, whether it be Corndell or someone else, he's made it personal. You and I both know that your father is next and last on the list. Which means, I might have to remove you from the case."

Gardener raised his hands to the ceiling. "Why does this always happen to me?"

Chapter Forty-one

Gardener and Reilly were on their way to see Corndell. If Gardener kept out of Briggs' way, then the DCI couldn't order him off the case. At the moment, that was unthinkable: there were too many unanswered questions for his liking, and he and Reilly had worked the case from the start, so he wasn't going to give it up easily. He wanted to see Corndell again, flush him out.

Despite having no concrete evidence, a lot of negative points were stacking up against him.

He was a master of disguise. He appeared incredibly intelligent. He supposedly wrote scripts. Couldn't he therefore be the author of the verses and puzzles? Corndell lived in an old-fashioned world and had an obsession with Lon Chaney. The man they wanted fitted that description as well.

Whether it was Corndell or not, there was the added pressure of his father's involvement to consider, not to mention his personal protection. Maybe it would be better if Briggs did remove him from the case, then he could shadow his father day and night.

There was still a lot of ground to cover. He needed to speak to so many people: Fitz, to see if any of the current cases matched previous murders; Fettle, to see if he could enhance their knowledge of Corndell any further than the bottom rung of the ladder; Colin Sharp, had he uncovered anything from Corndell's past that would satisfy their desire for an arrest?

Reilly brought the car to a halt outside the gates. Gardener jumped out and pressed the intercom. He glanced at the cloudless blue sky and wondered why they were having such reasonable weather for the beginning of April. Maybe global warming was to blame.

After a healthy wait, a terse voice replied to the intrusion. "Yes?"

"Mr Corndell? DI Gardener and DS Reilly, we'd like to talk to you."

"I told you last night that I didn't want to speak to anyone, and my views have not changed."

Another little point that irked Gardener: Corndell's perfect alibi for last night's murder was none other than himself. How could he have murdered Harry Fletcher? "I don't care what you want! *I* want to speak to *you*."

Their conversation continued over the intercom. "Mr Gardener, you're not listening to me. This is police harassment, and if you continue I shall be forced to call my solicitor."

"Maybe he should use his mobile," suggested Reilly.

"It's you who's not listening," replied Gardener. "Now we can do this the easy way or the hard way, it's entirely up to you. The easy way is to let me in and answer my questions. The hard way is for me to go away and return with a warrant, arrest you on suspicion of murder, and then turn your entire house upside down. Am I making myself clear?"

During the time he spent waiting for the reply, Gardener wondered if Corndell really had decided upon the second option.

Eventually, the intercom buzzed and the gates opened. Both detectives jumped into the car and cruised slowly down the drive. The door opened as they came to a stop. Gardener stepped inside to find Corndell still in his dressing gown. Underneath the gown he wore a pair of blue and white striped pyjamas, decorated with *Winnie The Pooh* logos. He knew better than to ask.

"Do you realise what time it is?" asked Corndell, pointing his mobile phone at them.

"Of course I do. I've been up since five o'clock this morning."

"I'm not surprised," replied Corndell, closing the door after Reilly had entered. "I do hope you've come to apologise for last night." Corndell held his head high and his nose in the air as he glanced down at the pair of them. He placed the mobile in the pocket of his dressing gown.

"I have nothing to apologise for."

"How dare you?" he shouted, jumping back, clenching and unclenching his hands. "You people have persecuted me–"

"I wouldn't say persecuted!" replied Gardener, cutting him short. He did not want the situation escalating beyond his control. He was here for a reason, and he was going to make sure they stuck to the point. With his temper close to boiling point, he chose his words carefully.

"We're investigating crimes of a very serious nature. We will conduct ourselves in a manner to which we see fit. Now if you have a problem with that, then you contact the police complaints commission, but quite frankly your case will not hold water."

"I do apologise, Mr Gardener," Corndell replied, his face softening immediately, childlike, "and please forgive my lack of manners. If you would like to come through to the conservatory, I shall make fresh tea for us all."

Gardener suspected he was being manipulated because of the sudden change in Corndell's manner. He told Reilly to join Corndell whilst the tea was made, not to let him out of his sight. Gardener stayed in the conservatory. Eventually, both returned.

"Now then, gentlemen, I'll pour the tea and you feel free to ask me anything you like."

All three sat down and Gardener removed his hat. "Where were you last night?"

"You know very well where I was," replied Corndell, sliding their tea across the table.

"After the show."

"You turned up here wanting to speak to me, but I wouldn't let you in."

"I know where *I* was. I'm asking *you* where you were. Answer the question."

"Of course. I was here, Mr Gardener, where else would I be? Has something happened?" Corndell banged the teapot on the table and stood up. "Has someone else been murdered, and you want me for a scapegoat?"

"Such a vivid imagination, Willie boy," said Reilly. "No wonder you write scripts."

Gardener ignored Corndell's question. "Perhaps your CCTV will show us what time you arrived back at the house, Mr Corndell?"

"It would if it was working."

"Oh, well now, isn't that convenient?" said Reilly. "Your closed-circuit TV system is on the blink the night you need to prove your innocence."

Corndell took a sip of his tea. "I beg to differ, Mr Reilly. It is you who has something to prove, not me."

Another condescending reply that made Gardener's skin crawl. As far as he was concerned, the man had guilt written all over his face, but what they lacked was concrete evidence. And at the rate they were going, they would never find it. "What's wrong with your CCTV?" he asked.

"That's a silly question, Mr Gardener. If I knew that, I wouldn't have called them out."

"Name of the company, please."

Corndell left the room but returned quickly, with a card.

Gardener read it, put it in his pocket, and then continued. "I'd like to ask you a few questions about our previous meeting... in particular, your phones."

"What about them?" replied Corndell.

"According to the information we have, you don't have a mobile number, and you've only received one call to your landline in the last ten years."

"Am I under arrest?" asked Corndell.

"No."

"Suspicion, then?"

"The very nature of your business means we have to carry out a detailed investigation," replied Gardener, before adding, "if for no other reason than to eliminate you from our enquiries."

"Perhaps it would be better if I phoned my solicitor, Mr Gardener."

"Something to hide, Willie? Use your mobile, why don't you?" suggested Reilly.

To Gardener's astonishment, that's exactly what Corndell did. He picked up his mobile and placed a call through to his solicitor and asked him to return the call when it was convenient.

"Give me that number," Gardener demanded.

Corndell did as he was asked and wrote the number down. He passed it to Reilly, who placed the slip of paper into his pocket.

With a smug expression, Corndell continued the conversation. "You see, Mr Gardener, your records must be incorrect. Most of my business is either conducted online or through my mobile."

"Our evidence doesn't support your statement," replied Gardener, making a mental note of the fact that Corndell used a computer regularly.

"Then I suggest you retrace your steps." Corndell took another sip of tea. "Now we've cleared that one up, what else would you like to ask me?"

Gardener was unwilling to show his annoyance, but he realised he was treading water. Without a warrant, he couldn't force the issue. "Let's talk about films. In particular, your cinema–"

Corndell stood up, beckoned them, cutting Gardener dead. "Say no more, Mr Gardener. I shall take you." Leading them out of the conservatory, he said over his shoulder, "I do realise that under normal circumstances you would have to obtain a warrant to do this, and we all know that if I push you hard enough, you will. I have nothing to hide, so I am now inviting you of my own free will into my cinema."

Gardener wondered if Corndell was recording the meeting. No one spoke like he did. They followed him up the stairs. He made a point of showing them his favourite film posters, informing them of their value and rarity. At no stage were his attitude or his expressions those of a guilty man. Before continuing up to the top landing, he turned and spoke to them.

"I think I should take you in here first, Mr Gardener, it's my make-up room."

Corndell opened the door and switched on a light. Along the back wall stood a range of mannequins dressed in a variety of guises. Gardener immediately recognised the costume from last night's performance of *The Hunchback*; the Phantom was also there, and others of which he had no idea.

"I don't recognise all of them. Enlighten me."

"Over there, is the Ape Man from the film *A Blind Bargain*. And there you can see the Clown from the 1924 film *He Who Gets Slapped*."

"Who starred in those films?" asked Gardener.

"Lon Chaney, of course." Corndell had made the statement so boldly that Gardener was convinced he was trying to rile him.

"I thought Lon Chaney only made horror films. What was the clown film about?"

"It shows how little you know about him, Mr Gardener. He was the greatest actor the world has ever seen. The film was based on a play by the Russian writer Leonid Andreyev. It had a successful run on Broadway in the 1920s. Chaney plays a struggling scientist in Paris who is betrayed by his wife and his benefactor, Baron Regnard. The Baron stole his essays, took the credit, and his wife. Disillusioned, Chaney eventually runs away and becomes a clown in a circus, changing his name to 'He Who Gets Slapped', because his fellow clowns slap him no matter what he does."

Corndell had thrown in details that very few people left alive would know. Maybe that's what Gardener needed, Corndell knocking nails into his own coffin. Perhaps now he could alter the course of the interview by turning up the heat and giving him the opportunity to hang himself.

"Fascinating," said Gardener. "Are they all Chaney outfits?"

"Not at all. That one there which, to you, probably looks like a bunch of rags, is in fact from the first short movie adaptation of a United States version of the film *Frankenstein* made in 1910, in which the monster is played by Charles Stanton Ogle. A very prolific film, Mr

Gardener, for which I probably have the only remaining copy. And that, may I add, cost me a fortune."

The atmosphere in the room was intense. The walls were dark. The floor was natural wood, stained and polished. Opposite the mannequins was a tile-topped table running the length of the wall, and above that a huge, dusty mirror. The tabletop was crammed full of paraphernalia: wigs, creams, face powders, jars of chemicals. The whole space had a distinctly unsavoury odour that he couldn't place, a sort of sour, spicy smell.

Corndell leaned forward and reached under the table. Producing a bin bag, he removed the clothes from the dummy wearing the Hunchback outfit.

"What are you doing?" asked Gardener.

"You'll want these for forensic testing, Mr Gardener. You have my permission to take them."

Gardener glanced at Reilly and then to Corndell.

"Do you require any samples of my make-up?" he asked.

Reilly answered the question. "What would be the point?"

"Evidence, Mr Reilly. After all, you are trying to eliminate me."

"Come on now, Willie, old son. You're only offering this lot to us because you know damn well that you've been careful and we can't prove a thing. On top of that, there's no evidence that the costume you've given us is the one you were wearing last night."

Corndell turned. "That remark, Mr Reilly, implies that I am your killer. If my solicitor were here, you'd have to retract that."

"But he isn't, is he, Willie?"

Corndell glared at Reilly. "If you would be so kind, Mr Reilly, as to please use the name my mother gave me. Now, gentlemen, is there anything else you require from this room?"

"No," replied Gardener.

"Then shall we move on to the cinema?"

Gardener followed Corndell up the staircase, into the room. He glanced around, impressed. It was long and angular, and stretched across the top floor of the house. The projection booth sat at the far end, while a screen covered the wall nearest to them. The films were placed in racks on the left- and right-hand walls. There was yet another odour in the room that Gardener also failed to place. "What's that smell?"

After a pause, Reilly replied, "Mothballs."

"Not quite, Mr Reilly," said Corndell. "What you can smell is celluloid, a plastic made from camphor and cellulose nitrate. But... as you so rightly point out, it does smell like mothballs, which were actually made from camphor many years ago." He smiled, and Gardener was growing ever confident that the man's pomposity would be his undoing. But had *he* realised it? Was he now playing games?

Gardener strolled slowly around the room, studying each and every one of the films on display. They were contained in a number of silver canisters banded together. He glanced at the titles, recognising some but not all, wondering how many of those featured Chaney. *The Hunchback* and *The Phantom* were obvious, as were *A Blind Bargain* and *London After Midnight.* But *The Dark Eyes of London* didn't ring any bells, nor did *The Invisible Ghost, The Black Castle,* or *Imperfection.* He wondered what the value of the whole collection was.

"The last time we were here, you said it had been a life's work trying to track down lost films from the silent era. I can see what you mean, now. It must have taken you years. How did you manage to find them?"

"It's my life, Mr Gardener. If it's something you're interested in, you'll pull out all the stops. They've cost me a fortune, but they're worth it. Take this one for instance." Corndell pulled the reels forward. *"London After Midnight–"*

Gardener cut him off. "Interesting you should start with that. Isn't it commonly known among film collectors as the Holy Grail of archivists?"

"That's one way of describing it."

"I was reliably informed that the film was destroyed by a fire in the 1960s. So how did you come by it?"

"You're talking about the fire in Vault 7 at MGM. That very well may have been the last surviving copy that anyone knew of, but my father passed this copy on to me. He had been the proud owner since the Thirties."

"Know the film well, do you?" asked Gardener.

"Like the back of my hand." Corndell's answer was sharp and his expression stern, as if his intelligence had been insulted.

From his inside pocket, Gardener produced the artist impression of the vampire, the one drawn from the eyewitness account on the night Janine Harper was killed. "Then how come you didn't know who this was the last time we visited?"

"Oh come now, Mr Gardener, it's hardly a likeness, is it?"

Gardener had to allow the man credit for not hesitating. "We have a witness who'd disagree with you. In fact, when we showed it to him, he knew who it was straight away."

"What are you trying to say?"

Reilly answered. "That either you don't know your films as well as you think–"

"I am the last word on Lon Chaney, young man," shouted Corndell, indignantly.

"Or, I *was* going to say before you opened your trap, you're leading us up the garden path."

"I am leading you nowhere. I am simply answering your questions to the best of my knowledge, as I have always done."

"If you're such an authority on Chaney," challenged Reilly, "why didn't you know who that was?"

"Because it looks nothing like the character from the film."

"There is a resemblance, you could have guessed," suggested Gardener.

"Guess, Mr Gardener? Guess? Where would we be if I were to guess all of my answers? Some innocent person would have been locked up by now, that's where."

Gardener ignored Corndell's outburst, trying to recollect the other connection to the film, Inspector Burke, and the film clip they had first watched at the hotel in Skipton. So far, he had not recognised anything that led him to believe that it had been filmed here. But then again, he hadn't seen the whole house yet. He walked up and down each side of the room, checking all the films. "Any of these yours, Mr Corndell?"

"They're all mine," replied Corndell.

Gardener sighed. "I meant, did you write any of them?"

"How could I have, Mr Gardener? As you can see from the titles and the dates, most, if not all, were written before I was born."

Gardener turned to face Corndell, leaving Reilly to continue writing the titles in his book. "Tell me again what it is that you write."

Corndell sighed, as if tired. "Stage plays. I told you last time, my work is regularly shown in America."

"Is it fair to assume that you would know other writers who have their material accepted in America? On Broadway, for instance?"

"Very possibly. It never hurts to be aware of the competition," replied Corndell, choosing to move away from the films and nearer the staircase that led down into the make-up room.

"Does the name Harry Fletcher ring any bells?"

"Can't say it does. Just starting, is he?"

"Couldn't really say. It's just that you seem to know all of the big names, Lon Chaney, Boris Karloff—"

"I actually met Karloff, many years back, just before he died, on the set of a film called *Targets*."

Gardener continued. "Wallace Worsley, Rupert Julian–"

"Don't talk to me about Julian," scoffed Corndell.

"Funny that. He *is* the one I wanted to talk about. Last time we were here, you were having a conversation with George about a director called Rupert Julian. If I remember correctly, you said 'either Rupert Julian stands down or I'll take my script elsewhere'. Do you remember that?"

"Well I would, wouldn't I?" replied Corndell. "It was me who said it."

"I checked out that name, Rupert Julian. He died years ago. Why are you writing scripts for a dead man?"

Corndell suddenly burst out laughing, a high-pitched screech in which he rocked so much he held his stomach and almost lost his balance. After he had regained his composure, he answered. "Mr Gardener, you're so funny. I'm not writing for *the* Rupert Julian who directed Chaney. I write scripts for his son."

Gardener laughed with Corndell. "Yes, you're right, I am a little odd. Must be the policeman in me. Where do you write your material?"

"In the study, downstairs."

"Do you have a computer?"

"Who doesn't, these days?" Corndell frowned. Gardener took it as a good sign. Time to capitalise.

"Good, because you're going to take me down there now, and you're going to show me some of the scripts you've had accepted. You're going to give me the titles of your most successful American plays, and then you're going to tell me where I can reach Rupert Julian Junior and your friend George, so they can verify your story. I also want to see bills from your internet service provider and your mobile."

Corndell's mood changed. Maybe the added pressure was paying off. Gardener noticed that Reilly had finished writing and was standing beside him.

"Why should I do that?"

"Because I'm a policeman and I want to check everything you've told me in order to eliminate you from our inquiries. If I find any differences, I'm coming back. And I'll bring a warrant and a team of forensic officers, and one by one, bit by bit, we are going to turn this whole house upside down, with or without the presence of your solicitor." Gardened paused and moved closer. "And should I find just one small spec of evidence which connects you to my investigation, Mr Corndell, I am going to wipe the floor with you. Am I making myself clear?"

Without warning, Corndell stormed down the spiral staircase to the make-up room. Gardener and Reilly gave chase. They followed him down the stairs and into the hall, which was where Corndell stopped, glaring at the front door. As Gardener and Reilly arrived at the bottom of the stairs, Corndell made as if to open it.

"I think you'll find your study is that way." Gardener pointed.

"I know exactly where it is, thank you very much, but as far as I'm concerned your interview ends here. I have co-operated of my own free will, Mr Gardener. I have provided you with evidence to clear my name, yet you continue to persecute me. From here on in, any interviews with you will be conducted in the presence of my solicitor, and if you want personal details from me, you can damn well provide that warrant you're talking about."

Gardener could tell they had physically rattled Corndell: his left eye twitched and his top lip trembled.

"I want you out of my house, now!" shouted Corndell.

"So soon, Willie boy," said Reilly. "Why the change of mood? A little too close to the truth, are we? Guilty after all, maybe?"

Corndell confidently strolled towards the door, grinning, reaching for the handle, all the while staring at Reilly.

"That's for me to know and you to find out, Mr Reilly."

Gardener stared at William. "Don't worry, Mr Corndell, we will. And the next time we pay you a visit, we will have that warrant."

"I can't wait, Mr Gardener."

Chapter Forty-two

Gardener pushed open the stage door. Reilly followed him down the steps towards Albert Fettle's office. Nothing had changed. The little spot of cleaning that Fettle had claimed he was doing last time was still unfinished.

He heard Fettle's voice before he saw him. The door leading into the theatre opened and he appeared with Paul Price close behind, the latter bearing a distinctively unhappy expression as he saw the two detectives.

"Hey up, how are you doing?" shouted Fettle. He continued without waiting for an answer. "You two know how to time things right, don't you? I've just brewed a pot of tea and I've some of my favourites to go with it. Nice packet of fig rolls."

"Can I reopen my theatre, yet?" asked Paul Price.

"Answer another couple of questions for me, Mr Price, and I don't see why not," replied Gardener.

"So, it's not me you want, then?" asked Fettle.

"All in good time, shorty," said Reilly.

"Come on, get yourselves in here, this tea's nearly mashed."

While Fettle continued with the tea, Gardener addressed Price. "How long have you worked here, Mr Price?"

"I'm sure I answered that question on your first visit."

"Then refresh my memory."

"Thirty years."

"Does the name William Henry Corndell ring any bells?"

Price hesitated. "As a matter of fact, it does, just can't think why."

"Has he ever worked here?"

"Not to my knowledge."

"Is it likely that he has, but under a different name?"

"That's always possible. I can check the files, if you could give me more details."

Gardener turned to his partner. "Sean, will you go and check the files with Mr Price, see what you can come up with?" He then added, "Leave me your notebook before you go."

"Here," said Fettle. "Best take your tea."

"You said I might be able to reopen, when will that be?" asked Price.

"As soon as you find out what we need to know."

Price gestured for Reilly to follow him. Gardener entered Fettle's room and took a sip of tea.

"You still chasing this Corndell bloke, then?"

"Any news from your friend at Her Majesty's?"

Both men sat down. "Aye, there is. He never played the part of the Phantom."

"He didn't?" questioned Gardener, curious.

"Not in so many words, no. He were given a trial run in the West End, more or less as the show were starting. He were Michael Crawford's understudy, and he only got that 'cause of his father, Wallace. Anyway, he was promising, knew almost everybody's lines. Apparently he's got a good memory, remembers facts and figures like there's no tomorrow. He turned up to every performance, and in rehearsals he was brilliant. Problems started when he were faced with an audience."

"In what way?" Gardener asked.

"He panics. He were given his chance in the main role one Saturday matinee. Crawford's car had broken down and he wasn't gonna make it until the evening performance, so they gave Corndell the green light. Apparently he were useless, fluffed his lines and wrecked half the scenery. The worst bit was when he was doing the scene in the graveyard on top of the big cross. He fell off and broke his leg."

Fettle slurped his tea and bit into a fig roll. "Anyway, it finished his career. But even if he hadn't fallen off and broken his leg, he'd never have got another chance."

"And that was his one and only time playing the main part?"

"As far as I know. After that, no one else in the West End touched him."

"Any idea what he did after that?"

"No."

"Okay, well that's something. He's reliable, this friend of yours?"

"Oh aye, he worked there for over thirty years."

Gardener took another sip of his tea. "Have you still got those film books?"

"Aye." Fettle left the table and reached into the cupboard. "What do you want to know?"

Gardener produced Reilly's notebook with the titles of the films in Corndell's library. "Do you remember any of these?" He passed the list to Fettle.

"I know those two. *The Dark Eyes of London*, that's pretty old. It was written by Edgar Wallace. It's about a bloke who runs a home for the blind, and he uses a giant to drown the insured victims."

"Another Lon Chaney film?"

"No, that was Bela Lugosi. And so was that one, *The Invisible Ghost*. That's about a bloke who murdered his wife and she comes back to haunt him, he keeps seeing her all over the place, before he goes mad."

"*The Black Castle*?" asked Gardener.

"Not sure about that." Fettle flicked through his copies of the *Film Review* before finally consulting the *Halliwell's Film Guide*. "Here it is, an eighteenth-century knight avenges the death of two friends who have attended a hunting party at the castle of a sadistic Viennese count. I certainly haven't seen that one."

"Are any of these real collector's pieces?"

"Doubt it. *The Dark Eyes of London*, maybe. Can't say I've ever seen a copy of that."

Gardener sighed and sat back. None of the films that Fettle had talked about bore any similarity to the murders that had been committed, so it seemed unlikely that the killer was copying an obscure film in particular. "Who was in *The Black Castle*?"

"Boris Karloff and Lon Chaney Junior."

"Karloff played Frankenstein, yes?"

"Aye, in 1931."

"Apparently Corndell has a US copy of the film made in 1910 starring a bloke called Ogle."

"Fucking hell," whistled Fettle. "That'd be worth a fortune."

"What about that one, *Imperfection*?"

"Never heard of it." After consulting all the books, Fettle drew a blank. "I can't find any reference to a film of that name. Do you know owt about it?"

"No, other than the fact that it's in Corndell's library."

"Well, it's not one I know."

"What about banned films, anything spring to mind?"

"There's been plenty of 'em over the years. *Freaks*, in 1932. MGM made it but disowned it. A lot of people said it was tasteless. I think it was because they used real freaks. A bit like that other film *The Sentinel*, in '76, they used proper freaks and that got banned."

"Do you know of a film that was banned by the local watch committee in Leeds in the late Seventies or early Eighties?"

Fettle thought long and hard. Gardener could almost hear the cogs turning inside his head. "No."

Gardener started to wonder about the title of the film *Imperfection*, and how well it defined Corndell. He needed to find out more about it. Was that the title of the banned film they were looking for? What was it about? Why had it been banned? And if that *was* the film, what connection did it have with Corndell and how had he managed to obtain a copy?

"Last time we spoke, I mentioned a director by the name of Rupert Julian. You said he was dead."

"Aye, he is," replied Fettle.

"Did he have a son?"

Fettle finished his tea and another biscuit. "I've no idea. I've never heard one mentioned, but I'm not as well up on directors as I am the films. You could soon find out."

Reilly and Price entered the room. Paul Price had a copy of a letter, which he passed to Gardener. "I thought I recognised the name Corndell. He sent me a letter a few months back."

Gardener took it but didn't read it. "What about?"

"He wrote and asked if he could have a tour of the place, quite some time ago now."

"Why?"

"He said he was an author and he was writing something new which he wanted to set in the Grand Theatre. Asked if I would mind showing him round so as he could get the feel for the place."

Gardener glanced at Reilly. "Why would he do that? According to him he's spent his life in theatres up and down the country, writes regularly for Broadway."

Price continued. "He mentioned his success in America. I asked him if he had a website, but he said he didn't. I was hoping to do a little checking myself. He also said he wrote his material under different names."

"Can you remember any of them?"

"I'm sorry, no."

"Yet you still met him and showed him round?" questioned Gardener.

"Oh yes. I didn't mind. I had some free time on my hands. The only thing I stipulated was that he should write nothing that would bring the theatre into disrepute. I also asked him of the success he'd had in America and he mentioned one or two titles, which I later wrote down on the back."

Gardener turned the paper over and studied the titles. He didn't recognise either. He then passed the paper to Fettle. He was about to ask Price another question when Fettle jumped out of his chair.

"Hey, I know that one, and it's not one of his."

"Which one?" Gardener asked.

"*Blood's Thicker Than Water.*"

"Who wrote it?" asked Gardener.

"Yon lad as worked for Playhouse."

"Harry Fletcher?"

"Aye, that's him. He wrote *Blood's Thicker Than Water*. I remember reading about it somewhere."

"Any idea what it's about?" asked Gardener.

"Not really, no. Summat about a feud between two brothers, which goes on for years until one of 'em's dying. I just remember reading a review, and it were taking the States by storm."

"That's one of them," said Paul Price. "That's one of the names he said he used. Harry Fletcher. I remember it now."

Another nail in Corndell's coffin: he said he didn't know Harry Fletcher.

Gardener's mobile chimed. He fished it out of his pocket and answered. After listening to the caller, he glanced at Reilly. "We'll be there in five minutes. That was

Fitz. Apparently, he's found something unusual connected to Janine Harper's death. He wants us over there now."

Chapter Forty-three

"Who found him?" Gardener asked the officer guarding the door.

"The prospective new owners, over there."

The couple's appearance spoke of wealth: camel hair coats, jewellery, the finest Italian leather shoes. The woman was blonde, slim, mid-forties with a long, deeply lined face. The man was stocky, perhaps early fifties with a good head of hair, tightly curled and grey. He was smoking a cigar. His wife cast glances about as if she'd rather be anywhere than a shopping arcade in Leeds that harboured a dead body, particularly one they were going to buy. And from her expression, the purchase was not her idea.

Gardener and Reilly suited up and entered. The interior of the shop was still gloomy, and despite the cleaning service having done their best, they had been unable to eradicate the smell of death, more the legacy of Janine Harper than the fresh body.

Alan Cuthbertson was laid on the floor behind the counter. He had been no oil painting in life, but death had decided he would be remembered with an expression that welcomed his fate.

"What time?" Gardener asked.

"About ten minutes before I phoned you."

"Who else have you told?"

"I phoned the station and they said someone was on their way. They told me to phone you."

Gardener turned his attention to the matter in hand. The shop had been stripped bare. Everything that had been on display on the night of Janine Harper's demise had been removed for forensic testing. Once the police had finished with it, Alan Cuthbertson had told them to burn it. Gardener had wondered about Cuthbertson's state of mind during that time period, his personal feelings at having seen his life's work tainted – if not destroyed – by the actions of a lunatic. The idea of returning to a building responsible for so much trauma was obviously too much. An empty pill bottle stood on the counter, as did the half-finished bottle of whiskey, and what he surmised was a suicide note.

"I wonder what made him do it?" asked Reilly.

"I hope it wasn't us," replied Gardener.

"We didn't do anything wrong, boss. We were doing our job."

Gardener glanced at his partner. "Maybe *he* didn't see it like that."

Briggs arrived, suited and booted, and then made his way into the shop, glancing behind the counter. "What have we got?"

"Suicide," replied Gardener.

"Anyone read the note?"

"Not yet."

Briggs tore open the envelope. With a confused expression he glanced at Gardener. "It's addressed to you, Stewart." He handed over the letter and studied the corpse.

"Why has he written a letter to you?" Reilly asked.

"I've no idea."

Gardener read it:

Dear Mr Gardener,

I appreciate you had a job to do and I want you to know that in no way do I hold you responsible for my suicide. It is fair to say that I have lost everything: the business I had spent years building, my assistant, who meant more to me than you'll ever know, and the lifestyle I tried so hard to keep secret, becoming public knowledge. There are two things you need to know: Firstly, I am not your killer and have no idea who is. Secondly, proof which backs up the first statement, I could never have killed my own daughter. Janine was my flesh and blood, born from an illicit affair. Though why the secret had been kept after Jack Harper's death I shall never know.

Gardener sighed and passed the letter over to Briggs. He read it. "Do you think she knew?" he asked.

"I've no idea," replied Gardener.

"I still can't understand why he'd write a letter to you," said Briggs.

"Maybe he didn't," suggested Reilly.

"Meaning what?" asked Briggs.

"I'll grant you it's not the killer's style, but maybe he staged all of this and then wrote the note to throw us of the scent."

"If that's the case, how did he know Janine Harper was Alan Cuthbertson's daughter?" asked Briggs.

"He knew enough about Janine Harper to kill her for the reasons he did," added Reilly.

"I appreciate your point, Sean," said Gardener, "but Alan Cuthbertson wasn't a member of the watch committee, and that's what this seems to be about. The watch committee and the banned film."

"Unless it isn't," said Briggs. "Do you know anything about this banned film yet?"

"I think I'm on to something, but nothing concrete."

"Then how do you know the murders are connected to a banned film?" asked Briggs. "I'm sorry, Stewart, but we're no nearer to solving the case now than we were at the beginning. So for all we know, Alan Cuthbertson's death might well be tied into it. For God's sake, this bloke moves around like a fucking spectre. No one ever sees him, and he's managed to commit the most brutal killings, and have time to write notes."

"It still looks like suicide to me, nothing more," said Gardener.

"Maybe Fitz can tell us," replied Briggs. "Which reminds me, where the bloody hell is he?"

Before Gardener had time to answer, his mobile rang.

Briggs and Reilly turned their attention to the corpse while he took the call.

"We're on our way," said Gardener. "That was Fitz. Apparently he's found something unusual connected to Janine Harper's death. He wants us over there now."

Chapter Forty-four

Fitz threw a folder on to his desk and ran his hands down his tired face. His expression was a mixture of fatigue and elation at having possibly found a piece of the puzzle. "Would you gentlemen like coffee?"

Gardener and Reilly nodded, and Fitz turned around from his desk. He reached for the percolator, a new addition to his office, and a much needed one from what Gardener could see.

"Smells good," said Reilly.

"So, what have you got for us?" asked Gardener.

Fitz sat back in his chair. "Janine Harper. You remember that she had a lethal cocktail of ephedrine in her system. I suggested that the killer may have perfected the technique."

Both men nodded, sipping their coffee.

"I've found some new evidence. I consulted Mathew Stapleton about it. He's one of the country's leading toxicologists up in Edinburgh. When I spoke to him, he was in London. The method unsettled him for a week. He'd heard of a similar case. He used the computers at the University College Hospital. Surprisingly enough there were no records, nothing in the archives, nothing on paper. Having said that, the paper files only date back to the Eighties. Anything further back had been stored electronically."

"Had the files been erased?" said Gardener.

"They think so, but they're still checking. You see, all other records of suspicious deaths around that time were still on file."

"Murder isn't the only technique he's perfected," said Gardener.

"Mathew spoke to his father. Turns out that one of his colleagues had performed the autopsy on the lady in question." Fitz opened his folder, removed the notes. "Her name was Elizabeth Cranshaw. She was sixty-one years of age and worked as a nanny for a well-to-do family who lived in Weybridge in Surrcy."

Gardener's heart sunk a little when he thought of how far back the incident may have occurred.

Fitz continued. "It was the next morning before the old lady had been found dead in her room, still sitting in her favourite chair with her novel resting on her lap. According to the report she looked quite peaceful, despite what she must have gone through."

"So, we're not talking exactly the same MO here?" asked Gardener.

"She hadn't been hung and brutalised, if that's what you mean," replied Fitz.

"So, the link is the ephedrine?"

Fitz nodded. "Elizabeth Cranshaw had suffered from asthma all her life. The results of the autopsy discovered sherry in her system, believed to be her favourite tipple while she was reading. Mixed in with the alcohol was a pretty hefty dosage of nuts that had been ground into a fine powder. A massive heart attack caused her death. In fact, the report confirms that her heart had been so overworked that it had literally exploded."

"Was the family she worked for interviewed?" asked Gardener.

"Yes, they were cleared. Apparently, Elizabeth Cranshaw had been to London on a shopping expedition. She'd been out of the house all day. The parents, who were normally at work, had remained home for the day to supervise their son. When the nanny returned, they went back to the studio."

"Studio?" Gardener asked.

"Pinewood, in Buckinghamshire. The boy's father was a film director."

Gardener's heart sank. In his confusion, his earlier calculation suggested that the killer should be in his sixties, which suspended belief. However, the other option was equally unthinkable. Could he possibly have started something so gruesome at such an early age?

"Who was the boy?"

"William Henry Corndell."

Chapter Forty-five

Colin Sharp had returned from London during the early hours of the morning. It was early afternoon before he'd found his way to Gardener's house for a meeting. Malcolm had gone to the cinema to see an old-fashioned black and white double bill that was right up his street. Gardener had asked his father to take a mobile with him, despite knowing he was under surveillance.

Gardener placed coffees on the table, sat down and cleared a space at the table. The files had all been neatly laid out.

Sharp took a sip of his drink. "That tastes good. You don't know what a relief it is to be back."

"Not keen on the Big Smoke, then?" asked Reilly.

"They do things differently down there. I'm not saying it's right or wrong, it's just different."

"What do you have for us?" Gardener asked.

"He's definitely an oddball, but there's nothing concrete here. Having said that, what I've found out might be enough to hold him for a while."

"Go on," said Gardener. He had a gut feeling that it was going to be one of those cases. William Henry Corndell was probably guilty, but lucky enough to walk free because what little evidence they did have wouldn't stand up in court.

"Nothing odd about his early life unless you count the fact that he didn't go to school."

"He must have been educated somewhere," replied Gardener. "From what we've seen, he's intelligent."

"If not a little loopy," added Reilly.

"Oh, he was educated," said Sharp, "just not in school. His mother and father paid for a private education at home. He had two different teachers, and they looked after him until he was about fourteen."

"Did you speak to them?" asked Gardener.

"Only one of them is still alive. The other one died in a traffic accident a few years ago. Anyway, she said the same as you, he was intelligent, but he didn't always use it, or show an interest. His pet subject was English. He used to love writing stories. They were always gruesome, but she blames his father for that. He used to take him to the film studio a lot, even bought him a make-up kit when he was eight. Eventually, Corndell spent most of his time at the studio. He worked with his dad on the films, and with the professionals in the make-up department by the time he was ten.

"And it was about that time Corndell discovered Lon Chaney, and how good *he* was. He was never away from the library, or the film studio's archives, reading everything he could lay his hands on. By the time he was twelve, he'd honed his skill so much that most of the professional actors preferred him to any of the regular crew. The private tutors eventually left, and his mother and father hired a new nanny by the name of Elizabeth Cranshaw."

"We already know what happened to her," said Reilly.

"The people I spoke to said she had a stroke," said Colin Sharp. "She was old."

"Age had nothing to do with it," said Gardener. "We've since learned from Fitz that Elizabeth Cranshaw was an asthmatic. She'd had a heart attack, which probably led to a stroke brought on by a lethal dose of sherry mixed with nuts that had been ground into a fine powder, creating the drug ephedrine."

"What does this have to do with Corndell?"

"Janine Harper was killed the same way."

"Interesting," said Sharp.

"Did you speak to anyone who knew both Corndell and the nanny? Someone who could verify what kind of a relationship they had?"

"Briefly. The old lady had a daughter. They were together on the day of her death, shopping in London. She said her mother never stopped complaining about Corndell. He was highly strung, bad tempered, would go out of his way to play tricks on her. She did say her mother could be quite hard to get on with, and she was a bit strict: maybe the lad was just rebelling against a disciplinarian."

"Not worth killing for," said Reilly.

"Well, after what you've told me, maybe there was more to it. Elizabeth Cranshaw told her daughter about Corndell's strange behaviour, and the fact that he hated authority, and she figured the only way to get her message across was through his make-up kit."

"What did she do with it?" asked Gardener.

"That much I don't know, the daughter never told me."

"She probably got rid of it," said Reilly. "That would send him up the wall, so it would. Especially if he was using it at the studio."

"I'm sure it would be reason enough for Corndell to kill her ... in his eyes," said Gardener.

"But he can't have been much more than ten or twelve," said Sharp. "Surely he wouldn't have had the know-how at that age."

"I wouldn't count on it," replied Gardener. "That's something we're all guilty of – underestimating him."

"What are you going to do?" asked Sharp.

"Show Briggs your evidence and see if he'll get us a warrant for his arrest. Did you delve into his bank accounts?"

"I did. We need to take a closer look. His father left him about three million pounds all told, if you take the property into account. All the cash was deposited into an account at a private bank in London. What with client confidentiality, and the fact that I didn't have a warrant, they wouldn't tell me too much. What I did find out was that he has taken out large sums of money, and the bank is either not sure what he's done with them, or won't tell me."

"Most likely the latter," said Reilly.

"In that case, use the computers and the banks up here to find out what you can. My guess is, he's set up accounts in different names and he's used them to finance his little ventures, perhaps to hire transport. How else would he get around and do the things he's done?"

"Makes sense, boss," said Reilly. "We need somebody to help Colin. The quicker we get this bastard off the streets, the better."

Gardener's mobile phone chimed, which he quickly answered.

"Sir, it's Frank."

"Hello, Frank, what can I do for you?"

"We've just had a call from Mary Phillips. She wants to speak to you urgently."

"She leave a number?" asked Gardener. Frank Thornton gave him the number and then mentioned that Briggs had been asking after him. Gardener called Mary Phillips.

"Oh, Mr Gardener, I'm so pleased you've called."

"Is there a problem?" he asked.

"A little one. You asked me if I'd look and see if there were anything missing from Henry's room, after you'd finished with it, like."

"Is there?"

"Yes, love. It's his mobile phone, I can't find it anywhere."

Chapter Forty-six

Gardener realised he still had no proof that Corndell had actually killed the nanny but it was stretching one's imagination to believe someone else had done it. Also in his favour were the murders with the puzzles, the use of a lethal cocktail as a weapon of disposal, and Corndell's genuine obsession with Lon Chaney.

Was that enough?

And where did the film *Imperfection* enter into the equation? He was convinced that it did... somehow. But even Malcolm had no recollection of such a film. A Google search revealed nothing.

That created another problem. Malcolm had been at the cinema all afternoon and Gardener had heard nothing from the officer trailing him, so everything must have been fine. Still, he hadn't been able to settle.

When Chris had arrived home from school, the pair of them had spent an hour in the garage sorting through the Bonneville engine components, checking what could be re-used and what couldn't. But even then his concentration was lacking. Eventually, Chris had finished up and gone to his room.

Gardener heard the front door open. He glanced at the kitchen clock. It was a little after six. He realised that he hadn't yet prepared anything to eat. But it wasn't the end of the world: worst-case scenario, they could all go out for a meal or phone for a take-away. As Malcolm entered the kitchen, he heard voices. "Stewart, I'd like you to meet someone."

Gardener glanced over his father's shoulder and noticed Martin Brown standing in the doorway.

"Mr Gardener," said Brown, nodding. "I didn't think I'd be seeing you again so soon."

"The feeling's mutual."

"May I come in? There's something I need to tell you."

"Of course, come and sit down."

"I'll make us a cup of tea," offered Malcolm.

Gardener was confused, concerned. His dad had gone to the cinema for an afternoon matinee. Having returned with Martin Brown, he suspected that something was wrong; but the old man appeared to be fine. "Is everything okay?"

"Depends what you mean by okay, son."

Gardener wasn't happy with his father's evasive answer. "Has something happened? Are *you* okay?"

"I'm fine. We're here, or should I say, Martin's here, because he thinks he may owe you an apology, and he may also have disturbing news for you."

Gardener sat back down and glanced at Martin Brown. If the man was here to speak, then he would let him.

"It's about Corndell," said Brown.

"Everything about him disturbs me. What's he done now?"

"I'm not sure that he has. I met your father this afternoon for the first time. I had no idea who he was." Martin Brown stopped talking while Malcolm put the tea on the table.

"We ended up in the cinema foyer during the interval," said Malcolm.

"What did you go and see, anyway? You never said."

"A Lon Chaney double bill, as it happens."

Gardener grew cold at the mere mention of Chaney. "Which ones?"

"*The Phantom of the Opera* and *The Hunchback of Notre Dame*," said Martin.

"*The Hunchback* was first," said Malcolm. "At the interval I went out for a coffee and a chocolate bar, I felt a little peckish. As I turned around, Martin here knocked into me and I spilt my coffee. He ordered fresh drinks and we started talking. It turns out that he was sitting directly in front of me."

"We talked about films in general, and Chaney, and how good he was," continued Martin Brown. "And then Corndell slipped into the conversation. I told your father that I was in charge of the entertainment at the university and about the fiasco earlier in the week. Your father then told me who *he* was and who *you* were and what you were involved in."

Gardener wondered how much his father had told Martin Brown. "Dad, you're not really supposed to discuss police cases. In fact, I'm not supposed to discuss them with you."

"Under normal circumstances I would agree, but these are not normal, and I am involved," replied Malcolm. "I haven't given away any secrets, but what we've stumbled across could prove useful."

"Go on," said Gardener.

Martin Brown sighed. "I booked William Henry Corndell because of what I'd thought had been a glittering career. Everything I'd heard, and seen for that matter, was nothing short of stunning. The man is an absolute genius with make-up. He can do anything. I've seen him on the London stage for *The Phantom*–"

"You actually saw him play the part?" interrupted Gardener.

"No. I had a friend who worked for the theatre, and I was given backstage passes to one of the performances. I was there on the morning Corndell was given his big break, and his rehearsal was nothing short of a revelation. He put so much emotion into the part that the stagehands reckoned he was better than Crawford."

"Did you use the tickets for the performance?"

"No, my wife, girlfriend at the time, took ill, and we couldn't make it. But I later heard he had an accident."

"It was a little more than that," said Gardener. "I found out that he's brilliant in rehearsals but no good in front of a crowd. During the matinee he fluffed his lines, wrecked the scenery, and eventually broke his own leg, blaming everyone but himself."

"I never heard that."

"Take it from me, it's true."

"That puts the night at the university theatre into perspective a little bit. If he is frightened of crowds, that's probably why he fell off the podium."

"Exactly. And he used the fact that we were there putting pressure on him as an excuse for his own incompetence."

"That's where the apology comes in, I think."

"Don't worry about that. What else have you got to tell me?"

Martin Brown appeared hesitant, as if he didn't want to speak.

"Martin, you're not under arrest, anything you tell me will be in the strictest confidence."

"Malcolm told me about Leonard White's death, and the quote on the dressing room wall. 'For long weary months I have awaited this hour.'"

Gardener's stomach tensed. "And?"

"I know which film that comes from; or should I say which two films. It's a quote from *The Phantom of the Opera*, the Lon Chaney version released in 1925."

"We know…" Gardener stopped talking when he realized what Martin Brown had said. "Two films?"

"Before we go any further, Mr Gardener, I need you to tell me if there were other quotes at the scenes of the other murders, and what they were."

"You do know I'm not obliged to tell you anything," replied Gardener.

"I'm only trying to help. Maybe it's my turn to inform you that anything you tell me will be in the strictest confidence. Do you want to catch your killer?"

Gardener struggled with his conscience.

"Your first murder was Leonard White," continued Martin Brown. "He was found hanging in a theatre." Martin Brown stopped talking, but Gardener realised he knew more. His glare forced the man to continue. "At the autopsy you found a puzzle carved into the man's chest."

Gardener left the table without saying anything and collected the file from a cupboard in the living room. Although the central heating was on, he felt a chill. Martin Brown had told him something that only the police knew. He sat back down and studied the file, then asked Martin Brown for the second quote.

"'The night passed, a night of vague horrors, tortured dreams.' The second murder," said Martin Brown. "You found the second body hanging upside down in a kind of reverse crucifixion. Furthermore, at that autopsy you found another puzzle about the case, in a test tube inserted into the victim's anus."

The blood in Gardener's veins had turned to ice. Either Martin Brown knew more than was good for him because of inside information... or he was their killer. And in all honesty, Gardener wouldn't know: he wasn't sure anyone else would either. He couldn't believe the tension in the room. It felt like time had stood still. No one was drinking. In fact, it didn't sound like they were even breathing.

"The third quote?" asked Martin. "Would it be, 'so far so good, for a house with a curse on it'?"

Gardener nodded.

"Your third victim was found in a locked room, suspended in the crucifixion position once again. However, this time the body was the right way up, naked, and his real head was missing, but he had someone else's in its place. Along with a puzzle in his right hand."

Gardener was mortified. His stomach ached, his legs felt weak. "How do you know all these things?"

"Each of the people killed was a member of the local watch committee and had been killed by an independent film producer because they had banned his film for being too horrific. The man was totally incensed because he was unbalanced. But the police couldn't catch him in the film because he was a master of disguise."

"What film are we talking about?" asked Gardener, as if he didn't know.

"A film called *Imperfection*, written by William Henry Corndell, and produced by his father, Wallace."

"Have you seen the film?"

"Yes."

"Where?" Gardener asked.

"An underground copy. The film never made it to the big screen. The one the censors issued an 'X' certificate for was not the film distributed around Leeds. Therefore, the local watch committee that your father sat on banned the film immediately, told him in no uncertain terms he had to make cuts. It was too violent, too graphic; he had to cut it and then re-present it."

Gardener glanced at his father. "But you weren't there that night. You didn't see the film."

"Corndell obviously doesn't know that," replied Martin Brown.

"So Corndell made a film back in the Seventies and has basically lived it out since then?"

"Sounds like it. He's killed everyone the same way as he did in the film and used quotes from Chaney's films because he's obsessed with the man. Three down, one to go, and we all know who that is." Martin Brown stared at Malcolm.

"Do you mean to say I've been going out, unaware that my life was at stake?" asked Malcolm.

"Actually, no," replied Gardener.

"What do you mean?" asked Malcolm.

"You've been under twenty-four-hour surveillance for some time. Every move you've made has been watched and monitored."

Malcolm's bottom jaw fell open and nearly hit the table. After he'd regained his composure, he asked, "Why didn't you tell me?"

"I couldn't, Dad. Firstly, we've never been sure of our facts from the beginning, and secondly, because of that we didn't want you worrying unnecessarily. Thirdly, we had to make sure everything you did was natural, so we could lull the killer into making an attempt and therefore expose himself."

"But I could have been killed."

"No you couldn't, we know what we're doing."

"I've never seen anyone following me," said Malcolm. "Corndell could have taken me anytime he wanted."

"He couldn't," argued Gardener. "You were being watched, and the reason you didn't know was because you weren't meant to; and the reason you didn't see him was also because you weren't meant to. That's how good a job we've been doing."

Malcolm didn't reply.

Gardener grabbed his mobile and scrolled his way through the contacts list.

"What are you doing?" asked Martin Brown.

"I think it's time I spoke to our friend William."

"I have his landline number," said Martin.

"It's okay," smiled Gardener. "We'll ring his mobile."

"But he doesn't have one," argued Martin Brown.

"Yes he does," said Gardener.

Chapter Forty-seven

Laura had left the house early in the morning, spending the best part of the day in the centre of Leeds shopping for clothes. She had returned to Yeadon about an hour later, depositing her carrier bags before popping back out again to pick up a parcel at the Royal Mail sorting office. Her intention had then been to drive back home, but the car had other ideas.

All morning her engine management light had been on, indicating a problem that the garage had been unable to find two days previously when it had been booked in for that reason. The excuse the garage had given was that their computers had been attacked with a virus which had somehow been passed on to the diagnostic machine they were using. She now wondered if it had transferred the virus to her car. She supposed it was possible, but would readily admit she knew nothing about computers *or* cars, so if you mixed the two together she was doubly lost. What she did know was that the car was not running properly.

Overhead, the rich blue skies were cloudless, creating yet another warm day for the time of year. Laura had her driver's door window open, and was listening to the radio. As she drove down Rawdon Road heading towards Horsforth, the car misfired. "Oh, Christ, don't do this to me."

Suddenly, the dashboard lit up, and the vehicle rolled to a halt at the side of the road. Despite having lost her power steering, she managed to guide it into a drive fronted by a pair of magnificent wrought iron gates. She tried in vain to start the engine, but it simply turned over without firing.

Laura jumped out of the car and reached back in for her handbag. She took out her mobile phone and glanced around in order to ascertain where she was. Phoning the breakdown service would be something akin to passing an X-Factor audition, and then she would probably have to wait about four hours before the tow truck arrived, which they would promise within the hour.

Laura took a peek inside the grounds of the house beyond the gates. "Someone's tight on security," she said to herself. After phoning the breakdown service, she also left Sean a voicemail message.

Laura pressed the intercom button and waited for an answer, which came quite quickly. "Hello?"

"I'm sorry to bother you, but I've broken down outside your gates. I thought it only polite to let you know."

"How unfortunate. Are you all right?" came the reply.

Laura recognised the voice, but she couldn't place it.

"Yes, I'm fine. I've phoned the breakdown service and they've promised to be here within the hour. Is that a problem?"

"Not at all. But we can't have you waiting out there by yourself in this day and age, you never know who's around.

I'm going to open the gates to allow you a little more room for the breakdown service. And if you'd like to take a walk down, I'll make you a nice cup of tea, er... I'm sorry... you never told me your name."

"I don't want to put you to any trouble," Laura answered.

She heard him laugh before he said, "Goodness me, that is rather an unusual name. It's no trouble." With that said, the gates silently opened.

She spoke back into the intercom. "Thank you. My name's Laura, Laura Reilly. I'll see you in a couple of minutes, Mister...?"

The intercom clicked off, but the man on the other end never gave his name.

The walk to the mansion wasn't as long as she'd imagined. When she arrived, the front door was open, which led her into a panelled hallway framed by film posters. She then turned and saw her host.

Chapter Forty-eight

Briggs stared at the file on his desk. It included everything Gardener could muster, along with the folder Colin Sharp had prepared, and details of the information everyone else had supplied. It had taken Briggs an hour to sort through it all, with the help of Gardener and Reilly who were now sitting opposite. "Well done, Stewart, Sean. There's a lot of information here."

"Enough to gain a warrant for his arrest?" asked Gardener.

"I don't see why not," replied Briggs, sitting back and folding his arms across his chest.

"Can I ask you a question, Stewart? And I'd like *your* opinion on this one as well, Sean," said Briggs.

"Go on."

"From everything we've seen, you're absolutely sure it's Corndell?"

The question knocked Gardener off balance a little. "As sure as I can be, why?"

"What about Martin Brown?"

"The thought did cross my mind, particularly when he came out with the information that no one else knew."

"You're barking up the wrong tree, sir," said Reilly. "If Martin Brown was our killer, then why didn't he abduct Malcolm at the cinema? There was nothing to stop him."

"Maybe he wanted to rub Stewart's nose in it," offered Briggs. "You know what these people are like. Brown takes the opportunity to befriend Malcolm at the cinema. They get talking, Malcolm takes him home to meet his son and therefore gain some more inside knowledge. You said yourself he gave you information that only we knew."

"From a film written by Corndell, one that he'd seen," protested Gardener.

"How long ago, Stewart? A bit of a good memory, wouldn't you say? Can you remember quotes from films you watched over twenty years ago?"

"I can't, but I bet my dad can. The point I'm making is that if you're a film buff, then maybe you would remember these things."

"And another thing, sir," Reilly said. "Laura knows Martin Brown. She's worked with him, so she has. She hasn't given me any reason to suspect him."

"And you still haven't seen this film anywhere, or come across anyone but Brown who knows anything about it?" Briggs asked.

"Actually, we do know who has a copy," said Gardener.

"Who?"

"Corndell," replied Gardener. "He has a canister in his cinema with that title on."

Briggs sat back and stayed quiet for a moment or two. "Okay, Stewart. I'll go with it. I'll get the warrant, you get him off the streets."

"How long will it take?" Gardener asked.

"Not long," replied Briggs. "But there is a problem."

Gardener's stomach lurched. "Go on."

"I'm afraid I can't let you handle the case."

Gardener knew it had been coming "Why?"

"Because whoever it is, whether it's Corndell or Martin Brown or someone we haven't yet come across, they've made it personal. Your father is next in line. How would you feel if I allowed you to drag Corndell in, spend all day interviewing him, only to find when you got home your dad was missing, or worse, strung up?"

"That won't happen if we get Corndell off the streets," said Gardener.

"I'm not taking that chance, Stewart. I appreciate all the work you've done on the case, but I still have to ask, are you one hundred percent certain? And the answer is no. Even now, your judgement may be clouded–"

Gardener was about to say something, but Briggs put his hand out to stop him. "What I want you to do is go home and spend time with your dad. *You* keep him under twenty-four-hour protection, at least until this thing blows over. Reilly and I will handle Corndell's arrest." Briggs stood up and nodded to Reilly. "Come on, let's go."

Gardener had no chance to reply.

Chapter Forty-nine

Gardener pulled his car to a halt opposite the stage door and switched off the engine. He glanced further down the street to where a road crew were unloading the trailer.

Through the stage door and down the steps, he heard Fettle humming to himself. When he came into view he realised why, the man was making tea. "Just in time," said Fettle. "Fancy a brew?"

"Do you ever do anything else apart from drink tea all day?" replied Gardener. "I'm afraid I don't have time this morning."

"Why's that then?"

Gardener felt heavy and hollow. He really wanted to be there to see Corndell's reaction when they arrested him, but he understood the reasons behind it. He told Fettle if he came across any more information to ring Sean and let him know.

Fettle nodded as Gardener turned and mounted the steps to the stage door. Before he reached the top, Fettle called him. Gardener came back down and Fettle was standing with two dog-eared copies of *Film Review* in his hands. "Thought you might like to show these to your dad. Might take his mind off things and cheer him up a bit."

"Thank you, I'm sure he'll love it. I'll get them back as soon as possible."

"There's no rush," said Fettle, returning to his tea and biscuits.

Outside, Gardener settled himself in the car and threw the magazines on the passenger seat. As he reached for the ignition, he changed his mind and picked one up, leafing through. He was about to put it back on the passenger seat when he came across a photo that made his blood curdle. His knees weakened, his fingers tingled, and he felt numb. Gardener fumbled for his mobile phone.

It couldn't be!

Chapter Fifty

Briggs launched himself towards the door, but it took another two attempts before it caved in. When it did, he jumped back into the hallway and held his nose. "Jesus Christ!"

Reilly covered his own and walked into the room. The place was a tomb. As he'd suspected by the view from the outside, the window had been covered with newspaper. The floor had no carpet, only bare boards. The walls were back to brick. An old-fashioned range adorned one wall; frames – which had probably hung for years – had been removed, exposing clean wallpaper. For what purpose, he had no idea.

In the middle of the room, tied to a rocking chair was the naked, headless corpse of the man they suspected was the real Trevor Thorpe, the profiler.

Briggs sighed. He'd taken a harried call from Gardener who had spotted the image of the Trevor Thorpe they had seen in one of Fettle's *Film Reviews*. The photo was in fact Lon Chaney in the lead role of a film called *The Road To Mandalay*: and the exact disguise Corndell had used for the incident room meetings. It had taken them almost an hour to find Thorpe's address and drive to the remote farmhouse.

Briggs stared at the emaciated body, bound tightly with cheese-wire, having been there some considerable time. He'd struggled to free himself, the congealed rivers of blood trailing down his chest attesting to that fact. Briggs glanced around the room for any notes or messages, but there were none. "What are we dealing with here?"

"One sick individual."

"How long do you reckon he's been here, Sean?"

"Hard to say... I reckon at least a month."

Briggs clenched his teeth. "If this is Thorpe, and I'm sure it will be, then the killer has been disguised as our profiler, and he's listened to everything we've had to say. What's more, he took us all for idiots, by throwing us duff information about the kind of person we should be looking for."

"He's a clever man, so he is."

"Either that, or he's lucky," said Briggs.

"No, sir, he's clever. And he's been allowed to get away with it because he's so damn good with a brush and paint."

"Corndell it is, then?"

"Too feckin' right."

Briggs walked outside for a breath of fresh air and checked the signal on his mobile, glancing up at the three-storey farmhouse. It was old and in need of repair with missing roof tiles, damaged render, leaking gutters, and rotting window frames. It was hardly befitting an ex-police profiler. He noticed the barns and outbuildings were no better.

"It's the middle of nowhere for Christ's sakes, Sean. Why the hell does he want to live here?"

"Who's to say he does?"

"What do you mean?" asked Briggs.

"The only letter we have is the one you received. We don't know anything about him, only his reputation. Who's to say he actually wrote the letter? Who's to say that's him in there?"

Briggs sighed loudly and called the station.

Chapter Fifty-one

"There's something wrong," said Reilly. He pulled the car to a halt outside the wrought iron gates.

"Why?" Briggs asked.

"Because the gates are open."

"Drive on, Sean, I'd like to have a look at this place, and the maniac that lives here."

Reilly put the car in gear and drove down the gravel drive, parking outside the front door.

Briggs opened the car door and heaved himself out, glancing around. "I can see why you'd want to protect the place." He turned to Reilly. "Have the gates always been closed?"

"Yes, you have to ring the intercom if you want to talk to him."

Briggs knocked on the door, retrieving the warrant for Corndell's arrest from his inside pocket. When there was no answer he knocked again, before eventually trying it. Stretching his legs, he walked around the perimeter. When he reached the back door, he knocked once more.

When Reilly tried the handle, the door opened.

He glanced at Briggs. "I'm not happy."

"Okay. At least let's take a look around while we're here." Briggs shouted Corndell's name, but there was no answer. He noticed that the kitchen was spotless and strolled through, glancing into each of the other rooms, which were equally as clean. There was no sign of life downstairs.

Briggs admired the film posters. Reilly pointed out the original *Frankenstein* poster with Boris Karloff, and told his superior officer how much it had sold for recently.

"What? For a fucking poster?"

"That's what I said."

"And that's what he paid for it?"

"No, he didn't say he'd paid that much, just that's what it went for when it sold recently."

Briggs sighed heavily. "Some people have more money than sense."

They covered the rest of the house, and Reilly showed Briggs the make-up room and the cinema. But the whole building was like a mortuary: no sign of life. Reilly fished a piece of paper out of his pocket, and then reached for his cell phone. "Shit, I must have left mine in the car, have you got yours?"

"Who are you calling?" Briggs asked.

"Corndell... who else?"

The phone rang, but no one answered.

Chapter Fifty-two

Back at the house, Gardener parked the car on the drive and let himself in through the front door. He went straight to the kitchen and switched the kettle on, placing the two *Film Reviews* on the table. He pulled two cups from the rack and started to make tea, wondering if his father was in the shed, his usual place of rest.

From a feeling of dejection at having been removed from the case, he was now elated at having found what he considered to be another nail in Corndell's coffin. The photo of Chaney in the *Road To Mandalay* – the person they had thought was Trevor Thorpe – had sent a chill right through him, but the sense of satisfaction that followed was immeasurable. He was pretty sure he'd receive a phone call soon to tell him Corndell was safely tucked away in an interview room, and that the next couple of days spent with his father would simply be a paid holiday.

Gardener checked his mobile, but there were no text messages or missed calls. He tried the handle of the back door and found it unlocked, which meant his father should be down the garden in the potting shed. The kettle boiled, so he poured the tea into the pot before going to find him.

Gardener was surprised that his father wasn't in the shed when he arrived. He tried the garage, and he wasn't there either. A wave of sadness passed him as he glanced at the Bonneville, which had been abandoned. He really wanted to finish the project.

Gardener checked every room in the house before running back out to the potting shed. He now had his mobile in hand, already ringing his father's number. A feeling of trepidation hung in the air.

Where was he?

The phone shrilled. Gardener heard it! His guts turned to ice.

The ring tone was coming from the shed. Gardener peeked in, and the phone was on the bench, his number lighting up the display panel.

What did that mean? Had he wasted too much time between the station and coming home? Shouldn't he have come straight home and not bothered to take a detour to see Fettle? Why had he done that? What had gone through his mind? Surely his father was more important than Fettle.

Had Corndell slipped the net? Had the call to Briggs and Reilly to inform them about Trevor Thorpe actually been the final nail in his father's coffin? Had they gone to check out that lead instead of arresting Corndell first?

Back in the house, Gardener was about to call the station when the doorbell chimed. In frustration, he threw his mobile on the nearest chair and ran into the hall. Opening the door he was confronted by a UPS van and the driver, dressed in the standard brown uniform. A parcel delivery was not high on his list of priorities, and only served to irritate him further.

"Mr Gardener?" asked the driver.

"Yes."

"Parcel for you."

Gardener thanked the driver, took the package, and walked back into the living room before a thought suddenly hit him. The man had not asked for a signature. Gardener picked up the parcel. It was rectangular shaped, about twelve inches by eight. There were no stamps, no UPS logos, and no writing other than his name. He ripped the package open and quickly scanned the contents: a photo and a newspaper clipping.

Dropping them on the floor, he ran outside, where he found the driver in the process of starting the van. The fact that it was a pleasant day meant he hadn't shut the door, which gave Gardener the opportunity he needed to pull the driver from the seat, drag him out of the cab, and throw him heavily against the side of the vehicle, so much so that he dented one of the panels.

"What the fuck—"

He gave the driver no chance to say anything else. Instead, he banged the man's head against the panel in an effort to subdue him. Only now did the driver's features register in his mind: he was a similar height to Gardener but much thinner, his complexion was tanned and he had a beard and moustache, which Gardener was trying to pry from his face in an effort to see whether or not it was real.

"What the fuck are you doing, man? You're ripping my face apart!"

"Who are you?" Gardener shouted, breathless, grabbing the driver's shirt and shoving him back towards the van again. The driver hit the ground in a sitting position with his legs underneath him. He wasn't going anywhere.

"I'm a UPS driver, for God's sake." He tried to push Gardener out of the way. "This is assault, I can have you arrested for this."

"We both know you won't. What's your name?" asked Gardener, his heart pounding.

"You tell me who you are first."

Gardener used one hand to release and flip open his badge without bothering to explain further.

"Oh, shit."

"Let's try again, shall we? Name?"

"Gary Barlow... and don't bother, I've heard all the jokes."

Gardener had no idea what he was talking about. "Show me some identification. Now!"

"It's in the cab, any chance you can let go?"

Gardener did so. The driver wasn't a threat, and he'd established that it wasn't Corndell. He handed over his ID for inspection.

"Tell me about the parcel."

"Nothing to tell," said the driver.

"Don't mess me about, otherwise I'll arrest you for conspiracy to murder and have you inside so fast you'll break the four-minute-mile by at least half. Now start talking."

"Look. I haven't killed anyone, and I don't know what you're talking about. Anyone in my position on my shitty salary would have done exactly the same." Barlow pulled his shirt back into place – as if it suddenly mattered – and sat on the step of his van.

"Done what?"

"I just did what he told me to. A couple of hours ago, a bloke asked me if I wanted to earn a few quid. I asked how much, he said five hundred pounds, in cash, and he had it in his hand. I asked him who he wanted me to kill, and all he said was he wanted a parcel delivering to this address, and asked if it was on my rounds. I said, for five hundred quid I didn't care if it was on the moon. For five hundred quid I'd take it."

"Where were you when he asked?"

"Horsforth."

Chapter Fifty-three

Briggs had called Gardener five times while Reilly drove through the centre of Leeds and finally out on to the road that led them to Churchaven. The phone remained unanswered.

Reilly eventually brought the car to a halt on Gardener's drive, noticing there were no other vehicles. Reilly knocked on the front door and walked in. Briggs followed Reilly into the kitchen, where they found a puzzled Malcolm staring at two teacups and a pot of cold tea.

Startled, Malcolm nodded and greeted both men.

"Have you seen, Stewart?" Reilly asked.

"No, but he must have been here at some point. Look at this lot."

"Where have you been?"

"Only next door. I was in the potting shed when Harry popped round and said he'd just brewed up, so I went for a cup."

"And you haven't seen or heard from him?" asked Briggs.

"No. Is something wrong?"

"We're not sure," replied Briggs. They all sat at the kitchen table, and Briggs briefly told them that he'd removed Gardener from the case and that shortly afterwards they had taken a call from him with some important information, which led to another corpse.

"Maybe we should ring him," suggested Reilly, fishing in his pocket for his mobile. "Shit, I've done it again, the bloody thing's still in the car."

"It's okay, Sean, I'll ring," said Briggs.

"You ring. I'll get my phone."

As Reilly came back in, he saw Briggs and Malcolm rushing round the living room trying to locate the ring tone from Gardener's mobile. They eventually found it down the side of a chair.

"Something's wrong," said Reilly. "Cold tea on a kitchen worktop and his phone stuffed down the side of a chair. He left here in a hurry."

"So, where's he gone, and why?" asked Briggs. "And why was it so important that he had to leave without calling us?"

"Christ! Would you look at that? My phone's not even switched on, so it isn't." As soon as it was, Reilly had a voicemail message. He listened intently.

"Is it your boss?" Briggs asked.

"No. Laura. Her car's broken down. But she hasn't said where, just that she's phoned the recovery people."

"Is she okay?" asked Malcolm.

"I'll give her a ring at home, she should be there by now." Briggs' concerned expression did little to abate the feeling in Reilly's mind. The Irishman disconnected after ten rings.

"No answer?" asked Briggs.

"No."

He called her mobile. On the third ring, a male voice answered. "Erik speaking."

"Erik!" repeated Reilly. "Who the feck is Erik?"

"Oh, Mr Reilly... I'm sure you know the answer to that by now."

The connection died. Reilly tried again but the phone had been switched off.

"Erik?" Briggs asked.

"Corndell!" Reilly threw the phone on the chair. It landed next to Gardener's. "That bastard has Laura somewhere."

"Why Erik?" asked Briggs. "Who does he think he is now?"

"I suspect he thinks he's the Phantom," said Malcolm. "From the film."

"Oh Jesus!" replied Briggs.

"Who he is or who he thinks he is, doesn't matter," said Reilly. "*Where* he is, that's what I want to know. When I find out, I'm going to kill him."

Reilly's temper scaled new heights, his fists clenching and unclenching. As far as he was concerned, Corndell had signed his own death warrant.

"Calm down, Sean," said Briggs. "Losing your temper won't help Laura."

"Won't help Corndell either, when I find him. So, where the hell is Stewart?" asked Reilly. "He must know something, which is why he's left here without telling anyone. He hasn't even left a note. That means he was in a hurry."

Reilly hoped so, because the only thing that would stop him wiping Corndell from the face of the earth was if his partner found him first.

Briggs phoned and informed the station before putting his mobile in his pocket. "I think I know where they might be."

Chapter Fifty-four

Gardener parked the car and switched off the engine. He remained in the vehicle, studying the building opposite: what was thought to be a disused warehouse. He now knew better. In the sodium glow of the streetlamps it resembled the mausoleum he imagined it would be inside. The sky was clear, and he noticed the start of a slight ground frost.

After the disagreement with the UPS driver, Gardener had gone back inside the house and forced himself to remain calm. It was the only way he was going to think rationally. It was obvious who had paid the driver five hundred pounds to deliver the package containing a clue as to whom he held hostage. But it didn't tell him where.

For that, he had to rely on his police instinct and his memory. The warehouse behind the Playhouse was where the watch committee had held their screenings, the very same group of people that had banned William Henry Corndell's film *Imperfection*. That's where he had to be.

He'd phoned the station to find out that Reilly and Briggs had gone to see Trevor Thorpe, after which they were going to Corndell's with an arrest warrant. Gardener figured they would have been far too late.

In the car, he glanced at the parcel he'd received and removed the photo and the newspaper clipping. The photo was of Laura. The clipping was the damning review she had written about Corndell's performance at the university theatre. So, it was pretty obvious that he had Laura in there. And during the time that Gardener had spent with Fettle, Corndell had probably taken his father. So, God knows what he was going to walk into.

Glancing at the dashboard clock, it was six-fifteen. He knew that he shouldn't walk in there alone, but calling for backup could waste vital time. Nevertheless, he owed Sean that much.

Reaching into his jacket pocket revealed he did not have his mobile. In that instinctive moment of panic he tried every pocket he had, before reaching into the glove compartment, even though he knew it wouldn't be there.

A picture suddenly came to mind: he had thrown the phone on to an armchair before he'd gone to see who was at the door. He obviously hadn't retrieved it. So now he had no choice but to walk blindly into the situation alone – seeing as public phone boxes were a thing of the past.

Annoyed with himself, Gardener stepped out of the car and locked the door. He saw little point in scurrying over to the warehouse. Knowing what he knew about Corndell and how security conscious he was, there would most definitely be CCTV watching his every move.

He confidently strolled to the building and opened the side door next to a roller shutter door. It was unlocked. As he thought, he was expected.

* * *

The first thing he noticed about the inside of the warehouse was the clinical silence. Standing still, he could hear absolutely nothing. That made things worse, because he would almost certainly telegraph his moves.

Glancing around, he saw what he presumed was the missing limo, and the large white truck parked in front of a corridor with rooms either side. As he crept forward and glanced in, the first office had a computer terminal and monitor, which was on stand-by. There was also a variety of other electrical equipment including, as he'd suspected, CCTV. As the screens revealed, it was also linked to Corndell's house.

Opposite that office was another. Standing on a tripod was a movie camera. The room had plain, bland walls, with a chair in front of one of them. There was no carpet. Gardener suspected it was the room where Corndell had donned his Inspector Burke make-up, filming the small clue he had left them.

Further down the corridor Gardener sensed a strong odour of leather before he came to the last two rooms. On the left, a small kitchen; on the right, a complete replica of the room in Corndell's house, featuring mannequins and mirrors and benches. A number of shelves were crammed with tubes and bottles of make-up.

Gardener walked inside and inspected the costumes. The Hunchback from the night at the theatre was there, complete with blood spatter patterns. The vampire costume Chaney wore in *London After Midnight* was also present, and it too had blood spatter. It was obvious now how Corndell had managed to do all he had without being caught. The warehouse was his centre of operations, not his house.

Outside the room he glanced to his right. A curtain blocked entry into the main warehouse. He waved it aside and stepped through, into another world. The view was magnificent, one to make Hollywood sit up and take notice.

Straight ahead was a French street scene reminiscent of yesteryear. The ground was covered in a fine layer of dust. Two circular pavements around ten feet in diameter had been constructed on either side, each with old-fashioned gas lamps. The street continued toward a brick pavement, where he noticed more traditional lamps. A swirling mist hung around the lamps.

Gardener's heart raced when he suddenly realised that hanging from those traditional lamps were a number of bodies. All were perfectly still, as if they had been in the building some time. Despite that, he ran forward to test the pulse of the first. As soon as he grabbed the wrist, it came away in his hand and Gardener breathed a sigh of relief as he realized they were mannequins. He checked two more with the same result.

Turning to study the remainder of the area, he realised that the warehouse roof had been raised in order to accommodate the showpiece, a huge gothic building that had been backlit very carefully in order to create an eerie ambience, particularly as the façade had been constructed with cylindrical columns and arches. A series of steps led up to a number of doors, each with a wire grille front save one. A glass dome sat on the roof of the building, and on each corner were a number of angels glancing in different directions.

Before he had any further chance to think about what to do, a spotlight lit up one of the arches. Approximately twenty feet high, standing in one of them was Corndell, as far as Gardener could ascertain. "At last, Mr Gardener."

The voice confirmed it all. He suspected a hidden microphone. Even at that distance it was crisp and concise. Gardener walked slowly forward as Corndell launched into his running commentary.

"The Paris Opera House is one of the most beautiful buildings in the world, Mr Gardener. It contains levels beyond levels of cellars, fountains, chandeliers – the history of which is very dark and very interesting. It even has its own ghost!"

It's talking to me, thought Gardener, with little idea what he was going to do, or in fact what he was going to say once he *was* up close. All he did know was that he was at an extreme disadvantage from the positions they were in.

Corndell continued unabated. "Part of the mystique of the opera house, Mr Gardener, is the levels that it inhabits underground. There are chorus rooms, green rooms, ballrooms, set rooms, cellars for props, closets, dressing rooms, and many more kinds of rooms making up the building. The underground levels contain all sorts of gruesome objects from various operas that have been produced. Of course, my replica is nowhere near as prolific, but it does contain a nasty surprise for you."

Gardener had reached the steps leading up to the only entrance door available. He had a much better view of Corndell, and the character he was playing, the Phantom. Even from where he was standing, the attention to detail was so intricate that Gardener felt lost for words.

Corndell's head was little more than a skull with an up-tilted nose. The dark shading around his eyes gave them a hollow-eyed expression, emphasised even more by the line of colour under the lower eyelashes. And his ears seemed flattened against the sides of the skull, so much so that at first glance, he didn't appear to have any. His face was very pale and the head itself bore very little hair save a few fine strands. Gardener was impressed, and at the same time disturbed.

"How do you like what I've done, Mr Gardener?"

"Where are they?" he asked.

"All in good time. Now, perhaps you can answer my question."

Gardener sighed. Whether he liked it or not he would have to play the game. "If you mean, do I actually enjoy watching lunatics mutilate people, leaving puzzles all around the city, I can't really say I am that impressed, Mr Corndell. It's people like you who make my job extremely unpleasant."

"I'm not talking about that, you peasant!"

He realised he'd touched a raw nerve because Corndell's left eye had started to twitch, something he had noticed only once before when he thought he was being threatened. Corndell gripped the sides of the arch in which he was standing, and Gardener found himself praying that he had not done too good a job when erecting the exterior: hopefully the whole fucking lot would collapse and kill him!

"But seeing as you brought up the subject, perhaps we can discuss what I've done... why I've done it? Isn't that what you shrinks are all about?"

"I am not a psychiatrist, I'm a police officer." Gardener was growing tired of the conversation, and he certainly wasn't about to pander to the whims of an egomaniac, particularly when he was holding two people hostage who were not necessarily here.

Corndell leaned forward. "You should be very interested in me–"

Gardener realised there was no stopping Corndell now, even if he wanted to. He had the microphone, and there was probably very little that could be done but let him have his finest hour. It would – after all – be his last, thought Gardener.

"Chaney was a true legend, Mr Gardener, and could only be admired. He was an inspiration, and I have taken his place: I am the modern-day master of the silver screen, the modern day 'man of a thousand faces'. Or at least I would have been if your father and his friends hadn't meddled. Who did they think they were? What right did they have to pass judgement on my masterpiece, to ruin my career? Well, let me tell you Mr Gardener, no r–"

Gardener cut him dead as he shouted, "If you've quite finished, I have no wish to stand here all night while you give me what you think will amount to your finest hour. I want to know where my father and my friend's wife are. Now, if you don't tell me in precisely ten seconds, I'm going to forget that I'm a police officer and fucking throttle you with my bare hands. Do you understand?"

Corndell burst out laughing. "Such language, Mr Gardener. I really don't think your superiors would take kindly to that. I do have rights, you know."

"His superior officer is having trouble with his eyes and ears at the moment," said Alan Briggs, appearing in front of the curtain at the back of the warehouse. "And as for any rights, as far as I'm concerned, you gave up those when you started murdering people all over the city, and then decided to kidnap one of my officers' wives." Briggs glanced at Gardener. "So, you go right ahead, Stewart, do what you have to, so long as you get the information we need."

Briggs walked slowly towards Gardener, who had never been more pleased to see him than now.

But where was Sean?

Briggs whispered to him. "He doesn't have your dad, Stewart. He's back at the station with a couple of junior officers. I left word with the desk sergeant to locate the rest of the squad and get them here, pronto."

Gardener turned and glanced at Corndell. He wore a long dark cloak with one arm swept across his chest. Even his clothes were covered in dust for emphasis. The other arm was reaching to something that Gardener could not see because of a low-slung velvet drape.

"Where is she?" asked Gardener. "Your time is up."

"How true that statement is, Mr Gardener," said Corndell.

Gardener realised how much confidence Corndell had. You couldn't do what he'd done without self-assurance. That thought alone was worrying, because right now, he was holding all the cards.

"You'll find what you're looking for inside. And by the way... best of luck." Corndell pulled the rope behind the low-slung drape.

Two things happened.

Firstly, he disappeared behind the curtain. Secondly, the front doors of the opera house clicked open.

Chapter Fifty-five

The warehouse lights dimmed, leaving only those of the opera house for guidance.

"Right, forget that mad bastard for the moment," said Briggs. "Let's get inside and see what we have to do."

Both men took the steps two at a time, and Gardener went through the door first. The inside was as magnificent as the outside, only much more disturbing.

They were in a graveyard. An earthy smell, and it being soft underfoot, told him that the maniac had used soil – and not for appearance. Peering into the distance, Gardener could make out a series of randomly scattered tombstones and, what he suspected were fake trees. On the extreme right and left of the building were in fact two shrines; on either side of the headstones were two angels staring down at the names on those headstones. A small amount of green coloured lighting added to the emotional scene. Other than that, there was very little light.

Gardener felt a breeze skate across the back of his neck, forcing him to shiver. He really didn't like it at all.

"Jesus Christ!" whispered Briggs. "How does he think of all this?"

"He's disturbed," replied Gardener. "He doesn't live in the same world we do. Everything about him tells you that." He moved forward and bumped into something solid, causing him to curse. Whatever it was must have grazed his shin.

"Steady, Stewart," said Briggs, before shouting, "he could have given us some fucking lighting to work with!"

Which is precisely what their host did.

Puzzled, Gardener glanced behind and noticed that he had bumped into a real tree stump. And that the headstones all around them contained names of all the people he knew: his father, the rest of the watch committee, even one for himself and Sean Reilly. The shrines bore the names of Corndell's parents: Wallace and Betty.

Corndell junior had a very sick mind. His masterpiece confirmed it: the inside of the opera house was more unsettling than anything he'd ever seen.

Gardener turned around again as a noise diverted his attention. Two halogen lamps cut the darkness to reveal a round column, rising up from the graveyard, leading into the rafters up above.

Gardener peered upwards. Although it was dark, he could make out the top of the column, which had a small round base. Though he couldn't swear to it, he thought he could see a pair of feet.

Chapter Fifty-six

Corndell chuckled to himself as he surveyed his handiwork from another arched box at the other side of the opera house. Two police officers completely out of their depth, unaware of the situation they were caught up in, and therefore unable to help. Something to which they were unaccustomed.

He turned, reached out and pulled a lever. The hum of an electric motor broke the silence.

Laughing even more, Corndell was thinking of how much he had enjoyed himself recently. But as Gardener had mentioned only minutes previously, his finest hour was yet to come.

The column descended.

Chapter Fifty-seven

The column suddenly moved, forcing Gardener to jump back. He would have lost his balance had it not been for Briggs.

"Steady, Stewart."

"Stand back," said Gardener, "I've no idea what's coming down but I wouldn't put anything past this freak."

The column continued lowering, sliding into the earth beneath them. As it did so, the feet Gardener thought he had seen grew into a pair of legs: wearing blue jeans and a pair of small white boots with a heel, certainly not suitable footwear for holding your balance. There must have been countless females in Leeds wearing those kinds of fashionable boots but he knew whom they belonged to.

The person on the column let out a whimper.

"Who the hell's on that?" shouted Briggs, peering upwards.

"Oh, Jesus," said Gardener, "it's Laura."

"What?"

She had now dropped low enough that they could see up as far as her chest. Laura's arms had been tied behind her back. As her face came into view, Gardener noticed she had been gagged and a noose had been tied around her neck. Her biggest problem was that the base upon which she was standing was perhaps only a foot in diameter, allowing little room for error.

"What the hell goes through this bloke's mind?" Briggs asked Gardener.

The slack in the rope was taken up and it started to tighten. Gardener realized – with a panic – that if they didn't do something, his partner's wife was going to be hanged right in front of them.

But what could they do? The column still towered above them – well out of their reach. It was impossible to climb because it was a smooth round pole. It was pretty much in the middle of the earth and he could see nothing he could use to gain any height: not that he thought he'd be allowed to anyway.

Gardener turned and glared at Briggs. "How the hell are we going to get her out of this?"

As he said it, the column stopped.

Gardener turned. Laura was still at least six feet above him. There was little or no slack left in the rope and she was now standing on tiptoes. She made no sound but he could see the tears running down her face and the imploring expression in her eyes, reminding him of the night Sarah died.

There was no margin for mistakes. She had to stand absolutely still for as long as it took for both officers to negotiate her release. But did she have the confidence to see that through?

Chapter Fifty-eight

A powerful beam appeared through the rafters, lighting up a theatre box to Gardener's left, illuminating Corndell.

"If she falls, she hangs," he shouted. "If you don't do as I say, she hangs. If you try to save her, she hangs. Not a lot to look forward to, has she, Mr Gardener?"

Gardener's temper was mounting but he knew at the moment he was the underdog. He held no cards. "Don't be stupid, Corndell, you'll never get away with this."

"Oh but I will, Mr Gardener."

"He's right, simpleton," said Briggs, "you've done enough damage, don't make things any worse."

The DCI stepped to his left, as if to show some initiative to rectify the situation.

"Take your inspector's advice, Briggs, and don't *you* be stupid. I am controlling the lever, so her fate is in my hands. You will not reach me in time to do anything about it. You will not get anywhere near your sergeant's wife, and you certainly won't save her life, so I suggest you stay exactly where you are."

Gardener could have heard a pin drop, which raised the tension. He glanced at Laura. She was still crying. She was also shivering and Gardener knew that it wasn't cold. He either needed to buy her some time and alleviate her predicament, or he had to save her, neither of which were likely in the short term. And time wasn't something she had a lot of.

Gardener glanced at Corndell. "What exactly are you planning, Mr Corndell? If it doesn't end well for Laura it certainly isn't going to end well for you. You're in enough trouble. You've already killed four people. You're looking at life, so how much worse would you like to make it?"

Corndell laughed hard, a high-pitched screech in which he rocked backward and forwards. "I don't think so, Mr Gardener."

"What don't you think?" shouted Briggs.

Corndell stopped laughing and stared at Gardener, as if he were a machine that could simply switch itself on and off when he wanted.

He leaned forward with his hands on the side of the box as if he wanted to fire his words at Gardener.

"I don't think I am going to get life. Let's look at the facts, shall we?"

Corndell raised his right arm and started counting off the fingers of his right hand with those of his left.

"Fact one: you have absolutely no evidence against me. Two: neither you nor anyone else has ever seen me kill anyone." He raised his third finger. "There is no trace of me at any crime scene. No sightings. Your witness statements will sound like they've been made up by Mickey Mouse. 'What did he look like, sir?' 'Well, your honour, a bit like a vampire with pointed teeth and wearing a dark cloak.' Any evidence you think you have is circumstantial at best.

"If you put me in front of a jury, Mr Gardener, you will be completely laughed out of court because you have nothing to back up your statements. My solicitor will have a field day."

Briggs had his phone in his hand and appeared to be filming the exchange. He stared at Corndell. "What's this if not evidence, sunshine?"

Corndell laughed at the superior officer. "By the time you have finished filming that and try to present it, I will be long gone."

"You think we're just going to let you walk out of here?" shouted Gardener, "after everything you've done, and still are doing?"

"I know so, Mr Gardener. You are going to let me walk free if you want to save the life of your partner's wife."

With that, Laura let out a strangulated cry. Gardener glanced upwards. She implored him to do something despite the fact that she couldn't move or talk. Her legs were trembling.

"She cannot possibly hang on much longer," said Corndell. "She's been standing like that for an hour. It's only a matter of time."

"He's right, Stewart," said Briggs. "We need to save Laura's life and we can't do that without him so whatever bargain he wants to make, go ahead. We'll pick him up later, he won't get far."

"He's managed to escape every other time he's killed someone," retorted Gardener, unwilling to play his game. "What's different now?"

"He can't slip back to this place any longer. We know about it. As soon as he leaves here, we can set up roadblocks and we can have men on stations and airports. He's going nowhere fast, so give him his moment of glory."

"Listen to him, Mr Gardener. He's talking sense." Corndell stood with his arms folded, as if he had already won the battle.

Laura whined. One glance at her and Gardener knew Briggs was right. She could not hold that stance very much longer.

Gardener ran his hands down his face, thoroughly frustrated. *Where the hell was Sean Reilly when he needed him?*

Gardener raised his hands in the air. "Okay, you win, Mr Corndell. How are we going to play this?"

Chapter Fifty-nine

Corndell chuckled, he had them where he wanted them. And they hadn't seen the half of it yet.

He drew his right hand toward his pocket, reassuring himself everything was in place, and that he maintained the advantage. He wondered how far he would be able to push it, making them dance to his merry tune.

Glancing at Laura, Corndell realized there was a slight amount of slack in the rope around her neck: time to ramp up the tension.

He turned. As he reached out for the lever, he had a shock of his own to deal with.

"No you don't, sunshine," said Sean Reilly, punching Corndell straight in the mouth, more than once.

Corndell fell back, crashing into the side of the box.

Reilly punched him once more and Corndell fell flat on his arse, winded and slightly dazed.

The Irishman grabbed Corndell by the scruff of his neck. "I haven't finished with you, sunshine. I'm going out there to free my wee wife and then I'm coming back in here to finish you off.

Corndell's head was swimming. He felt like he'd been hit by a battering ram.

Reilly grabbed his right hand, quickly handcuffing it to the rail running around the box.

"You're going nowhere."

Chapter Sixty

Gardener heard the crash as an aluminium ladder was thrown over the side of the box, landing in the soft earth with a clump. "Where the hell's that come from?" Gardener peered up toward the box. He couldn't see Corndell.

"What the hell are you up to, Corndell?" shouted Gardener, tramping forward, which wasn't easy due to the soil underfoot. Was he about to play another game: allow them to try and save Laura but perhaps lower the column at the last second?

The silence was condemning.

"What fucking perverse game is he up to now?" Briggs asked Gardener.

"He isn't up to anything," said Reilly, appearing stage left. He headed straight for the ladder.

Gardener lurched forward and helped his partner part the ladder despite it being nowhere near stable enough to climb.

Briggs ran to help. "Where the hell is Corndell?"

"Don't worry," replied Reilly, "he isn't going anywhere."

Knowing his partner better than anyone, Gardener wondered if he'd already killed Corndell. It was a fleeting thought, so he doubted and dismissed it.

"Sir," said Gardener to Briggs, "grab the other side of the ladder, let's do the best we can. I doubt it will be stable enough but Laura has very little time left."

The first time Reilly attempted to climb it, the ladder fell toward the pole, rocking it slightly, causing Laura some unnecessary panic. Gardener glanced upwards and his heart flew into his mouth as Laura rocked forward. Thankfully, she kept her balance.

"Jesus Christ!" shouted Reilly. "He's a dead man when I'm through here."

Briggs ignored the threatening comment. "It's okay, Sean, just get up there and get your missus."

Despite the rocking motion, he finally made it to the top of the ladder. Gardener didn't figure he would have any chance of being able to stand on the podium with Laura but the ladder was almost as high and Reilly was slightly taller than his wife.

But it was a tense few seconds whilst he managed to loosen the noose.

Gardener heard a sigh of relief as he unhooked Laura's neck.

But then they heard a scraping sound from the box to the left.

Gardener turned.

"Good effort, Mr Reilly, but not good enough."

Chapter Sixty-one

In his left hand, Corndell held a small oblong box, about the size of a TV remote. His face was bloody from a cut to his mouth and Gardener could see his right hand.

"What's he holding?" asked Briggs.

"I'd hate to think," said Gardener, aware of how precarious their situation was. Reilly was still at the top of the ladder with Laura slumped over his shoulder. He and his senior officer were stuck in mud.

"It's all over, Mr Gardener, you're out of time."

Corndell screeched with laughter as he raised his left hand.

Gardener was suddenly reminded of the mad scientists in the old horror films, those who went down screaming, taking everyone else with them.

There was no further time for a reply or a thought.

Corndell pressed the button on the oblong pad and the first explosion rocked the place.

Gardener had no idea where it came from but the force was enough the blow them all sideways. The ladder came down on top of him, cracking his forehead and scraping his face. Thankfully for him, Briggs disappeared in the opposite direction and not on top of him. Reilly and Laura punched the earth next to him. He heard his partner exhale loudly.

Another explosion to their left rang through Gardener's ears, nearly deafening him. Flames shot toward the box in which Corndell was standing.

The Phantom screamed and fell backwards.

Reilly jumped up and started to make his way to the left-hand side of the theatre.

Corndell was shouting something but Gardener couldn't hear it clearly enough.

Gardener grabbed Reilly's arm. "What are you doing?"

"I want that bastard up there," shouted Reilly.

"You'll never make it, Sean."

Popping and crackling sounds flashed around their ears. The flames grew higher and as Gardener peered at the box, he could not see Corndell.

"Trust me, Sean, you'll never make it."

He could tell that Reilly would not be satisfied until he had Corndell's throat between his hands.

"He's right, Sean," shouted Briggs, "that scum isn't worth it."

Laura had managed to make it to her feet. "For God's sake, look at this place." She pointed upwards as another mini explosion sounded above them.

In the blink of an eye the roof beams were aflame, and in no time at all the building was set to become a raging inferno.

"He needs to pay for what he's done."

"Fuck him!" shouted Briggs, "we need to save our own skins."

One of the roof beams fell down behind the pole on which Laura had been standing. No further warning was necessary. All four of them tramped through the thick earth underfoot, finally making it to the steps of the opera house. As they almost fell down them, a creak and a slam made Gardener glance behind him. The only door that had ever been available for entry and exit had slammed shut.

Corndell had planned everything down to the last detail.

But what had happened to him; where the hell was he?

Gardener bent forward with his hands on his knees, breathless, unable to believe how lucky they had been.

"Stewart, move yourself, for God's sake," shouted Briggs.

Like an alarm in his head, he realised that if Corndell had triggered the opera house doors to lock, he may well have triggered the main doors of the building in the event that they had foiled him.

Gardener and the others bolted for the entrance. The doors were still open. Once on the street, they ran across it to where their cars had been parked, and Briggs called the fire brigade on his mobile.

Epilogue

It was close to midnight when the fire chief pronounced the warehouse safe and secure. Standing a little way from the two officers, Gardener heard the conversation between the chief and his colleagues. The building had been reduced to a shell.

All four of them had sat beside the car listening to the cracking and banging as the timber joists fell, the windows exploding as the fire raged out of control.

A crowd had gathered shortly before the fire services had arrived, some of them asking if they were okay. God only knew the impression they must have given. One of the assembled onlookers had even gone to a burger bar around the corner and brought back tea and coffee and snacks for them.

Laura and Sean had stuck together like glue, before he had finally taken her home around nine-thirty. The pair of them had had enough.

"You never did tell me where Sean had got to," said Gardener to Briggs.

His superior officer was a picture: the lenses of his glasses were so thickly coated with grime it must have been impossible to see through them, his face had been covered in soot and soil, and even a vagrant would have turned his nose up at the clothes he was wearing. But he figured he hadn't fared any better himself.

"I wasn't really sure myself," said Briggs, taking a sip of coffee. "When we got out of the car, he told me to go inside. He said that if Corndell saw all of us together, he would have the advantage. And he would probably be cocky enough to think that we were stupid enough not to have split up."

Briggs paused, staring at the shell of the burnt-out warehouse. "He also said he would be much more use to

Laura if he couldn't see the state she was in. At least he wouldn't be distracted."

Briggs glanced at Gardener. "He was on a mission, Stewart. I've never seen determination like it. Even if I'd argued with him it wouldn't have mattered, he'd have done what he wanted anyway. As it was, I didn't get time, he was away around the building well before I had chance to think about what he'd said."

Gardener remained silent, thinking about what his partner had told him regarding the situation in the box. He'd handcuffed Corndell to the side to prevent him from escaping or grabbing the lever to inflict further pain on Laura. The position Corndell had ended up in had been unfortunate. He'd become a victim of his own games. None of them could have known he'd planted explosives.

Gardener thought about him being trapped in the box. Surely he couldn't have escaped.

Could he?

The fire chief approached them both. "Which one of you is in charge?"

"I am," replied Briggs.

"Fire Officer Marshall." He shook hands with Briggs. "Everything's safe and sound for tonight. The council will be here in the morning and decide what further safety measures to take."

"Did you find the body?" asked Gardener.

"Body?" repeated Marshall.

"Yes, I'm afraid we couldn't save him," said Gardener, his heart in his mouth. Surely the bastard had died. There couldn't possibly have been any escape.

The expression on Marshall's face was not a good one. "We found three."

Briggs glanced at Gardener, horrified. He waited until the chief was out of earshot. "Who else was in there?"

Gardener thought before replying. "Did you see the names on the two main shrines?"

"Can't say as I did," replied Briggs.

"They belonged to his parents... but I didn't think the bodies would be there."

Briggs said nothing.

Marshall bade them goodnight and rejoined his team.

"I'm all done in, sir. I'm going home."

Briggs nodded. "You take care, Stewart. You did a good job in there." Briggs turned and walked in the direction of his car.

Gardener stood by his, glancing at the warehouse, thinking about everything that had happened. He realised how fitting the title of Corndell's film had been.

Imperfection.

It really did sum him up.

If you enjoyed this book, please let others know by leaving a quick review on Amazon. Also, if you spot anything untoward in the paperback, get in touch. We strive for the best quality and appreciate reader feedback.

editor@thebookfolks.com

www.thebookfolks.com

ALSO IN THIS SERIES

**If you enjoyed IMPERFECTION, the second book,
check out the others in the series:**

IMPURITY – *Book 1*

Someone is out for revenge. A grotto worker is murdered
in the lead up to Christmas. He won't be the first. Can DI
Gardener stop the killer, or is he saving his biggest gift till
last?

IMPLANT – *Book 3*

A small Yorkshire town is beset by a series of cruel
murders. The victims are tortured in bizarre ways. The
killer leaves a message with each crime – a playing card
from an obscure board game. DI Gardener launches a
manhunt but it will only be by figuring out the murderer's
motive that they can bring him to justice.

IMPRESSION – *Book 4*

Police are stumped by the case of a missing five-year-old
girl until her photograph turns up under the body of a
murdered woman. It is the first lead they have and is
quickly followed by the discovery of another body
connected to the case. Can DI Stewart Gardener find the
connection between the individuals before the abducted
child becomes another statistic?

IMPOSITION – *Book 5*

When a woman's battered body is reported to police by
her husband, it looks like a bungled robbery. But the
investigation begins to turn up disturbing links with past

crimes. They are dealing with a killer who is expert at concealing his identity. Will they get to him before a vigilante set on revenge?

IMPOSTURE – *Book 6*

When a hit and run claims the lives of two people, DI Gardener begins to realize it was not a random incident. But when he begins to track down the elusive suspects he discovers that a vigilante is getting to them first. Can the detective work out the mystery before more lives are lost?

IMPASSIVE – *Book 7*

A publisher racked with debts is found strung up in a ruined Yorkshire abbey. Has a disgruntled author taken their revenge? DI Stewart Gardener is on the case but maybe a hypnotist has the key to the puzzle. Can the cop muster his team to work some magic and catch a cunning killer?

IMPIOUS – *Book 8*

It could be detectives Gardener and Reilly's most disturbing case yet when a body with head, limbs and torso assembled from different victims is discovered. Alongside this grotesque being is a cryptic message and a chess piece. A killer wants to take the cops on a journey. And force their hand.

IMPLICATION – *Book 9*

When a body is found in a burned out car, DI Stewart Gardener quickly establishes that a murder has been concealed. But with a missing person case and a spate of robberies occupying the force, he will struggle to identify the victim. When the investigations overlap, he'll have to work out which of the suspects is implicated in which crime.

IMPUNITY – *Book 10*

After a young woman passes out and dies, the medical examiner makes a grim discovery. Someone had surgically removed her kidneys. Detective Stewart Gardener must find a killer evil enough to think of such a cruel act, let alone have the gall to carry it out. It looks like revenge is a motive, but what had the victim, by all accounts a kind and friendly girl, done to anyone?

All FREE with Kindle Unlimited and available in paperback.

THE
BOOK
FOLKS

www.thebookfolks.com